To Mik
poker plac
brother! U Karen was a blast
with ya!

A DIFFERENT BREED
OF BROTHER

A Novel

By

N.K. STEPHENS

Milligan Books   California

Published by:
Stephens Publishing

Distributed by:

Milligan Books
1425 W. Manchester Ave., Suite C
Los Angeles, CA 90047
(323)750-3592
http://www.milliganbooks.com

Formatted by Black Butterfly Press

First Printing: March 2000
Second Printing: May 2001

10 9 8 7 6 5 4 3 2

ISBN   0-9700572-0-2

Milligan Books
1425 W. Manchester Ave., Suite C
Los Angeles, CA 90047
(323)750-3592
http://www.milliganbooks.com

Be not deceived: God is not mocked:
For whatsoever a man soweth
that shall he also reap.
Galatians 6:7

Walking through life at such a pace

Many hopes and dreams may go to waste

The faces we see

The hearts we cross

Often lead to the love we've lost

But as a man

We pretend to be strong

Facing the consequences of the things we have done wrong

Some lives can be repaired

Some decisions may never be clear

But the burden of our choices is a cross we must bear

So be careful of your choices

And be thoughtful of the voices

That may prove to be the ending

Of the life that concluded with your descending

Rathel C. Robinson

DEDICATION

Dedicated to the loving memory of
<u>Mrs. Mable, and Vanessa Smith, and Mrs. Marie Faulkner</u>
(My Grandmother and Aunts) I miss you all very much.

<u>Special thanks to the following Investors in my Dream</u>

Ricky Barnes (You invested in my dream when others would not, and I love you for that. I look forward to many future projects with you. You are the man!)

Lon and Ruth Briggs *(Of The Rocky Mountain Chocolate Factory in the Wigwam Outlet Mall, Goodyear Arizona). Thank you both so much. I hope everyone who reads my book goes into your store and buys a treat)*

Marsha Lanette Stephens (The reason I call you Marsh— it is because you don't take any from anyone. I love you)

Rachelle Renee Stephens-Overby (I love you very much and miss you too)

Janice "Sugarfoot" Gary (You have always been special to me and I hope in the future I'll get the chance to show you how much. I am also very proud of you)

<u>Much love to my publisher and supporters</u>

Dr. Rosie Milligan (Publisher for Milligan Books in Los Angeles. I didn't realize how sweet you were until we met. I look forward to many future projects. Thank you for all of your advice, assistance and patience.

Mrs. Victoria Christopher Murray (Your seminar inspired me to complete my story; also thanks for all of your help and for being on-line.)

Michael Carr of Michael's Design's and Sheron (Your friendship has grown to become one of my most valuable)

Crystal M. Stephens (Big Sis, I owe you so much. This book wouldn't be anything with out you. I love you from the bottom of my heart and I'm proud to be your brother.)

Ricky Barnes (Pretty Ricky, Zack, H-Town Productions) and Crystal

Black Stream News at http://www.aisalinger.com **(A source for informed African Americans)**

Proof Readers: **Chris Torres, Jeanette Stephens, Cora Moss, Trina Jenkins, Karen Sanders, Tim Deramus and Robin Robinson**

Much love to the Tom Joyner Morning Show

KMJK Majic 106.9FM Phoenix AZ and Power 92.3 FM Phoenix AZ

(Both Stations are keeping it real in Arizona, much love!!!!!)

<u>*Much love to Mary J. Blidge*</u> *For your "My Life" CD it got me through some tough times and I love you for that! Thank you.*

ACKNOWLEDGMENTS

Thanks to God above for giving me the strength and the courage to complete this project. I also thank him for Nathan and Joyce, my parents. They found a way to raise six children in the rough streets of North Philadelphia without anyone of us joining a gang or being sent to prison. We were all raised to be God-fearing and streetwise.

To my dear friend Karen Donovan (Kd), thanks for always being there for me, I love you very dearly. Much love to all my sisters and brothers: Crystal-We might as well be the twins; Kevin—God blessed me to have a special brother as well as a twin (I love you so much); Rachelle-I love you; Marsha—You're the strongest sister in the world; Mark—I'm glad to see you headed in the right direction.

Christopher Stephens: You are the son that I never had. I'm sure when you decide what you want to do in life, you'll make me even prouder to be your uncle. Uncle Rob and Janice Gary—You just don't know how much all of your visits helped me (I love you both). Snoop, Bobby, Rodney Marqueese, and Sugar Foot, Uncle Jerome, Uncle Bootsie, Aunt Rosalyn, Uncle Butch, The Stephens' Family of North Philadelphia. My cousin Cheryl. (I love you all very much). Chucky-My first cousin who could've made Kevin and I triplets. To all of my other relatives, there are so many of you, I love all of you from the bottom of my heart. I hope you are all proud of me. Jeanette-My brother married an Angel, and you gave him a prince in Wendell II. Mrs. Finger (My favorite Mother-in-law, I love you very much) and to all of the Finger family members I hope we can become closer because I realize how much I love Jeanette and it's because of you that she is now my sister!

Tonya Monroe (I pray to God everyday hoping you are "The One" that will make me a different breed of brother. God Bless Mom (Rita) and Dad + the Family + Cuz). Calvin, Rhonda, Corey, Lil Calvin, and Calil, you are the only friends in Philly whose number I still know by heart.

Calvin, I love you, man! Mr. and Mrs. Bishop R. Walker Jr., Kevin and Karen, Mary and family. Mr. and Mrs. Roy and Evelyn Mitchell and Roy, Byron, Erny, Benggy, Nora, Andre, and Derrick. Elder U. Goode, Earn, Veldi, Tannya and Nashay, Ryan, and Robert and Terri Fields. Sharonn (I left you all those years ago and when you remembered the date, month, and year, it made me realize how insensitive I am). Dwayne Hansberry- I was lucky to meet you, you're like a brother to a brother, I love you, man! To Keon-You're the bomb, girl, George is a very lucky man. To Christine Torres-thanks for being my sensitive proofreader, you're my little angel. I hope God blesses your marriage. To the following folks, I love you: Boomer (You be thinking about me?), Brandon (What's up doggy, dog), Ebony ("Can I have some candy?"), Terrace (The best husband in the world and homey), the JBs (John, Janice, and Jayden, I love you all, eventhough I have to be playing ball to visit), Cora Moss (the most down to earth woman I've ever met and my boo!), Julia Davis (you are always there for me and I'll do the same), Joyce Palmer and family (Joyce, you're the best, God bless You, James and Jamil), Robinski (You're the bomb, girl, why couldn't I just scoop you up? You helped tremendously with finalizing this book, I owe you big time, congratulations on the new addition), Susie and James Lewis (I love you both, thanks for all your help. God bless the entire family of new additions. This project should help me pay you back). Rathel Robinson (Thanks for the poem brother. I know you are just like me wanting to be a different breed of brother, God bless the girls). Richard "Coco Love" Cosom. Constance Miller (I miss you). Tannya Blue (We should've just gotten married and said to hell with all of the haters). Bridgett Cunningham (I miss you and Ashley, hope mom is doing fine also). Chocolate bar (Linda Ross glad we met). Mark Donovan (Love you man!), Bob and Shelly Morehouse, Malerie, and Ashley (I love you all). Stewart Cassidy and Hausaan (You're both like my nephews, I'm glad Chris has friends like both of you!). Kyle (My young boy) and Victoria Sanders (you guys make me feel proud of how Karen has raised you). Patrick, Me'Oshea, lil Patrick and Temp (you are very special, thanks for making me feel just like one of the family). Donald Lair (Pook) and Pat (love ya both). The Cracker Barrel Restaurant (Store#277, Especially Mark Lausman and family you're all #1 and I love everyone). Christine Hemingway (My first love, I miss you!), Terricita (My sweetheart, I don't know why we fight so much? Maybe one day we can go to the lake and figure that out, if I don't drown you first), Yo (You're still my girl) Sheila Nelson (I guess I was afraid of the differences we had), Bridgett Nelson (Thanks for treating me just like a son and a friend), Stephen Ridley (My cool brother), Timothy Deramus (#1 Colgate smiling brother, thanks for everything), L. Kim Dismuke (No one knows why I stayed with you so long, I do), Brenda Dismuke (the best mother-in-law I wish I had), Suzanne, Ryan, and Brandi (You made me appreciate dating a single parent), SMSgt Byron Stringer (God sent you my way and I'm truly grateful, thanks for everything), SMSgt Cargill (thanks for helping me with my writing skills, I would never have had the confidence to take on this project without your help). The Pulleys (Thanks for all the caring and sharing), Lillian Robinson (I owe you and Mark so much but most of all I'm sorry. I pray we can one day sit down together and laugh like before). Carol (I wonder what would happen if I never went to California? I miss you and Deaden). Dr. Dionne McClain (You thought I left you out, I'm saving some carrot cake for you sweetheart, hope your marriage lasts forever!). Ms Tamashea Thomas ("Oh my Goodness") and Ms Stephanie "Leggs" Spann (my sweet heart). Mrs. Susan Messick (You helped correct a ton of my mistakes, thank you so much. I wish every writer could take advantage of your talents). Ms. Stacey Eleby (Maybe someday you would like basketball). The entire Klemstein Family (God bless you for treating me just like a son, I Love you all). Much love to the Luke AFB Falcons (Neiko, Chris, Norwood, Tee, Eddie, Duron, Jamal, JJ, Boogie, Blue, Pook, Stew, Kyle, Casey and Stretch). To all of the Skynights of Mather AFB in Sacramento (Money, Walker, Tee, T-bone, Twin, Sherman, Shelby, Early, Joe Piscapo, Don, Kenny G, I love you all like brothers). Big props to all the folks at Luke AFB, especially the Legends (D Bledsoe, Chicago D, Bam, Rich, D Lang, Jack, Big Mike, E, Marcus, Porter, Juan, Searge, Tom, Chuck, Barney, EL, Much love). A special thanks and apology to all of the women that I have ever had the pleasure of dating. I know that for whatever reason we didn't work out but without those many experiences I could never have gotten to the point I am now. I can honestly say that today, with your help, I know how to treat a woman.

ABOUT THE AUTHOR

Master Sergeant Nathan K. Stephens has been a member of the United States Air Force for over 18 years. He was reared by his parents, Nathan W. and Joyce Stephens in North Philadelphia along with his sisters Crystal, Rachelle, and Marsha and brothers Kevin (Twin) and Mark. At 36 years of age, Nathan has managed to remain single with no children. He has a long and distinguished career in the US Air Force. He is currently serving as an Education and Training Craftsman at Luke AFB in Arizona.

He received an Associate in Applied Science Degree in Education and Instructional Technology through the Community College of the Air Force and is working towards a Bachelor's Degree in Human Resource Development.

Always the consummate storyteller, Nathan has recently completed his first novel, *A Different Breed of Brother*, which promises to be a "bestseller." His hobbies are basketball, cooking, singing, sewing, movies, reading and of course, writing. His dreams are to become successful as an author and help other authors get their works published, as well as helping friends and relatives with bringing their dreams to reality.

DIFFERENT BREED OF BROTHER

My story is dedicated to all of the women in the world who have had their hearts' broken by a man. It depicts the attitudes, and attempts to break the silent code of conduct governing the heart breaking African American male in the United States today. Most women spurned will say that all men are dogs. This maybe holds true, depending on how you interpret the data.

You see there are several breeds and categories of dogs. The Poodle is the manicured and pampered pooch, with an attitude to match. He is similar to the kept man. The Mongrel or crossbreed has several genetic strands of various breeds, each one edifying itself in different situations. The male counterpart to this pooch has about as many women as genetic variations. His allegiance to his mate is questionable at best. This is the one dog women have to be careful not to feed, since they're hard to get rid of.

A few others are the Rottewiler or Pitt bulls. Both of these dogs are purchased for protection. They are big, strong, extremely violent and uncontrollable. They must remain on a very tight leash, the slightest bit of slack and someone will get bit.

You can pick any women in an abusive relationship and nearby will be the distant male relative of the two above-mentioned breeds.

Women will be able to read my story and find some similar characteristics to the man she has at home or possibly just broken up with. This story should enlighten, caution, persuade, predict, and often times restrict female actions in future relationships. Just remember the different guys in my story and see how many men in your life seem like they are represented. I'm sure I don't know them personally, however the specific male personality exists throughout the world. Just like the pooches that you pick up at your local pet shop there is always a "Different Breed of Brother"

To my brothers who are doing the right thing and treating their women with respect and dignity, big props to you all, keep on keeping on. For the brothers who are continuously disrespecting our "Nubian Queens of the Nile", please stop tearing the sisters down. Lets find a way to build them up and make amends for the vast amount of years they have been placed in subservient roles. This book is my cleansing powder and I'm getting back to treating all women with love, respect, and dignity.

To all of the brothers that read my story and gain a little insight on fidelity, and monogamy, much love. Any brother that changes and becomes a different breed as a result of my words will make me a better brother myself.

CONTENTS

BEGINNINGS

<u>*MARCUS*</u>

At 6'9", you would think I was a ball player in the NBA. Well, I hate to say it, but my ass is terrible at basketball and just about any other sport, except football. I'm pretty well coordinated. I just never got into sports. I played football in high school just to get next to the ladies. That backfired on me. There was this one big rivalry game and I was starting as wide receiver. I never wanted to start, but at the time I was about 6'4" and I could leap over defenders and catch the football.

I decided this was a pivotal point for me. If I excelled out there, scouts from all over would be knocking at my door to send me to some college to continue playing this barbaric sport that I didn't even like. I went out on the field as usual, avoiding the helmet smashing linemen getting pumped up for the game. I remember the team was driving downfield and doing pretty well, then it happened. They called my number for the next play. It felt like I had just been through an earthquake or a plane crash. I was petrified. I ran my route just as smoothly as in any other game.

The quarterback delivered a perfect pass and, just as I went up over the defender to catch it, I remembered my distaste for the game of football. I dropped the pass and to everyone's surprise, including my own, no one said a word. I caught a few passes and would let the defense catch up and tackle me. I wanted my purposely bad playing to seem convincing. I dropped a total of four potential touchdown passes that day. Our team lost the game by one touchdown and everyone in the stadium knew that if I had caught any of those passes, it would have been a different game. When I got to the locker room, nobody said anything to me. All of the guys stayed out of the shower until I had finished. As I finished getting dressed and headed out the door to go home, there was the coach. He was giving everyone a pep talk as they left with their heads hanging. I wanted so badly just to get by him without him saying anything to me.

Just as I approached, he called out my whole name: "Marcus Harold Turner II. Get over here."

I paused for a moment and walked over to him. He was rambling on about how football was like life and, if you give up in a game, you'll probably give up in life. I just agreed with him and headed out the door, never to play football again.

I had a different agenda after football. It was time to concentrate on women full-time. Getting women had always been pretty easy for me. I was blessed with a nice grade of wavy hair, just like my mother. My father passed on his straight white teeth. But, I didn't have the benefit of growing up with a dad. The last time I saw my father was the day my mother nearly killed him.

My childhood was filled with abuse. Whippings by my father were a weekly routine. Sometimes he would beat my ass for no reason at all. Then there were the times when he would knock my mother around. He would come home drunk and start bitching about whatever—no food, or no beer in the fridge—anything to start a fight. It was never much of a fight anyway. Dad would smack mom around a few times, until she was black and blue, and then go fall asleep. This got progressively worse before culminating one day. That particular day, daddy came home drunk again and attacked moms. He beat her really badly this time.

I was always too young to do anything but cry. There was no way I would dare let pops ever see me cry, either. He always said men shouldn't cry or show emotions. He was a man and I guess kicking my mother's ass every chance he got was confirmation of that fact. I knew if I started crying, the next ass getting whipped would be mine. I felt so helpless. A frail thirteen-year-old, I couldn't even think about trying to fight him. Instead of getting whipped, I'd probably get killed. It was around 2:30 in the morning, and the noise mom and dad were making woke me up. I heard him yelling and screaming at mom in the kitchen. I got up and cracked the door to my bedroom to get a better look at the fight. I wanted to do something this time, but I felt helpless. All I could hear was daddy yelling at mom.

"Mrs. Turner, where the hell are you?" he shouted. He always called mom by Mrs. and his last name. This was probably his way of letting her know she belonged to him.

I noticed his clothes were wrinkled and rumpled like he had just slept in them. His body reeked of whiskey, which clouded the air in the apartment when he walked through the door.

"Mrs. Turner, where is my fucking dinner?"

"I made it earlier this evening, and then I put it in the fridge."

"Why don't you just wait until I get home before you put my food up, bitch?"

"It would never be hot. Can't I just get it out of the refrigerator and heat it up for you?"

"No, it's too late now. I want to eat when I get in the fucking door, not when you want me to. I'm going to kick your black ass now."

From the doorway of my bedroom, I could see both of my parents having this ridiculous debate about dinner. My mother stood there shaking like a scared kitten. She headed towards the refrigerator to appease my father and get his dinner ready.

"I'll fix it for you. Only please don't hit me anymore. I'm tired of you always beating on me."

"Watch your fucking mouth, you bitch. I'll continue to kick your ass until you get your shit together. Go in the room and get my favorite belt."

"I'm not going to get your belt. Why are you always beating on me?"

"Shut up and get my belt, bitch."

Mom stood as still as an ice sculpture, not moving an inch.

"Are you testing me, bitch?" he said.

"No, I'm not testing you," she answered.

Mom retreated to the bedroom, and I assumed she was going to get the belt. When she returned, I felt my heart jump at the sight of her eyes. They were as large and bright as lanterns. Then I noticed she had not returned with a belt. Instead, she was carrying a gun.

"What the fuck are you doing with a gun, bitch?"

"I told you I'm not going to let you beat me up anymore."

"You better put that gun down, or your ass-whipping will be worse than you ever had before."

Mom closed her frightened eyes and pulled the trigger. The gun went off with a boom that rang in my ears long after the shot.

Daddy hit the floor. We thought he was dead. It turns out mom had shot him in his chest, just below his heart. Any higher and daddy would have been history. He lay on the floor shaking, and there was blood everywhere.

The whiskey must have thinned his blood because it was coming out of him like sweat. I could see the carpet turning a wet burgundy color right under his body.

Dad was rushed to the hospital. The police handcuffed mom and took her away. I couldn't believe the police were taking my mother away. They had never taken my father away when the neighbors would call them while he was hitting my mom.

Some child-protection lady took me to this foster place for the next few days. There were never any charges filed against my mother, and she was released a few days later. I guess they reviewed her hospital records, which were as thick as some perpetrators' wrap sheets. I haven't seen my father since that day.

Mom and I moved away to live with my grandmother in Sacramento, and I've been here ever since. I've always had a hard time when it comes to dealing with women who have children. I guess I resent the fact that my dad wasn't there for me. I'm not interested in being there for someone else's child.

Whenever I hook up with a single mother, I always wind up dogging her out. I don't need to be raising some other man's kids. My dad wasn't there to raise my ass. Every kid should suffer just like me. I'll wait until I'm ready to make my own child. I know my child won't want for anything. I've got a good job making about $80,000 a year.

I had a friend who worked at the airport and, when I turned 18, he hooked me up with a job as a skycap. It took me about six months to learn the ropes and get my hustle on. After a year, I was only working about four or five hours per day and making about $50 per hour.

I would show up at about seven or eight in the morning and start helping travelers with their baggage. People would travel with all kinds of shit. Luggage, boxes, trunks, skis, anything they can check through to their final destination. I would check their bags, check their identification, toss their bags on the conveyer, get my tip, and point them to their gate. This was the easiest money in the world.

I would average about two to five bucks per transaction and each one only took me about ten minutes. Then I was on to the next customer. I know a lot of the brothers that are working at the airport would be pissed if they knew I was discussing our little hook-up. There were days when I would leave work with about six hundred dollars cash in my pocket. That's undeclared cash money.

The best part about working at the airport is the women. I've met more women by working as a skycap than I've met at any club. There were all kinds—professionals, vacationers, visitors and freaks. You name it; they came through the airport. I would scope them out, pass all of the other passengers, and take care of their bags. I was rolling out the red carpet for all good-looking women. Once I got the phone number, I would double as their tour guide to Sacramento. This was the best hook-up in the world. I was fucking a new woman almost every week. I was having a ball taking advantage of these women. I was scheming them out of money, clothes, and one even bought me a car. Most of the brothers were puzzled at the fact that my shit worked on almost all women. The ones it didn't work on weren't worth my time anyway.

TAJ

Everyone calls me Taj instead of saying my whole name, Timothy Alexander Johnson. I'm twenty-two years old, six foot six with a seriously muscular frame. I've always been a gym rat. I grew up watching all of those bodybuilding shows on television, wishing I could get a body like Arnold Schwarzenegger in the movie, "Pumping Iron." I figure I'm getting really close to that body, and I'm still young enough to use it to get just about any woman I want.

It's kind of crazy watching women salivate when I walk my tall ass by them and flash my cut-up, chocolate arms in their faces. My mother used to call me her little Hershey's kiss. Now I'm as big as those African slaves, whose presence caused a ruckus amongst the plantation owners bidding and salivating at the very sight of such a statuesque being. Some people say I'm arrogant. Well, that's true. I don't really give a shit about anybody or anything.

My mom decided when I was very young that I should go live with my punk-ass father. I ran away from his ass when I was thirteen. I spent most of my time on the streets and in juvenile homes. I finally got my shit together at around sixteen when my fifth foster family took me in. It was a lawyer and his wife. They had this wild idea of giving back to the community by taking a foster child in. I was one of the worst out there, but they somehow got me straight. She would spend time helping me read, and he provided me with the father figure that I had never known. Now I'm in college, and I owe it all to them. I still can't get over my obsession with fucking over women. I'm not sure why I just try to hook up with women who don't seem to want me. When I hook up with them, I always wind up dogging them out before they reject me. I guess it's my way of getting back at dear old mom for abandoning me.

I got into Georgetown University in Washington DC, and I was maintaining a modest 3.2 G.P.A., which would've been better if I could concentrate on the information instead of the many women just waiting for the chance to mount my particularly large frame. I would sit in class for hours just lining up potential targets I wanted to conquer. The women I pursued were always attractive and, as I mentioned earlier, usually not interested in me, not at first anyway. Most of the time, it was some young lady who thought she was too smart or good for the likes of such a muscular, possibly intellectually inept, individual.

Cynthia was probably the smartest sister in the class. She was also the finest. A strikingly tall 5'9" psychology student with a Flo-Jo body and a Vanessa Williams face. She had smooth brown skin that reminded me of fresh-picked pecans. Her eyes were a natural hazel color that I first thought came from contacts. She always wore slinky skirts, and outfits that showed her curvy body. Most of them, although revealing, were tasteful and left plenty to the imagination.

A member of Georgetown's world class track team, the girl had a body that made most men want to run in the other direction. Her good looks, cunning intellect, and muscular yet very feminine physique intimidated them.

Cynthia thinks she's all that. I can't wait to figure out how to get with her. I'm definitely not your normal brother. She will be holding onto me, like she holds her breath moments before the gun goes off for a race, real soon. I'm not even really attracted to her; she turns me on because she isn't throwing herself at me like the other women in this class.

Class is over and several women scoot by my seat and drop little sticky notes as they go by. I'm sure each note has a name and phone number, along with a promise to do some interesting trick with a part of her body. I give them each a weak smile, until Cynthia attempts to walk by.

"Hello, Cynthia, my name is Taj."

She pauses with this disinterested smirk on her face.

"How do you know my name?"

"I asked one of your girlfriends in our class."

"The next time you want to know something about me, just ask me."

"Is that an invitation?"

"No, Taj, it's not an invitation and I wouldn't give you any information about me anyway. Why don't you go chase one of those groupies who are always dropping their numbers on your desk?"

"Obviously, I'm not interested in them, since I'm standing here getting a hard time from you."

"I'm not twisting your arm. You can walk away anytime you want. On the other hand, that sounds like a good idea to me. Goodbye, Taj."

She thinks she is so smart. It may take a while, but I'll get that ass soon enough.

I've seen Cynthia twice today, and both times she rolled her eyes and looked the other way. She won't even stop and talk to me. We were in psychology class and I took the seat directly behind her. She never even acknowledged my presence.

Cynthia was wearing these tight black Lycra leggings with a matching top that exposed her midsection. I noticed she had her navel pierced and, I don't know why, but even that turned me on. I also smelled her perfume as she walked up. Whatever it was, I could tell it was expensive. It grabbed my attention like a slap in the face, yet caressed my nose like fresh roses.

Today the subject in class was the different psychological theories which determine why humans behave the way they do. What Cynthia doesn't realize is that I got hold of one of the term papers she handed in. It was on the Humanistic approach to understanding and predicting human behavior. After class, I went up to Cynthia with a worried, yet curious, look on my face.

"Hello, Cynthia. I have something to ask you."

"Dear God, what in the world could you want to ask me, Taj?"

"I was doing some research for a paper in our Psych class. My question is, why do most people drop Sigmund Freud's name like he is the Einstein of Psychology when there are several psychologists and theories out there that make his view seem archaic?"

"So you expect me to believe you know anything about psychologists, other than maybe Freud?"

"Sure, one of my favorites is Abraham Maslow. He is the founder of the Humanistic philosophy, which refutes the Freudian idea that personality is ruled by unconscious forces. Humanists believe in free will, our human ability to freely make choices. These choices, based on past experiences, govern how fulfilling our lives will be."

If you could've taken a picture of Cynthia, when I finished this line of bullshit I got from scanning her term paper, you would have a prize-winning photo. I could tell she was impressed. We continued the conversation for another twenty minutes, then she gave me her home phone number and hurried away to her next class.

I was determined to call Cynthia up and see if I could hook up with her. I dialed her number and the phone rang about six times. I waited for an answering machine to come on so I could leave her an intellectually stimulating message. She picked up and caught me off guard.

"Hello, Cynthia?"

"Yes, this is Cynthia."

"This is Taj and I just wanted to call and make sure you didn't give me a number to a phone booth or something."

"I wouldn't do that to you, Taj."

"You sound very sexy tonight, what are you doing?"

"I just finished taking a bath and I'm about to kick back and watch a movie."

"What movie are you going to watch?"

"It's called, 'Soul Food'."

"I heard it was a good movie."

"You mean you haven't taken one of your little groupies to see it, Taj?"

"No, as a matter of fact, I haven't even seen it."

"Well, I hope you don't think I'm going to invite you over."

"Why must you give me such a hard way to go, Cynthia? I'm just trying to get to know you."

"I'm sorry, Taj, I did give you my number, didn't I?"

"You sure did"

"So, can I come over and watch the movie with you?"

"Sure, Taj, I'll give you my address and directions."

The directions Cynthia gave me were right on the money. It only took me about twenty-five minutes to get there. She lived in this apartment complex in Rancho Cordova, a suburb of Sacramento. I always thought that was a low-income area, however these apartments were very expensive looking. I parked in one of the uncovered parking spaces and roamed the grounds of the apartment complex until I found her apartment. I have to admit it was a very clean and well-kept place. Cynthia answered the door on the first ring.

"Hello, Cynthia. Nice place you have here."

"Thank you, Taj. Excuse the mess. I haven't had any company in a long time. Would you like something to drink?"

"Sure, what do you have?"

"I have beer, wine, or Gatorade."

"I'll take some wine if you'll have some, too."

"You are just too smooth, Taj. You think I'm just going to sit here, pretend to watch a movie, while we get drunk on wine?"

"No, you're the one with the wine, if you didn't want me to have any, why did you offer it?"

"Sorry, Taj. You make me nervous. My last boyfriend did a number on me. And it always started with some wine. I guess I shouldn't even have any around considering what it does to me."

"What does it do?"

"Wouldn't you like to know?"

"Let's just have one glass, watch the movie, then I'll go home."

"Okay, that sounds good to me. Would you like some popcorn, Taj?

"Sure, if it's no trouble."

"Okay, I'll pop the corn and you can pour the wine."

"Sounds good to me."

We watched the movie, and it was actually pretty good. It was about this family, and the way their mother raised them. She kept the family together with soulful Sunday meals at her house. Whenever she cooked soul food, everything was all right. It made me miss my grandmother, who had died a few years earlier. When the movie was over, I have to admit I was a little choked up.

"Man, Cynthia, that movie really got me. It reminded me of my grandmother, and it also made me extremely hungry."

"I liked it also, Taj. But that popcorn was too salty, and I think I drank too much wine. I think you better go now."

"Can I stay for one more glass of wine?"

"Just one more glass, Taj, and then you must go."

"Okay, just one more."

"What are you doing, Taj?"

"What does it look like? I'm trying to kiss you. I thought it was a good idea since you're so sexy. Mmm, you smell good, Cynthia."

"Thank you, Taj, and you feel good. Damn, I shouldn't have had all of that wine. Taj, do you have any condoms?"

"Yes, I do."

"Could you please put one on and make love to me?"

"I thought you'd never ask."

Cynthia rips all of her clothes off, like a cat clawing at a couch. She ripped my shirt while undressing me. It seemed like she had been sex starved and needed some immediate nourishment. She could hardly wait for me to put the damn rubber on. We started out in the missionary position. She was kissing me the whole time I was inside her. We rolled around the couch, then the floor, and we eventually made it to her bedroom.

Once there, she threw me down on the bed like a sex crazed-animal, holding her prey. She mounted me and gave me the ride of a lifetime. She grunted and groaned and seemed to be coming for the third time in about 30 minutes.

Cynthia was truly a freak. I couldn't believe that a few glasses of wine could change her like that. I began doing her doggy style. She said she didn't like it that way because it's not a very affectionate position. She may have thought that before today, but she sure didn't complain.

I held that sexy race track ass, and I went for broke. Her groans grew progressively louder. Her groans of pleasure were actually making me give it to her harder and harder. She yelled that she was coming again, and I started pumping her faster.

"Ahhhh!" She let go of a scream that rivaled the shower scene in Alfred Hitchcock's "Psycho."

I wondered if the neighbors would dial 911. Somewhere in the middle of all that, I got off myself. She lay there on the bed in a puddle of sweat, breathing as if she'd just finished a 440-meter relay.

I began putting on my clothes and shoes.

"Don't you want to stay the night, Taj?"

"No, I can't, Cynthia, but I'll take a rain check."

"Sure, you just say when. I'll keep things warm for you."

I put my clothes on and headed out the door. When I got outside, I started laughing and saying, "I'm the man." Not so long ago, Ms. Cynthia wouldn't have given me the time of day, and now she has just given me all of her power.

I saw Cynthia in class the next day, and I didn't even say "hello." She comes up to me while I'm talking to this little red bone I'd been checking out earlier.

"What's up, Taj?"

"Nothing much."

"Is that all you have to say to me after last night?"

"Look, I came over to watch a movie, and things got a little out of hand."

"You mean you didn't want anything to happen? Did you even enjoy yourself?"

"I sure did, Cynthia, but I'm not looking for a relationship, just a friend. Don't get me wrong, the pussy was truly good."

"Taj, you are an asshole! I hope you drop dead!"

She was just like most women who give the pussy up too fast. Most men will be on a mission to get it on the first date. When women give in too fast, how can we give them any respect? She becomes what we players refer to as a "booty call," nothing more, nothing less. Little did she know, she'd be calling me for an encore fuck real soon. I was absolutely sure of it. I laughed to myself about this latest victory.

JOE

My name is Joseph Ronald Williams. I'm twenty-six years old, six foot five, with a smooth, Jordanesque baldhead. At first glance, I might remind you of an African-American version of Mr. Clean. The famous ammonia-scented cleaning concentrate your mother used to clean everything. I even have a large hoop earring in my ear, which emphasizes the resemblance.

Most women call me names like high yellow, redbone, or light-bright. Some women are offended by terms like that, however fair-skinned brothers, like myself, have been using their beige coloring to get over on women for years. Whatever women seem to say about my complexion, the fact remains they are calling me and calling frequently.

I'm no dummy either. I graduated from the University of Michigan as a business management major. While I was at school, I pledged Omega, otherwise known as the "Q-Dogs." College was a playground. It was the equivalent of allowing the fox to finally move into the hen house with his own private room. All I can say is that I've always loved women, all women. Becoming a Q-Dog was like getting a Ph.D. in dogging women. My choice of women encompassed short, tall, slim, or even chunky. These last sisters I termed "fat but fuckable."

If the women I dated knew the depths to which I stooped to get a piece of ass, they would have cringed.

I was obsessed with getting laid. I wanted it all the time, and the only weird stipulation is it had to be with a different woman. I lived by that old adage, "variety is the spice of life."

I used my fair skin to break into the famous Wal-Mart store management team. After working for a few years as a manager of a small sporting goods chain, "Champion Sports," I had the perfect background to move into the big time. At the time, less than one percent of Wal-Mart's management staff was African-American. I was black enough to be hired and light enough not to be too shocking to the status quo.

When I applied for the job, I beat out more than 50 other applicants. I figured it would be because I'm intelligent and I had the experience. I knew that once I got to the interview process, I would be a shoe-in. God blessed me with a silver tongue, which allowed me to breeze through most situations with the calm of a cat burglar.

I did just that, skated through each interview, leaving each subsequent interviewer with nothing but good things to pass on about this promising young man. During the last interview, in which the company was prepared to make a salary offer, I was not prepared for what happened. It was then that I realized that I had finally arrived.

On the day of that final interview at Wal-Mart, I must say I was a little nervous. I hadn't seen even one other brother during the entire process. I know they thought because I was so light-skinned, seemingly well mannered, and articulate, that they had found a real token. I had news for those assholes. I was the white man's worst nightmare, a brother who could blend. I'd sit in their meetings, listen to their boring speeches and stupid-ass stories. I'd sit back, watch them fuck over a few brothers and then become the star witness for the prosecution in the class-action anti-discrimination lawsuit.

I was trying to figure out what to wear to the damned interview. I'd already worn some of my best suits to the previous ones. But the final one was the most critical because it would be about the Benjamin's. That's right, how much money they're going to pay me. I wanted to bust off in there in my FUBU baggy pants and bomber jacket and really shock them. Instead, I decided to wait until I'd been there a while before I let them catch me in my cooling out gear. Besides, they would have probably made me an offer I'd have thrown back in their faces if they had seen me in my round-the-way clothes.

I found a nice gray flannel suit in the back of the closet that still fit pretty well. I used to wear that one all the time for formal meetings at Champion. The other managers wouldn't even recognize me since all we wore at work were athletic clothes. I had my suit on, and my smell good was starting to make me smile. I jumped in my 'Vette and headed down to the interview to see exactly how much or little the white man was going to offer the token brother.

I arrived at the same building where all of the previous interviews had been held. I was just a little early. I thought the company would have saved money by holding these interviews at the nearest Wal-Mart. I guessed that wouldn't have been wise as they had to keep up appearances until they had decided who was going to be hired. They rented out office space just to do the hiring for a new store opening in Citrus Heights, which is a suburban city only minutes from Sacramento.

My appointment was for ten o'clock and I intentionally arrived at about 9:40 a.m. I figured they were watching everything, including what I wore, said and the time I showed up for my interviews. A receptionist was always there to greet me and note the time I arrived. That was probably to gauge how prompt I would be after they hired me.

The receptionist escorted me to the interviewing room. I'd been in all of the others in the past week, but this one was different. It had an executive touch to it. There were three leather chairs, two on one side of a cherrywood table and one on the other side. I guessed the side with one chair was for the interviewer since it was opposite the door.

I sat back in one of the leather chairs. They were quite comfortable, probably to put interviewees at ease so they would slip up during the interviews. The slightest misstep can ruin a job interview. My father had always told me to answer the questions and not to offer any information.

I remembered a friend of mine who didn't listen to that advice, and it cost him a good job. He was probably the most qualified person for a position at a printing company. He had cinched the interview process until he ran his mouth too much. He rambled on about some manager that he used to work for and how he punched him out before he left the company. He told me the person conducting the interview was laughing with him, and then all of a sudden they had made someone else a job offer.

Brothers need to learn to shut the fuck up sometime. A man's two biggest assets are his mouth and his ears. One should always remain quiet while the other sums up the situation and prepares a detailed road map for the other to follow. I sat back and waited for almost twenty minutes. That's how corporate America treated newcomers. Job-seekers were expected to be as punctual as Swiss watches, but they could keep you waiting just to see if you flew off the handle or cursed them out.

Twenty minutes after the set meeting time, in walked a manager who I hadn't seen before. He was a short little character who reminded me of a tax auditor. He was a real geek with large, wire-rimmed glasses and a pocket protector full of pens. He came in and greeted me as if he were early and had just shown me into his office. I waited for him to acknowledge the point of this interview: to make me a salary offer. I watched him stumble through some papers, as if he were trying to find a particular form. He stopped, looked up at me and took a long deep breath.

"Mr. Williams, the Wal-Mart family is very pleased with your recent series of interviews and your very impressive resume. We are prepared to offer you a management position at our new

Citrus Heights store. First let's try to get an idea of what you were thinking about making. Please write down your expected salary. Be sure to give me a high and a low."

He handed me a pen and small piece of paper. I took the piece of paper and wrote down $39,000-$50,000. I folded the paper and passed it back to him. It seemed like we were transferring illegal documentation and someone was watching us. He opened the paper and paused. I thought for a moment that I should have given him a smaller high and a lower low. I knew I had asked for too much. Even if they gave me the low, it would be about $3,000 more per than I made at Champion Sports.

"Mr. Williams, I think we can come to some kind of happy medium." He scribbled what looked like two figures on a piece of paper and folded it just as I had. He then passed me the piece of paper and sat back in his chair.

I opened the piece of paper, and I almost screamed. My eyes popped out, and I had to catch myself.

We had definitely come to a happy medium. His figures were $42,000 and, after one year, I would move up to $46,000. That would be $10,000 more a year than I was making before. I know some college buddies that went to law school who aren't making that kind of money. They also had tons of benefits to go along with the salary. If I decided to get married, my wife would automatically be covered. I loved the fact that I chose to move on over to the Wal-Mart family. Daddy Wal-Mart was being awfully generous with the funds today.

I woke up today with a butt-ass naked woman lying beside me. I tried my best to remember what happened the night before, but I was still a little drunk. I couldn't remember a damn thing. I remember trying a new drink, Alize and tying one hell of a drunk on. My head was throbbing, and I felt like a boxer on the receiving end of a Mike Tyson punching assault. The pain in my head wouldn't allow me to remember how this woman even got to my apartment last night.

I decided to ignore my curiosity about how she got here or who she was. I began admiring her body. She had these long, curvy, butterscotch brown legs and I could see this sister was good-looking, using only the soft light flowing through the window. I started rubbing those long legs, thighs, and her nicely round butt. It didn't take long before I rolled her over and slipped my very hard nature inside of her.

She woke up with a groan of pleasure that made me even harder. Her name was Mercedes. Her parents must have named her that since that was the only way they could say they had a Mercedes at home. She mounted me and rode me like she was a champion bronco bull rider. There were several quarter horses in the Kentucky Derby that would have come in behind this sister.

We both reached our sexual peak and collapsed onto the bed in a pool of fresh sweat. I looked over at the clock and suddenly realized I was late for a meeting with Trina. I gave Mercedes some weak excuse for having to rush her off and said I would definitely call her later. Mercedes would eventually find out that I wouldn't call her right away. I might call her in a few months, if at all. She would simply be another one of my conquests.

"Whew! That was some damn good poontang. I'll have to put a star next to Mercedes' name in my black book. She'll be a definite second or third option one night."

It's 9:50 a.m. and I'm pushing my black Corvette at about 75 in a 55-mile-per-hour lane. I can't even slow down to see if a cop is anywhere in sight.

"Shit! I'm running late, and Trina is going to kill me."

The thought of being late to our meeting has me sweating bullets. Trina is five feet five inches of dark chocolate, brown-eyed sister with a centerfold body and a hitman attitude. She's twenty-eight, single and has no children. She's always wanted a family, but her career and marriage had to come first. Once she was successful in those areas, she would contemplate children.

She graduated with honors from one of those high-priced private colleges whose name you would have a hard time pronouncing, much less get into. Trina's a successful businesswoman who takes her career and life much too seriously. Trina is the consummate professional, and she's quickly surpassed her peers. She is the type who goes out wearing the most provocative dress, yet dares any man to whistle at her. Trina is mean. The epitome of the superwoman who doesn't tolerate shit from a man. She actually went a couple of rounds at the local boxing gym with some heavy hitters. After one bout, she told one guy he hit like a bitch.

You couldn't look at her and tell she was such a tough little sister, but I knew. I knew that being late to the appointment would have serious repercussions. Trina was one sister who has Joe the stud in check. It's 10:10 a.m. and I turned that last corner almost on two wheels. Trina is outside, looking angry.

"Joe! You son of a bitch. Where the fuck were you?"

Trina is clearly pissed. We are engaged to be married in three months. This was the wedding planning meeting that Trina had pulled several strings to get scheduled.

"I overslept, honey," I said, getting out of the car explaining. "You should have called me this morning to remind me of the meeting."

"Remind you? Joe, we have only been planning this wedding for about four months. What the fuck do you mean I should've reminded you?" The thought of having to remind me of a meeting that we had discussed for the last four months was making her even madder. She decided that we shouldn't keep the wedding planner waiting any longer, grabbed my hand and yanked me inside.

The planner was very understanding and offered me a drink. My head was still throbbing from last night and a drink was the last thing I needed.

"No, thank you," I replied, as I sat next to Trina. The place was exquisitely decorated with sample wedding invitations, linens, photographs, and plenty of catalogs. The place seemed fitting for a million-dollar agent for the potential broom-jumpers of America. Her services came with a very high price. The fee included her recommendations for the spare-no-expense wedding experience of your life. In fact, her fees were only surpassed by the top dollar suggestions, each of which Trina seemed to love.

I wanted so badly to have her give us one of those Las Vegas strip menus. Those allow you to pick a number that corresponds to the number of items you want with your special wedding. Everything from pictures, videotape, rings, even a fresh corsage. They make you feel good about how far your dollars stretch. It's like going into McDonald's and ordering a #3 value meal without the onions, but super-sizing the fries.

I was sitting there wondering why I even had to be present. This woman was becoming the biggest pain in the ass and wallet I'd ever seen. She made me feel so inadequate and cheap. She told Trina that I could use a lesson in manners, right there in front of my face. My first reaction was to show her my manners; yeah, just whip it out right there and watch her mouth drop. Trina would've tried to kill me, so I just smiled at the thought.

Trina didn't refuse a single one of her expensive suggestions. This was going to be an expensive event. The only upside to it was that Trina's father was footing a large chunk of the wedding bill. I know he hated the fact that his darling daughter was hooked up with the likes of me. The fact that I would be reaping some of the benefits of his hard-earned money was also probably hard for him to swallow.

Her daddy was rich and never hesitated to remind me of this fact every time he could. He also made sure I didn't think the fact that I managed to get his precious only child to marry me was going to somehow make me the son he never had.

Her pop really hated me, and I think I knew why. I'm sure he saw a lot of himself in me. I could tell he was a player in his day. He must have married Trina's mother after he knocked her up. He put up a good act, however I knew he really didn't care about his wife.

Trina and I eventually got back to her apartment where she hauled off and slapped the shit out of me. The sound made it seem worse than the slap itself. Wapow!

"What was that for?"

"That was for being late to one of the most important meetings in my life. You better not do that shit on our wedding day, or I swear I'll kill your ass, Joseph Ronald Williams."

"Baby, you know I wouldn't do that to you. I'm crazy about you, and all I want is for us to be happy. Come here and give me one of those juicy kisses of yours."

"Stop, Joe. Stop. You're making me wet, and I'm supposed to be mad at you."

"Let's see how hard you can ride me when you're mad."

We began rolling all over the sofa and eventually I was in her bedroom, forgiven and fucking for the second time that day. I'm keeping this woman because of the way she loves me one moment, then is ready to kick my ass, and the next minute, she's grabbing that same ass and calling my name out like I'm the man!

Trina would be good for any guy's ego. She gets wet when the phone rings, and you know how women like to talk on the phone. It doesn't even take much to get her off. A kiss here, a lick there and she's telling me, "Hold it right there. I'm coming!" One time she had four orgasms in a twenty-minute nooner we had decided to squeeze in because she was so horny at work. She came the first time shortly after I entered her.

If she knew I was fucking around behind her back, my ass and whoever I was fucking would be dead. I do love her and I don't know why I continue to sleep with other women. I hope I stop once we are married.

For some reason, I just like to have a variety of sisters that I'm sleeping with. It probably sounds doggish, however I look at it like I'm getting training. I'm trying to acquire as much training as I can, from as many different women. That way, when I do settle down and get married, the sleeping around will be out of my system. When Trina and I finally get married, there won't be any reason for me to wake up with another woman on my mind or in my bed like this morning.

CK

My father won out over my mother in picking my name. My first name belonged to my father's best friend, my second was his brother's and, of course, I had his last name: Calvin Kevin Kelsey. Everyone I grew up with called me CK for short and I guess that really stuck. I really love my parents, especially my father. Ours was one of only two families in the neighborhood with a father at home. My father was pretty strict and didn't take much shit. Moms always went to church. She was pretty quiet while raising me and my two brothers and three sisters. I was always a good-looking kid and got into trouble just like any other boy growing up in South Sacramento. I was pretty spoiled during my childhood and, even though I had a big family, I got almost everything I wanted. My grandmother made sure that whatever my parents didn't get, she bought it for me.

Now here I am twenty-five years old, six feet tall, which is taller than my father and brothers, and about 180 pounds. I've got my mother's hair, which is soft and curly as well as her smooth brown skin and dark, charcoal eyes. My grandmother told me that my mother's side of the family had some Indian in it. They all hail from Lumberton, North Carolina where silky haired black brothers are plentiful. I'd never been down south and after growing up in Sacramento, I had no desire to go down there to discover my roots.

Fortunately, I was always a good student. My parents didn't tolerate bringing home anything less than a B on any report card or that was your ass. I remember that once I failed three courses on my report card for non-participation. My father hit the roof. When he found out that one of the courses was wood shop, he beat the shit out of me. I thought he was tripping for beating my ass, but now that I'm older, I'm glad he forced me to pay attention and pass those damm classes.

It was because of my parents that I was able to attend Sacramento State University and graduate with a Bachelor of Science degree in Human Resources Development. My degree, along with some pretty good internship programs, helped me to have a really strong resume and land a good job with the state. Right now I'm making about 42K per year. This is not bad pay for a single black man just hanging out, trying to find himself and doing the dating thing. It seems my creativity along with my ability to talk to almost anyone in any situation has made dating women of various degrees of education and financial status effortless.

Most women would say I'm a smooth talker with the gift of gab. My mother said I could sell sand to an Arab, ice to an Eskimo, or fish to a fisherman. Well, you get the point. I know I'm a catch, and I'm not afraid to act like it when I meet a woman. I've managed to remain single, without kids. That seems to be a large attraction for most women to qualify me as the perfect man to walk down the aisle with. The fact that I don't drink or smoke makes me appear saintly; however, they should beware that I'm nobody's angel. There is one catch to this marvelous package.

I'm spoiled, and I live my life by my own rules and regulations. I'm like the trader with insider information waiting to take advantage of the market, and rationalizing the profits as a certain moralistic survival of the fittest. I can't say that I date with a particular purpose.

I'm on a quest to acquire the experience of dating different women of different races. Yes, I have the fever. "Jungle fever" is what folks call it. "Jungle fever" isn't that weak-ass Spike Lee depiction of adultery. His movie was simply a married black man committing adultery with a sexy, tempting white co-worker. You see, true "jungle fever" is when you have two single people of different races. These individuals are very eligible to date within their race, and for some reason choose to date another race, almost exclusively.

I've dated several sisters and a few relationships actually got pretty serious. No matter, I still find myself in a new situation with a white woman regularly. I would often sit and wonder why this is. Could it be that I'm actually discriminating against my Nubian Queens, mothers of the Nile? That is possible, however the weird thing is I'm very much attracted to black women and when I'm dating them, I treat them with more respect. The fact remains that I rarely date sisters. It is almost like some subconscious, twisted interpretation of affirmative action. One sister every now and again keeps me grounded and keeps the other brothers and sisters off my back. However, I date whomever I want and no one has any say in it!

Man, I'm hungry. I haven't eaten in about five hours. I could eat a small horse or a large chicken, whichever comes along first. Speaking of chicken, some Kentucky Fried Chicken sounds real good. I'll just jump in the ride and go pick some up. I know there's a KFC around the corner from this club I went to last week.

What the hell is that in my rear view? Aw, shit! It's the cops.

"Excuse me, sir, could you roll down your window and turn the music down a little?"

"Why are you stopping me, officer? Can't a brother drive down the street in a Lexus 400 without being harassed?"

"So, this is your car?"

"Are you kidding me or what? Yes, this is my car, here is my registration and insurance."

"I stopped you because we have had a number of car jackings in the area."

"Do I really look like a car jacker, officer?"

"Actually, you don't, but let's just pretend some car jacker took your beautiful Lexus at gun point, and I let him just whisk by me while you find a phone to call 911. Now wouldn't that make you just a little pissed?"

"Well, I'd never looked at it that way. I'm sorry I got so defensive, officer. I haven't eaten in a while."

"No problem. You're free to go. Just remember, not all policemen are bad. Most of us are God-fearing men with families who're just trying to enforce the law. Sometimes the efforts of the police cause people some occasional inconvenience, but I think it's worth it when we deter crimes."

"Thank you, officer, and you have a nice day." Damn, that was the first nice cop that I've met in my life. I guess they do exist. All right, there's KFC. I can finally get my grub on.

I always get hungry right after I break up with a woman. When my girlfriend and I were having our final conversation, all I could think was "damn, I'm hungry."

She chose to do it over the phone, however I had set the stage for her to break up with me long before she had dialed my number. Most of my previous break-ups had been pretty nasty. The process usually dragged on for a few weeks of getting angry calls and her showing up on my doorstep, trying to catch the other woman. Why do women always think it has to be another woman? Don't they realize a brother might just get tired of them?

My girlfriend's name was Denise and she initiated the whole split. Of course, I was becoming such an asshole lately, hoping to force her hand to break up with me. She finally called.

"Hi, CK?"

"Hello, Denise. How are you?"

"I'm fine. And how are you?"

"I'm hanging in there. What's happening?"

"I really need to come over and talk to ya."

The way she said "ya," made me realize the situation was serious. You see "I want to talk to ya," signifies a sort of indifference, in preparation for an inevitable talk of separation. A woman can learn a lot from her man or soon to be ex-man. If he goes along and is very rational and accommodating, he wanted to dump you also. He just didn't have the guts to do it first. This keeps his male sensitivity intact, not to mention that if he broke up with you first he has the "what goes around comes around" stigma to carry into his next relationship. I told Denise that I was really busy and that what she had to tell me, she could say over the phone.

"I just wanted to talk to you in person and tell you how much I care about you."

"I care about you too Denise. So, what's really going on?"

"There are so many things going on inside my head right now. I just need some time to figure out what I really want. Is that okay with you, CK?"

"Sure, honey, I realized you had some issues, I just didn't know how to help you through them. If it means stepping aside so you can clear your head and concentrate on the things you want the most out of life, I'll do it."

"You know I really love you, CK."

"I love you also, and I hope we can still be friends."

Now guys will say this and a woman must be careful of the insinuation. "Let's be friends," to a guy means an occasional booty call when he strikes out that night at the local club. Women, on the other hand, sincerely want to just be your friend. They tend to feel sorry for leaving you, even when it was their idea. The whole scenario drives me crazy. I wish there was a "What do you really mean?" rulebook out. The problem is so many women react to situations differently. Brothers don't want to get into the drama. The simpler the break up, the better.

MARCUS

Today is another day, which brings with it another woman for me to conquer. I can't seem to figure out what in the hell makes me dog women the way that I do. I guess it's because I can. You see when you get down to it and break it down, decent, single men are a commodity these days. Let's just put men into categories, start each one with 100 points, and then take points away for being in one of the negative categories. These are what women would consider undesirable situations for a single man to be in:

- Unemployed (30)
- Gay (90)
- Prior Imprisonment (75)
- Habitual Drug User (75)
- Uneducated(35)
- No Vehicle (20)
- More than one Previous Marriage (15)
- More than one Kid (10)
- Insensitivity (50)

Choose any of the above categories and subtract it from your original 100 points. If you get a score of more than 50 points, chances are you can have her if you want. Anything less than 50 points remaining and she won't even continue the conversation. Most women qualify a man for marriage within a few moments of meeting them. Most men qualify a woman for sex within a few moments of meeting them. That was just a very short lesson on male/female psychological dating attitude 101.

Brothers can get over on sisters so easily; we can't help but do their asses in. Once I can remember running about three sisters at the same time with the same game. I was living with a couple of homies and didn't want to bring anyone around them. I would use the excuse that they were all dogs and had no respect for women. That would keep most sisters away from visiting, like I just told them my roommates had the plague. My main girlfriend Janice was the only one that ever came over to the apartment around my boys. Anyone else would eventually get acquainted with my other apartment.

I tell women that it's my father's apartment. It really isn't my pop's apartment, but it turned out to be the sweetest hookup in the world. My partner is a real estate agent on the other side of town and one day we got to talking about properties and investing. He started talking about the Section Eight government housing program and how he was making money-renting homes through this program. He explained the whole program and I got this idea to apply for one of those properties.

The funniest thing happened. I actually qualified and received a nice one-bedroom place. It was very well built and in a nice neighborhood, unlike most of the houses in the program. Most section eight houses that I'd seen were roach-infested, rat vacation homes, with occasional plumbing and no modern amenities.

But mine had a small, well-groomed lawn, enclosed backyard and a carport for my ride. Inside of the two-story apartment was a tiny kitchen with a stainless steel sink, working refrigerator, dishwasher and garbage disposal. The living room was very cozy, complete with a matching camel colored sofa and love seat.

Someone took time to decorate the place extra special. Wall-to-wall carpeting and curtains coordinated like a spread from Better Homes and Gardens. A flight of solid wood stairs led to the second floor, I'm no expert, but it looked like some sort of expensive redwood or cherry. There was a master bedroom and additional bathroom. My total out of pocket cost was only about $150 a month, including utilities. This was less than my part of the rent I paid living with the brothers on the other side of town.

I went upstairs and was shocked by the size of the bedroom. It was similar to a master suite that hotels downtown charge $200 for one night's stay. There was a nice, sturdy queen-sized bed with matching curtains and a comforter. It was great. The bathroom was just as big. It had a separate bathtub and shower, and the toilet had its own area with a door. Shit, the toilet room was bigger than my closet at the other apartment. This whole thing made me consider driving to my other apartment, getting all of my clothes and moving into this spot today. I decided that I wouldn't be giving up my primary residence just yet.

I got this wild idea of using this place as my out-of-town father's crib. No one will ever realize that dear old dad would never be coming into town. I went all out with this idea. I got pictures of my mother, and some old photos of my father's tired ass. I placed these around with a few old albums and left out some old eight-track tapes that I picked up at a thrift store to complete the effect.

It was the perfect lie. I would meet a young lady and tell her that I'm just in town staying at my dad's place for a few days while he is out of town. If I met anyone else I would get even more creative. My dad is in the hospital and I'm watching his place until he gets better. Women were eating this shit up. They loved the fact that a black man in today's society actually had a relationship with his father. I can hear them now. "You're so sweet, that is the nicest thing I've ever heard." This would lure them right into my trap. It wouldn't be long before they would be admiring daddy's room with their legs up in the air on his bed. I was in heaven and the sweetest thing was my girlfriend didn't have a clue.

I remember one of the first conquests I had at the house. Her name was Claire. She was around twenty-two, 5'5", and blonde with a short-cropped haircut that kind of bounced when she walked. She was one of those woman you see in the gym all of the time. She had the nicest body you ever wanted to see and legs to match. You could tell she worked very hard to maintain her figure and most guys would turn their heads when she walked by. Like most of the men that saw her I was imagining what it would be like to see her body naked. I finally got my chance one-day after trading smiles at the gym. She walked right up to me and started a conversation.

This was very interesting, considering how enticed I was by this woman. We made plans for dinner and after a nice meal at a local restaurant we wound up at my "fathers" place. Just like all of the women she fell for the "this is my father's place story." We began having sex in the bed where many other women had surrendered to my charms. Of course, her body was even sexier without clothes. I was so excited I couldn't stand it. Claire was quite a freak. She was talking shit the whole time we were going at it. She was yelling things like "Yeah, right there," "Harder baby," and "Is it good to you?" I matched her word for word.

Then, the funniest thing happened. I had this little shelf-like stand over the bed with a pot of potpourri on it. I know that was a dumb ass place to put something like that, however I never had a reason to move it until today. You can probably guess what happened. The damn thing fell off the shelve and smacked Ms. Claire right on top of her head. There I was humping away and bam! At first I started looking around for the person that threw the pot on her. Of course I realized we were by ourselves. I got up, still excited, and there she was holding her head, which was bleeding, and she was covered with potpourri. I asked her if she was all right and she didn't answer me at first. There was blood all over her face and it scared me for a minute. She went into the bathroom and wiped her forehead and it turns out it was a small cut that bled a lot. I ran downstairs to the kitchen and got a towel and some ice. I stood there holding the towel on her head trying to hold back the laughter. I let it out after she started laughing. Once we both realized she would be okay we both had a good laugh. Of course that was the end of the sex, it seemed to be a dangerous endeavor at the time. We lay on the couch and she eventually fell asleep.

I woke Claire up around eleven in the evening and told her that I had to go rescue a partner of mine that was having car trouble. She got dressed and left. The real reason I had to get her out of there was so I could get back to my apartment. I had to be home in case my girlfriend called or wanted to spend the night. Claire left with the biggest lump on her forehead that I'd seen in a long time. I have to find another gym to attend, since I don't want to run into Ms. Large forehead. The beautiful thing about having a side house is women can't just drop by. Besides if Claire ever showed up again I'd just freshen up the potpourri!

A Bit More

<u>CK</u>

Today, I did something that brothers consider charity work. Charity work, community service, volunteering, pro bono, whatever your particular definition is: that's what I did.

You see most brothers consider hooking up with some butt-ass ugly woman, and not getting caught, charity work. It's a brother's way of giving back to the community, without anyone knowing of course. Most women who are considered unattractive usually have a difficult time dating, especially dating a handsome brother. They are usually very sweet and considerate, however they've had their feelings hurt several times by those handsome guys.

I hooked up with this young lady one day while kicking it at happy hour at one of the Black Angus clubs in town. Her name was Shaniqua, ugly women always have one of those hard to figure out names that end in "qua." She had a sexy figure with the nicest butt I'd seen in a while. Her dress was red and that special Lycra material that clung to her body. I approached her from behind and when she turned around, my stomach almost did a turn too. I had never seen such an ugly woman in my life. She had her hair done up and from behind could have passed for Anita Baker. When she turned around she looked like she needed a leash.

I paused for a second and realized my departure would be a little difficult, considering I'd approached her. I initiated the conversation with a simple hello.

"Hi, my name is Shaniqua. What's yours?"

"My name is CK." This was my first mistake. I normally use an alias when I'm talking to someone so dreadfully unattractive.

"Are you having a nice time tonight?"

"I am now. And don't you look handsome tonight?"

"Thank you, you look nice also. What are you drinking?"

"I'm just drinking a little Cognac."

I asked the bartender to hook us up with a Cognac and a coke.

"A coke? You mean you don't drink?"

"No, that's one habit I have never started."

"That's fine, I love a man who can handle being separate from the crowd."

"This sure is a nice place, isn't it?"

"I know, it sure is."

We pause for a moment and I'm hoping no one I know comes up to me while I'm talking to this monster. I break the ice by telling her that I'm just going to mingle a while, and to save me a dance.

"I sure will, and you do the same for me," she said.

I do a little mingling around the club and next thing I know Shaniqua is beside me asking for that dance I promised.

"Sure, Shaniqua, lead the way."

We get on the dance floor and man, I'd never seen a sister move so smoothly. We were doing the two-step like we were studying dance together. She was the perfect dance partner and I caught myself having fun. When we finished I could tell she was a little tipsy. I asked her if she would be okay getting home.

"Is that a proposition, CK?"

"I'm just trying to be a gentleman. I was just offering you a ride home."

"I came with my girlfriend and she would be pissed if I left with someone I just met."

"So tell her I'm an old friend."

"She won't believe me, she thinks she knows all of my old friends."

Shaniqua goes over and lets her girlfriend know she is getting a ride from an old friend. It turns out her girlfriend was getting her own groove on and basically blew her off.

We jump in my ride and head for her house. On the way we make small talk. The whole time I'm happy no one saw me leave the club with her ugly ass.

"This is a really nice car you have, CK."

"Thank you, Shaniqua. It's not the nicest, but it's paid for."

"I don't think I've ridden in a Lexus before."

"It's no different from any other vehicle."

"So what's a handsome man like you doing in the club by yourself?"

"I'm kind of in between relationships."

"What does in between relationships mean, CK?"

"It just means I am not really dating anyone right now."

We wind up at her house. It was located in a very nice section of town. I'm wondering why this lady has such a fine place in such a nice part of town with no car. We get up to the house and she invites me in.

"I'll just come in for a few minutes."

"So, CK, would you like a nightcap?"

"No thank you, I don't drink, remember?"

"Okay, I'll get you another coke, while I get me another Cognac."

"That sounds good."

"Can I get you anything else, CK?"

"No, this is fine, thank you."

"Would it be too bold if I went and put on something more comfortable?"

"No, go for it," I said. I sat there wondering if I should wait until she went into the back to change and make a mad dash for the door. I decided to wait and see if her body was as good as it seemed with her clothes on. She came back and did a little spin as if to suggest I check her out.

"So, what do you think, CK?"

I couldn't believe my eyes, this girl could never have been in a relationship with a real brother. She came out in a beautiful brown teddy that showed off her sexy shape and the nicest pair of breasts that appeared to be real. The thing that shocked me was the knee-high white tube socks and the high-topped Puma sneakers she wore with the teddy.

What the fuck was she thinking about? I didn't even realize they still made Puma sneakers anymore. Was she trying to begin and kill the mood all at once? I didn't know whether to bust out laughing or tell her just how stupid she looked standing there. I wished I had a camera so the brothers could see this shit for themselves. A simple description would not do the moment any justice. She must have realized something was wrong, it could've been the expression on my face. I think it was kind of a dumbfounded look.

"What's the matter, CK?"

"Oh, nothing's wrong."

"You don't act like there's nothing wrong. What is it?" she said.

I couldn't hold back any longer. I took a deep breath and let her have it. "What in the world made you put those fucking knee high white tube socks and those sneakers on with that teddy?"

"I don't know, I was just a little cold and the sneakers were the first things I saw. I just wanted to be with you and have you want me."

She started crying and I'm sure some tears dripped on those white Pumas. I decided to apologize for being so hard on her. "I'm sorry, Shaniqua, you just shocked me on the way you completed your sexy outfit."

"That's okay, and I'm sorry I put them on. I'll just take these socks and sneakers off."

"That's a good start." Now I wished she had left both of them on because she had some serious elephant feet. How could a woman with such a beautiful body not take care of her feet?

I figured I had invested enough of my precious time on this woman. Also I wasn't sure if someone had seen us leaving the club together. I decided to invest in a little bit of her sexy body. All I had to do was stay away from her face and her feet. Kissing was out of the question and I figured that if I did her doggy style I wouldn't have to look at her either. We got to doing the nasty and the girl actually had some good stuff. It's a shame it was hidden under such a monstrosity. The sex was good and I represented myself very well, not that I was worried. I had no intentions of getting with her ugly ass again anyway. This was a one shot good deal for a woman I would never even give the time of day to under normal circumstances.

We said our good-byes and I took her number with the promise to call. I knew that was a lie when I said it. There would never be another contact between us. Sorry, when you give to charity it's usually only once a year around tax time!

SISTAS

TAJ

Sisters can be so dumb sometimes. I'm not saying all sisters; however, the vast majority of stupid ass sisters make it bad on the few with a little sense. Let's forget for a moment that they have this high threshold for pain when it comes to having children. They can endure nine months of pregnancy, 24 hours of labor, and the whole time all they take is a few Tylenols. Also, sisters have the talent to search the trashcans of the world, scraping past the normal brothers, only to find the garbage on the bottom.

Don't get me wrong, this isn't a sister-bashing situation. I'm sure most brothers like myself still have a large amount of respect for our sisters and the plight that they are in today. There are a whole lot of sisters out there raising the kids of brothers who don't know or don't want to know their children. You see a lot of brothers grow up with their mother and possibly some sisters in the house. This is his first representation of the black woman. His interpretation of how to deal with this strange ass species is directly proportional to this early experience. There are a few different types of women playing the mother role that affect the brother growing up.

One mother is the one who lets the little so-called "man" of the house do whatever he wants to do with very little accountability. He'll grow up and eventually disrespect the same mother that bore his ass. This disrespect will continue throughout

He will more than likely have an extra-marital affair and rationalize the behavior as "that's how I've always been." Of course dear old mom condones all of his actions.

Another type of mother is the strict disciplinarian. She is protective, and instills in her son an intense reverence for the female gender. He must display respect for his mother and sisters at all times while growing up. She also allows him to become an independent individual by giving him a lot of responsibility. He will grow up respecting women and have the intrinsic motivation to defend their honor whenever necessary. Chivalry will be his calling card. His love will be nurturing and honest. His ultimate goal is to continue this relationship until it culminates in marriage and a family.

Finally the "mamma's boy." This brother will grow up with his umbilical cord still attached to his mother. His every decision will be made with or by his mother. Every endeavor has to have her stamp of approval, no matter what. He considers his mother to be the end all opinion for everything, even if dear mother doesn't have a clue.

These brothers will have a large amount of respect for their sisters, until a decision needs to be made. It is at this point that the sisters need to beware of the "cord." The cord can take many forms. It can be a phone cord, with speed dial and memory call button, straight to dear mother. It can be a car, or house, that conveniently has dear mother's name typed on the title. Whatever the situation, you can be sure these brothers will spend the rest of their lives asking mother what to do.

The sisters that our brothers grow up with are also products of their mother. However, they seem to grow up in denial and constant confrontation with their mother. This denial continues until they have matured, or have a family of their own. All of a sudden they go back to being like mother. You see, mother is their enemy while growing up. The sisters have all of the pressure in a household. They must learn to cook, clean, sew, iron, take care of their bodies and hair, and cater to daddy, if he is around. They also must remain responsible at all times. They're expected to dress respectfully, act like ladies, and bring the best grades home from school.

They make their parents proud until they encounter their first brother outside of the home. As soon as a sister hooks up with her first brother, all sense of reality rushes from her highly intellectual mind. This brother, in a few days, has the power to make her break all of the rules she has spent years living by. She will stay out late, talk back to mom, change her ladylike attire, and possibly start having pre-marital sex. All of this to the disappointment of dear mother, who realizes, her daughter has just repeated her own life's scenario.

This sudden loss of mental faculties continues well into her adulthood and manifests itself in every relationship with a man. This may be the reason for the plethora of dumb-ass sisters in the world today. I'm only interested in the minority of smart ones. I target them and see if I can convert them to the same type of low-self-concept sister I mentioned above. This is my way of sort of converting them over to the other side.

CK

My girlfriend, Janice, is a registered nurse, and she works all the time. It seems that I have to make a reservation to talk to her, sit down with her, and eat with her, and sex is just hit or miss. Nursing is a lucrative career. However, if a brother ever decides to date an RN, he had better be prepared to play second fiddle to her job or plan to fuck around behind her back. We started dating about a year ago and eventually fell in love. We made all kinds of compromises to spend time together.

We would hang out together, go to dinner, and make love all the time. Something changed when she got a promotion to head the nursing section of the hospital. Once she got that damned promotion, she was hardly ever home. She would work her normal shift, which was about twelve hours, hang around the hospital a few more hours, then she would be on call the rest of the evening. Anyone who has ever had a job where you're on call knows that the job will definitely call, no matter what. We weren't living together and that made it even more difficult for us to hook up.

After several months of being miserable, I met someone on the way home one day. She was struggling with some boxes as she headed to her car. She must have been moving, or rearranging her office. Maybe she had gotten fired.

"Hello, my name is CK. Can I help you with your packages?"

"No, that's okay. My father told me to beware of guys with initials for names."

"Okay, my name is actually Calvin Kevin Kelsey, but my friends call me CK."

"Nice to meet you, Mr. Kelsey. My name is Tammy Kavitz."

"Nice to meet you, also."

I just offered to help her out and before I knew it we were making plans to do lunch. Tammy was fine as hell. She was about 5'7" with long blonde hair and the cutest blue eyes you've ever seen. She had a nice slim body and a butt that made me want to watch her walk. That was the first thing I noticed on her. It wasn't too big or too small, it was just perfectly round and athletic looking.

I kept wondering what her butt would look like in the nude. Not only was she good-looking she was extremely intelligent. It turns out she had a B.A. Degree in French with a minor in Business. She worked from 7:30am to 4:30pm and was never on call. This turned me on all by itself. Tammy had a good paying job as a paralegal.

The next day we were supposed to meet for lunch and I knew we would hit it off simply because I already had a woman. It never seems to fail, when you are hooked up with someone you always meet a ton of sexy, fine ass women who are ready to mingle. I arrived at the place she picked and I was early. I wanted to get there first so she wouldn't have to wait one second for me. Women seem to count minutes like hours when they're waiting for a man. I went inside of the restaurant and placed my name on the waiting list.

It seemed a bit crowded but the hostess said the wait was only twenty minutes. I sat in the lobby and started checking the place out. It was a nice, clean, romantic restaurant with some fancy name like "La France." It was French cuisine and the place was famous for couples seeking a discreet rendezvous. The décor was straight out of France, at least it was convincing enough for anyone who has never been to France.

The waiters and waitresses were dressed in the French eatery attire, complete with unique little holders on their sides for vintage wines. I could never imagine a French restaurant without a massive wine list. These people have wine with everything, they must have a massive wine cellar.

Just as I'm picturing their huge wine cellar, Tammy walks by the front window of the restaurant, headed inside. It seemed like everything stopped and started moving again in slow motion. I could see several guys' heads moving to catch a glimpse of my date. She looked absolutely stunning. She was wearing a slinky, white spaghetti-strap dress, which was cut low enough to show her nice set of perfect breasts. Her dress clung to her fit frame and stopped midway down her thighs. This showed off her extremely long legs and brought a smile to my face.

I was thinking of how wonderful it would be to have those same legs wrapped around me. I met her at the entrance, this was to prevent any of the men with their mouths open from getting a word in. At this point I was the proudest man in the entire place!

"Hello, CK."

"Hello, Tammy. How are you?"

"I'm fine. This is really a nice restaurant, I've never been here before. How did you find such a place?"

"Some friends told me about it. I was just waiting for the right time and the right company to come here."

"The right company, would that be me, CK?"

"Yes, that would be you, Tammy. You are one of the sweetest visions my eyes have ever focused on."

"You didn't tell me you had a romantic side, CK. I hope to see some more of that, I love the attention."

"I hope to have an opportunity to show you more, Tammy. Are you hungry?"

"I'm starving, and I know such a beautiful place has got to have good food."

"What are you going to have, CK?"

"I thought about having spaghetti, since I saw your spaghetti-strap dress."

"How observant of you, CK, and you're pretty funny, also."

She thinks I'm funny. That's it, keep them laughing all the way to the bedroom.

Ms. Tammy doesn't realize this meal is just an installment on the ultimate plans I have for her. I can't wait to see this woman undressed and wet. Now I'm getting horny instead of hungry.

"CK? CK, are you okay?"

"Oh yeah, I'm okay. I was just picturing how perfect this afternoon was, and I wanted to savor the moment in my head."

"Well, is it savored, CK?"

"It sure is, so let's eat."

We finished lunch and said our good-byes. She had to get back to work and I told her that I had to also, which was a lie.

I kept thinking that I should tell her about Janice, however things were going too smooth for me to ruin things by telling Tammy about my girlfriend.

We went to lunch several times. It took about two months, but I did finally get to see Tammy in the nude. It was very intense. I thought that if I were a little less selfish, she could even qualify as a significant other. Ever since the night we spent together, she has been so clingy. I can't move an inch without her wanting to spend time with me and making plans for almost every single weekend.

She's very romantic. She would write me notes in French and tell me what they meant in English. It always sounded better in French. She still doesn't realize I already have a girlfriend. I'll probably wait a little while longer and then break up with Janice and then I'll be ready to start seeing Tammy full-time. I hadn't seen my girlfriend in so long, I'd almost forgotten I was in a relationship.

JOE

Today is the day. I decided this is it. No more sleeping around with every woman who gives me a hard on. I'm getting married, and I need to practice being true to my fiancée, Trina. My resolution lasted all of one day. The very next day I ran into this woman named Brenda.

Brenda was one of those strong willed sisters that knew what a man wanted and could handle being the other woman. You know the other woman is the one that gets treated the nicest, and she sure gets more attention than the main squeeze. She gets more things like flowers, candy, and gifts. Most of the time it isn't even her birthday, it's just because. Maybe it's brothers' way of rewarding her for keeping her place and not causing any trouble with the main woman. It may also be a way of paying her to keep her damn mouth shut. Brenda was the type of woman who knew enough to ruin a lot of brothers' relationships.

She was definitely fine. Brenda was about 5'5'', had a fairly athletic body, the biggest, roundest, juiciest ass in the world, and a tiny waist. She had this confidence about her that just pulled you in. Brenda also knew exactly what to say to a brother.

When we first met, it was at a cookout. I was with my girl, Trina, and Brenda knew it. Women can be so conniving. They see something they want and find a way to have it. It can be at the expense of another sister. To them, it really doesn't matter. Brenda came right up to me and asked me my name and what type of woman turned me on. I couldn't believe it. This woman was coming on to me while Trina stood only a few feet away. If Trina caught me getting my Mack on with Brenda, she'd kick my ass right in front of Brenda and I knew who'd be next.

Of course, I was glad to tell such a beautiful woman my name, and I added how very sexy I thought she was. We struck up a quick conversation while Trina was mingling with some of her girlfriends from college. Brenda goes into her purse and pulls out a business card with her home number on the back. It was like she came prepared to hand her number to a brother on the down low. This appeared to be a routine occurrence for her. I managed to leave without causing any drama between her and Trina.

A few days later, I decided to call Brenda up and after our conversation we had a dinner date. At first, I couldn't figure out how I was going to pull this off. Trina always kept pretty good tabs on me. However, it worked out perfectly.

Trina called me and said she would be leaving town that afternoon to attend an office training session. Trina would occasionally go out of town on business. It was never a big deal and she would just give me a call when she got wherever she was going. This was so that I wouldn't worry. She would also call when she was about to come home, so I could pick her up from the airport. It was perfect. I would always use her absence to catch up with the brothers and hang out.

They always gave me shit about being whipped or getting a kitchen pass. Once in a while, I would stumble across some new booty to get into while she was gone.

As soon as I hung up the phone with Trina, Brenda called me out of the blue. I was kind of shocked since I never gave her my number. She must have used call return from when I called her earlier. She was calling to confirm the time I was going to show up. I told her about six-thirty since Trina was leaving for the airport by five.

I arrived at Trina's place around 4:00 pm. She wasn't ready when she answered the door. I could tell from her undone hair, bra, and panties that this was going to be a long wait. Taking her to the airport was only the first thing I had to accomplish before my dinner date with Brenda. I still had to rush home, shower, get dressed before I drove over to Brenda's place.

Trina finally got dressed and packed for her business trip. We left and had to fight through rush hour traffic to get to the airport. When we arrived, she checked her bags curbside and gave me a kiss goodbye. I waited by the car for a few moments, trying not to appear to rush our separation. Then I checked my watch. It was almost five o'clock, which left me one hour and a half to do what I had to do and make it to Brenda's.

I made it home in record time, illegally using the carpool lane to cut down my travel time. There were just too many single-person vehicles using the regular lanes. I got home, showered, got dressed, and headed back out towards Brenda's house with the speed of "The Flash."

It was about six o'clock and the rush hour traffic was as thick as black smoke, however it was supposed to be only a ten to fifteen minute drive. Brenda gave me pretty good directions and I made it to her place in about twenty minutes, even with the traffic.

She lived in a nice, quaint neighborhood. There were plenty of trees and it was noticeably clean. They must have one of those fancy homeowners' associations.

Her place was a white fenced-in ranch house with a huge pecan-colored oak door that looked out of place. I walked up the driveway and noticed she had a well-kept older Ford Mustang. I rang the doorbell and after a few moments Brenda opened the door. I took one look at her, and my mouth almost hit the floor.

I had on a sports jacket, black slacks and a nice cream colored shirt. I wanted to make a good impression on our first dinner date. I anticipated us going to some nice restaurant and sharing some interesting conversation over good food.

She opened the door and all she was wearing was this scarlet teddy complete with matching stockings, garter belt and thong panties. She was even more beautiful than I had imagined and now I realized she was especially bold, greeting me at the door on our first date dressed like she was. I got excited while standing there at the door, wondering what to say. I was as hard as a piece of hickory wood. I could tell by the mischievous smile on her face that she knew she could have me.

You see a woman looks for these non-verbal signs of exciting a man. Once she realizes she has your interest you can kiss your self-restraint goodbye. She invited me in and led me to the kitchen, which was softly lit with candles. I had to pause for a moment to adjust my eyes. I then realized that dinner would be eaten right here at her house.

The dinner table was decorated with place settings, and a red candle, which matched the color of her outfit. It filled the room with a cinnamon aroma. It reminded me of the days when my mother would make sweet potato pies, only moms never dressed like this. Brenda also had one red rose, and I remember thinking that was just enough.

Brenda had already prepared spaghetti with meat sauce. She sat me down to a large helping of noodles and sauce. I have to admit it was actually pretty good, even though the noodles were overcooked. I was a little nervous during my meal, because while I was eating she had propped herself up on the table with her crotch only inches from my plate. This was one of the longest meals of my life. I'd eat a few helpings of my food while viewing this voluptuous woman in front of me. She instructed me to eat every little drop of food before I could even speak. She would be my dessert if I finished all of the food she'd put on my plate. You can guess that I wiped my plate clean with the bread she gave me. When dinner was over, she was, in fact, desert.

Brenda began straddling me right in the chair. She started kissing my chest, and slowly moved down until her head was buried in my crotch with me inside of her mouth. She took all of me, which is a lot, and I was pretty damned impressed. This was one night I knew I'd remember for a long time. We did it in so many positions, I thought I needed a program to keep up with all of them.

Brenda was definitely a completely confident woman. After all of the sex I started feeling obligated, like I owed her something for making me feel so special. Isn't that funny? I was feeling committal, go figure. She made me feel like no other woman I'd ever been with, even Trina. You see my whole objective is to leave women feeling special. Leave the woman thinking she's the only person you could make love to so good. We both had some sort of connection. I'll be damned, if she didn't make me feel just like that.

Even though I'm engaged to Trina, Brenda and I continue to sneak around behind Trina's back and get together for an occasional booty call. I can't seem to break it off with her. She's a beautiful woman, and I know she's a freak. Most of us players love a freak, however, that isn't the girl we want mommy to meet. I had a close female friend tell me that a woman's pussy is like her power. If she gives up her power too soon, she's doomed to be dogged by the very one she so quickly gave her power to. I think the whole concept is pretty funny. I know I took a lot of power from a lot of women on the first date, and I eventually dogged them out. That night with Brenda, I was the one who gave up the power.

I'm a typical man put on this earth to get as much poontang from a variety of women as quickly as he can. It probably makes most women sick to hear such a thing in this day and age of diseases and AIDS. I can't help it. Better yet I don't want to help it. I'm addicted to sex and the main stipulation is variety. "Variety is definitely the spice of life," and I'm spicing my life up before I get married. She could be tall or short, light or dark, have long or short hair, healthy (not fat) or slim (not on crack); it really didn't matter to me at all.

When I finally marry Trina, I want to say that I tried a little bit of everything, except white girls. I don't go that way. A lot of brothers are rolling around selling out to those blonde haired, blue-eyed bitches. Most of those white girls are trying to get a tan or get their lips injected with that collagen shit in an effort to emulate sisters. Well, I'm here to tell you that there isn't any booty like some sister booty. Before I finally say, "I do," I'm going to try and get as much of it as possible.

CK

My mortgage is two payments behind. My car note, pool payment, insurance, phone bill, electricity, gas and Levitz furniture account are all at least one payment behind. You might wonder how this happened. The answer is very simple. I got caught up going to Lake Tahoe playing blackjack. It is a simple game of twenty-one; however, no one told me how simple could turn to disastrous in a matter of weeks. It started out very well. I was winning about $700 a week. The more I won, the more I wanted to go up to Lake Tahoe in an effort to win again.

Soon, I went from twice a month to twice a week and, eventually, four times a week. The winning was short-lived. I wound up losing my seed money and gambling with bill money. Soon, I was writing checks to cover the losses that I incurred with a little extra to gamble some more. Every bill collector I could imagine was calling me up and trying to get paid. They were also getting creative. Most of them would call and ask to speak to Mr. Kelsey. I would answer the phone and reply that Mr. Kelsey wasn't at home. They would occasionally leave a message, but of course I never returned them. Soon they would call and simply say "Calvin"? Of course, that would get them the same response as asking for Mr. Kelsey. But, one day, a woman working for the company that financed my car called. I answered on the second ring.

"Hello, is CK there?" she asked.

"Yes, this is CK, who is this?"

"This is Susan from the McKinney Financing Company. I'm calling about your past due account on your car."

I was dumbfounded. I couldn't even reply for a few moments.

"CK, are you still there?"

"Yes, I'm still here, and I realize that I have a past due account."

"So, what are we going to do about that past due amount?" she asked.

"I plan to make a payment on the first of the month," I said.

"You realize that that is five days from now," she said.

"Yes, I realize that. What do you think I'm stupid?"

"No, I just think you need to start owning up to your financial responsibilities."

They always start talking to you like you're a little kid when you are in debt. How dare this perfect stranger call me by my initials so that I would think she was a friend! She then proceeds to chastise me like a child who should've known better. I decided to do the respectable thing and talk out a payment plan with this lady. She was probably going to get some sort of incentive award for finally getting to talk to an evasive client.

"CK, I need to know what you plan to do to bring your account to date."

"I plan to make that payment in a few days and another payment fifteen days later."

That seemed to suffice for her. She updated her computer and hung up the phone. I could tell I was starting to get deeper and deeper. This gambling thing doesn't hit you all at once, it sort of sneaks up on you after a while. When the checks bounce the fees cost you more and more. Past-due notices get more stringent with their language, and when the dust finally settles, your debts outpace your income. You know you're in trouble then.

The more you try to catch up on a gambling debt, the worse it becomes. The hardest thing in the world is to admit you are obsessed with gambling. It's the same thing a drug addict or alcoholic probably goes through. I thought I had the situation under control. Thinking that as soon as I start winning again, I'd raise enough money to pay all of the past due bills and get my life back together. Unfortunately, before that happened, I began looking for things around the house that were valuable. I needed some quick cash to gamble and make some money. I started with my bicycle, rationalizing that I never ride it anyway. I got about 1/3 of what it was worth, about $75. This pissed me off, but something was better than nothing. I continued to find little things like appliances, and knick-knacks; anything that was worth a few dollars. Soon I was out of stuff to sell and out of money also. One day I wrote a check, knowing full well that I didn't have the money to cover it, to go gambling. I lost the entire amount and didn't know how I was going to cover the check.

All kinds of things ran through my head. I realized how people get into a rut and rob a bank or a liquor store for that quick buck. I was determined not to slip down that road. I decided to take the only other option and that was to milk a few silly ass women for their money. I picked women who I'd just stopped talking to or dumped, particularly those who'd told me that they would do anything for me or be there for me when I needed them.

I made up a list of about six different women and wrote their names and phone numbers down. Their names were Janice, Stacy, Gloria, Dianne, Alison, and Mary. It just so happens all but one of them, Janice, were white women that I had dated at one time or another. I started with Dianne since she was the one I had most recently broken up with and I knew she still had feelings for me. I dialed her number and it had been changed, however the recording gave me the new number.

This was just like Dianne, she was always very thorough and always dotted her "i's" and crossed her "t's." She must have moved to another apartment. I dialed her new number.

"Hello?" she said.

"Hi, Dianne. This is CK. How are you?"

"I'm fine, and to what do I owe this marvelous surprise, CK?"

"Well, I don't have time to beat around the bush. You remember when you said you'd be there for me whenever I needed you?"

"Of course, I remember, CK. What's going on?"

"I need some money and I need it real fast. Can you help me?"

"I can't do much, CK. I just moved into a new home. I had to pay all kinds of closing costs and I had to have a pool in the back that cost me $17,000 cash. How much money do you need anyway?"

"I need about $5,000."

"I'm sorry, CK, I can only afford about $500 right now."

"If that's all you can give me, I'll take it," I said.

This scenario was repeated with Janice, Stacy and Gloria. When I was finished I had raised some attitudes, with my nerve of calling women that I hadn't talked to in a while. I also managed to raise about $2,500. This wasn't too bad considering how long it had been since I'd slept with any of them. I was getting the cash and didn't even have to give up any loving. Now that is pretty damn good if you ask me.

The last phone call was to Mary. Now Mary is kind of special. We met at this club about three years ago and all I could think about was how freaky she looked. She's about 5'9'', tall, with long, bright red hair, and she was sort of big-boned. I remember wondering if the red was all the way down to her spot. Guys tend to think of wild things like that when we meet a woman. Women wonder if the guy they just met would make a nice husband, maintain a job and take care of the kids. The brother just wants to know whether or not she can dance. If she can dance pretty well, she'll be able to do some other things good too. I finally ran up on the tall, wild looking, red head that turned me on and said hello.

"Hi, my name is Mary. What's up?"

"What's up?" I thought to myself, is this one of those "I look like a white girl but wish I was a sister" acts? Just then her clearly black girlfriend walked up and said hello. Her name was Tamara and she was also very good looking. She looked familiar at first, but I realized I had never gotten any of that booty so I just said hello back. They whispered in each other's ears and then Tamara left.

I asked Mary, "What was that all about?"

"Oh, just girl talk. Would you like to dance?" she said.

I quickly said yes and we headed for the dance floor. I couldn't help anticipating this sexy looking red head white girl who wished she was a sister getting on the dance floor and not knowing her right from her left. When we got on the dance floor I was amazed at how smooth the girl moved. She was spinning around me and grabbing my shoulders and pretending to go down on me. This was one dance guys wait a long time for. You know a woman who dances this smooth and erotic has got to be a freak in the bedroom.

After several records on the dance floor we decided to sit and talk. We begin talking about simple stuff, like what each of us liked to do. Then here comes her girlfriend. She pulls Mary to the side and they begin that silly whispering again. I just sit there like the worker at the end of a shift who just missed the bus, and the next one comes in 30 minutes. Mary interrupted my thoughts by grabbing my hand and asking to talk to me.

"I thought that was what we were doing before your girlfriend came along," I said.

"No, I really need to talk to you. Can we go outside?" she asked.

"Sure, can we get back in if we go outside?" I asked.

"It doesn't matter. Where is your car?"

"My car is parked out back." I hoped this wasn't one of those "I hope he has a nice car so I can date him" deals. Women can be so materialistic. I'll just play along but I know the deal. We get to my car and her mouth drops.

"This isn't your car. It's a Lexus," she said.

"What's the matter? A black man can't own a Lexus?" I said.

"I'm sorry, you just didn't seem like the type of guy that owns a Lexus," she said.

"What do you mean by that?" I asked.

"Most of the guys that come to the club who own Lexuses find a way to let you know while you're in the club. They may wave their Lexus key chain in your face, tell you some lame story that stars their car, or flash a Lexus wallet pretending not to have anymore business cards. One way or another, they'll let you know. You never led on that you even had a car, much less a Lexus."

"It's just a car. I just happen to like the smooth ride and dependable record that the Lexus has."

"Could you give me a ride home?"

"How did you get here?"

"I drove my car."

"Then why do you want me to give you a ride home?"

"I gave my keys to my friend Tamara. She wanted to drive over to some guy's house who she just met, and fuck his brains out."

"Are you kidding me or what?"

"No I'm not kidding, so can you give me a ride or not?"

"Sure, I'll give you a ride home."

Before I could say another word Mary pushed up to me and stuck her tongue in my mouth. I have to admit the girl could kiss. This reminded me of another thing that the brothers always say. A woman that can kiss well gives head even better. My nature was getting hard just thinking about this. She stopped kissing me and looked at me for a moment. It was like she was trying to get her focus back. I wanted to kiss her again and again, and possibly the whole night.

There was something about Mary that caught my attention. She had a kind of arrogance, yet a carefree attitude about herself. I later found out that her parents were very well off and dumped money on her like there was no tomorrow. Now, I was faced with a deficit of $2,500 and only Mary left to call. I dialed her number and got the answering machine. I began to leave a message and all of a sudden she picked up. She was clearly screening her messages, just like a player.

"Hi, Mary, what's up?"

"Nothing, much, CK, how are you?"

"I'm fine."

"I know you need something. You haven't called me in almost three months. What is it, CK?"

"Why are you acting like that, Mary, I'm just calling to ask what you've been up too."

"You're full of shit, CK. Don't be trying to play me, I know your ass too well. Just tell me how much money you need."

"Okay, Mary, I need $2,500."

"CK, I'm not going to keep bailing your ass out. Have you been gambling again?"

"Yes, I am, but I'm going to stop."

"You'd better stop. I really think you need to go get some help with this problem. They have programs to help you through this gambling addiction. I swear, CK, this is the last time I'm going to give you a dime to bail you out of some gambling debt. Also you're going to pay me back every penny you've borrowed from me!"

"So you're going to help me?"

"Yes, but God be my witness, this is the last time, CK, the last time!"

I hung up the phone with a real sense of accomplishment. In only a few hours I had raised $5,000. That's more than some public officials can raise in a day. Mary was a little pissed and I can't blame her. She's bailed me out so many times it isn't even funny. I know she said this was the last time she'd help me, however that's what she said the last time I needed her help. I do still care for her, and I don't know why I'm always calling her when I'm in trouble. If everything were going fine, I probably wouldn't even think about her. I know that's really foul, but it must be the dog in me. The bottom line is that I got the money I needed to bail my ass out. Now there is no reason to go to counseling. I'll be fine until the next time I have to make some "calls for cash."

TAJ

I woke up today and decided I was going to my mother's church. I found one of my nice suits in the closet and spent about an hour trying to find a tie. I got dressed and actually looked like I'd been to church recently, which was definitely not true.

I should've knocked on the door since I hadn't been in about two years. I actually remembered where it was. My mother's church was huge and the parking lot was packed. I found a space, parked and went up to the front door. I paused at the front doors and waited. I'm not sure what I was doing, maybe waiting for a sign from above that it was okay to enter. Finally I just opened the door, went inside and had a seat in one of the back pews. I don't know what possessed me to wake up and attend the services today, I guess God just puts things like this on your mind.

I always enjoyed the Sunday service scene. There were your usual sisters with their large hats decorated with lots of fruits, vegetables, and flowers. Everyone was trying to outdo one another with nice white dresses handsewn by the church seamstress. There were even a few modern day women in the church. They were wearing above-the-knee dresses and clinging skirts. None of the attire I was used to seeing when I grew up. The church was a little different from the last time I was there. They had clearly made some improvements inside. You know every church has a continuous tax-free building fund. Each Sunday, they would take up a building fund offering and I know it was over a $1,000, since the church was filled to the gills. Of course that was only one of many offerings during a typical service. The pastor would make everyone feel guilty if they didn't forget about gas in their cars, bills at home, and dig deep into their pockets and donate. The usual understanding is that God will give whatever you give back to you about ten-fold.

One of the church sisters recognized me. She came over in the middle of the service, kissed me on the cheek and said hello. She left me with a God bless you and come back more often. This is one of the things about the church that I missed a lot. The people are genuine and real, not like those fake ass people you meet in the club scene.

I also came to see all of the beautiful saved sisters in the church. I may be filled with the devil himself, but the Lord knows He has a host of fine women in the church. There seemed to be a lot of young women also. I figured they had returned to the church after listening to Kirk Franklin songs in the local clubs. I remember the first time I heard his hit, "Stomp," when I was in a club downtown. I started dancing to the song and after a couple of verses I listened to the words.

> *"Lately I've been going through something that's really got me down. I need someone, somebody to help me come and turn my life around. I can't explain it, I can't obtain it, Jesus your love is so, it's so amazing, it gets me high, up to the sky, and when I think about your goodness it makes me wanna stomp. Makes me clap my hands, makes me wanna dance and stomp. My brother can't you see? I've got the victory. Stomp!"*

The entire time I was listening to the words, I couldn't understand why they were playing it in the club. It made everyone get on the dance floor and do his or her own version of the "Stomp."

But, Kirk Franklin didn't have anything on the choir in this church. The choir was marching forward to sing some of their songs, and there must have been about fifty members. I always enjoyed the choir at my mother's church. They always sound like they are singing for the Lord and He is right there in the church. There was one special young lady who would lead most of their songs. Her name was Angelica Houston, and she sounded just like Whitney Houston with a pair of angel's wings. When she sang a song like "Amazing Grace," or "His Eye Is On The Sparrow," there wouldn't be a dry eye in the house. I mean in the church.

The choir sang about two songs prior to the first offering. Anyone who attends a Pentecostal church realizes that there will be approximately five or six offerings during the service. The first one was for the pastor, then the building fund (like I mentioned earlier), the sick and shut in, Tithes, the consecrated prayer offering, and the choir instrument and robe offering. All of these offerings will leave the average worshiper poor and tired. It must have taken about 30 minutes to get them all in. The choir was singing so good everyone probably thought they had just paid for a live concert. I put my fair share into the offering and then some.

The time came for the preacher to come forward and give the gospel of Christ. He started with a simple passage of prayer. He then wanted everyone to turn their Bibles to the passages he had prepared the week prior. Now I knew there was no way the preacher knew I was coming to church today, but his words singled me out in the midst of every saint in the house.

Our first passage was the first Book of Galatians 5:16 and he read the following: *"Verse 16: This I say then, Walk in the Spirit, and ye shall not fulfill the lust of the flesh."*

He then made us turn to 1 Corinthians 6:12-20. And it spoke of similar things such as lust and sins of the flesh. He talked about the body being a temple of the Holy Spirit and said sins against the temple would be dealt with more harshly than other sins.

He continued to read each verse, and I felt that the whole congregation turned to look at me like they knew he was talking to me. It seemed that every time I attended church the preacher's well-prepared sermon was directed toward me. I could pick a church that I'd never been to, and sure enough, the sermon would almost have my name on it. I just wanted to show up and blend in.

The preacher was in rare form with the traditional Pentecostal dramatically delivered sermon. It was complete with the organist induced fiery emphasis on each word he uttered. I just sat there sinking in my seat. He was talking about everything that I was doing now in my life. Fornication was an understatement. I was getting with as many women as I could and had the same thoughts about the many women here as I first walked in. Now the preacher had attacked my conscience and my character, since it was me who was living the words he was speaking. The preacher finished his sermon; it had lasted almost an hour. The man could definitely talk and talk long. He gave the benediction and all I could think about was getting out of there.

I left the church with a feeling of guilt similar to that of a person caught red-handed stealing. I'm sure I'll come back but not until I decide to get myself together. I would rather the preacher talk to someone else.

JOE

The brothers and I are getting together for a few drinks and to plan my bachelor party. CK decides to show up even though he doesn't drink. We hook up at this happy hour spot and I began by asking them what type of party we should have?

Taj lets us know what he wants right off the bat. "I'm down for some fine, big ass sisters wearing next to nothing, and a few hours later nothing at all. They have to be freaky and down for whatever. No white women, though. You hear me CK?"

"What the fuck you mean no white women, Taj? I didn't know you were the one picking the flavors for the party. I think we should have a few types of women and sample a little of everything," CK said.

"Well, I'm sorry, CK, I am strictly down for the dark mocha chocolate coffee my brother," Taj said.

"I'm down for the same sisters, Taj. I just don't mind if a little cream gets added to my coffee," CK said.

Marcus jumps in with his two cents.

"I'm with CK. It don't matter to me what the hell color the woman is, as long as she is a freak. She can be White American, African American, Spanish, German, French, English, Asian, or whatever, just as long as she is down for whatever. Besides you brothers are making a lot of decisions, why don't we ask the man of the hour what he wants?"

"I was thinking of doing something different from the normal bachelor party," I said.

They all looked at me and said, at the same time, "Something different?"

"Yeah, I've thought about us getting together and doing some new, ultimate bachelor party shit."

CK immediately bursts out, "Joe what type of freaky shit do you have in mind?"

"Just listen up for a minute. I thought since I am about to ruin my life and become a married man, we might do something unprecedented instead of a typical bachelor party with strippers. You are all my brothers and each and every one of us is an outstanding player in his own right. Isn't that right?"

"Yeah, yeah," the brothers all say together.

"Well, Trina, my dear fiancée, wanted us to do this bachelor thing one week prior to the wedding, so that I wouldn't be late for the wedding. In that case, I thought we could get creative on my bachelor weekend. I thought we would drive up to Lake Tahoe and spend the weekend doing the bachelor thing."

"Why would we have a bachelor party in Lake Tahoe? Isn't that a place for gambling, Joe?" Taj asked.

"I know you can gamble there, but we're not going to gamble. There will be a bet involved, but no gambling.

"This is what I want to do. We go up for the weekend and each of us will get a hotel room. I know it'll be expensive, but hear me out. Once we are all checked in, we spend the next two days finding out who has the tightest game."

"Do you mean what I think you mean, Joe?" Marcus asked.

"You all know what I mean. I want to spend the weekend with my brothers trying to find out where I fit in the pecking order among some players who have skills. I think I can get more ass in a weekend than each and every one of you."

"You're kidding, right, Joe? I know I can get more women than your whipped ass. That's why Trina got your ass walking down the aisle. You can't Mack like you used to homey," CK said.

"Fuck you, CK, I know my ass will wind up ahead of you, even if Lake Tahoe has a bunch of white women," Joe said.

"This shit is crazy. All of you know that I am the darkest, sexiest, most physically superior being in this room," Taj said.

"All you brothers are dreaming. You know when I walk into any room with you brothers the women notice my 6'9" ass first. And once they notice me, the rest is history. There is no way they're going to look down at you little Negroes," Marcus said.

"I got your Negro, right here!" Joe says, grabbing his crotch with his hand. "So, since all of you are talking shit, what's up?"

"I'm down. My game is tight," CK said.

"Bet, you'll be sorry for coming up with this idea, Joe," Marcus said.

Taj just looks at all of us and starts laughing.

"What the fuck is so funny, Taj?" Joe asks.

"I'm laughing because all of you brothers are going to be calling me the man, when this shit is over."

Joe began with the rules of engagement for the weekend.

"The way the shit will work is for each piece of ass you get, you have to keep her panties.

"If you get the booty and forget to get the panties, it doesn't count. Each pair of panties counts as a point. The one with the most points at the end of the weekend is the winner of the contest and will be the man! Also the winner gets to choose one favor from the rest of the brothers that they must do. Is every one down with the rules?"

They answer with a unanimous, "Hell yeah!"

MARCUS

I'm chilling out at my actual apartment with my roommates, Shawn and David. They're just two brothers who wish they could be players like me. After watching some TV and playing cards, we all decide to go hang out at the mall. They just finished building this massive mall about twenty minutes from our apartments and we hadn't checked it out yet. I got dressed in some of my best FUBU gear and LUGZ boots, and I was ready to get my Mack on.

My two roommates were looking equally cool. Shawn was one of those Rastafarian, Busta Rhymes looking brothers. I never thought he was good looking at all, however he kept plenty of women. There are a lot of women who like that roughneck type and Shawn fit that bill to a tee.

Now David was another story. David had that slim, Steve Erkle thing going on. Of course, the women in his life were few and far between. Most of the time he would just hang around and wait for the leftovers from Shawn and I. Usually, he got leftovers from Shawn, since I rarely shared any woman I'd had. The only time I would share is if we had some freak of mine over for a two-on-one. That has happened with Shawn and I. David was never brave enough to take part in the festivities. However, he probably listened in on us while he jerked off.

We took Shawn's ride, which was a dilapidated Jeep. The kind that the consumer reports always gave bad ratings because it frequently rolled over on drivers when turning at high speeds.

It was an extremely hot day, despite having the jeep's top off and getting a nice wind. The temperature was about 80 degrees and the humidity was almost as high. The trip to the mall should have taken twenty minutes but it took almost an hour because of the heavy traffic. I don't know why we waited until 4:00 in the afternoon to go to the mall when every one in the city was getting off work. Everyone seemed like they had road rage. There were people waving their hands out of windows, shouting obscenities and honking on their horns. I guess this was how they unwound after a hard day's work in Sacramento.

We got to the mall, and the parking lot was just as crowded as the traffic we'd just gotten out of. It took us about ten to fifteen minutes to find parking. I almost made Shawn park in one of the handicapped spots. Judging by his jeep, mall security would have thought some wounded Vietnam veteran had parked there. We caught an old couple leaving the mall and followed them down one of the lanes until they got into their car. They must have thought we were going to rob them or something because they pulled out in a real big hurry. We did look like a bunch of thugs. We all climbed out of the jeep, and it seemed to take a lifetime for us to get to the front doors of the mall. The only thing I wanted to do was to get something to drink.

"Where is the food court, Shawn?" I asked.

"I've never been to this mall, remember. We'll have to go inside and find out where it is. That's where all of the ladies hang out anyway. They'll be standing around nursing a coke for hours. The first female that asks me to buy her some fries or anything else, I'm going to go off on her," David said.

The Mall was supposed to be the largest in the city. It had about 175 stores, shops and restaurants and, like most malls, complete with all of the booty you can watch in a day. We got into the mall and the air conditioning felt extremely good after the heat of the day.

There were all kinds of women and they were all over the place. They were young, old, white, black, Hispanic, and a few other foreign flavors as well. That's why we enjoy going to the mall, it's like a booty-watchers convention.

Our first order of business was to find something cool to drink. We walked up to one of those fancy lemonade stands, the one with a bunch of lemons floating around in a large dispenser. I always thought that was a ploy to get you to think that the lemonade was fresh-squeezed. I still say the shit is concentrated, with a few fresh lemons thrown in for aesthetics. The drinks cooled us off pretty well.

Shawn and David began shopping and booty watching. Most of the shops in this mall were for those 90210 teenagers who are buying clothes to go see some group like NSYNC or The Back-Street Boys. Backstreet, my ass, the closest things those pretty white boys have been to a back street was a backdrop on a video shoot.

I'm chilling at this lemonade stand while my two roommates gawk and whistle at several young ladies passing by. I notice this fine sister coming out of Victoria's Secret on the second level of the mall. She entered the glass elevators and descended to the same level I was on. I was hoping she had to pass my way, however I was prepared to give chase if necessary.

She was extremely tall, about 6'1", and it seemed like her legs belonged to a thoroughbred stallion. She had flowing black hair that touched her slender shoulders. Her athletic figure was accentuated by the clingy brown sweater dress she was wearing. I yearned for an up close and personal view. She was almost close enough for me to touch and then I realized how I must look.

I was looking like a broke rap artist, and she was as classy as a baby grand piano. I was ready to retreat and then our eyes met. There we were looking at each other, as she seemed to glide by. We never took our eyes off of one another, and it seemed to take ten minutes for her to cover the short distance to the exit door of the mall. Then she just stopped and looked at me like she was calling me over. I answered her call and walked up to her. We exchanged pleasantries, and I introduced myself.

"Hello, my name is Marcus. What's yours?"

"My name is Angelica. It's nice to meet you, Marcus."

"No, the pleasure is all mine. If you don't mind me saying, you are the most beautiful woman I've seen in a long time."

"Thank you, Marcus, that was very sweet of you to say."

"That's the truth. So are you just catching up on some shopping?"

"I just stopped in my favorite store to pick up something to spoil myself."

"I can see any man wanting to spoil you, including myself."

"You're just full of compliments, aren't you, Marcus?"

"I'd like to be complimenting myself by being with you."

"That sounds good. So tell me, Marcus, are you a ball player or something?"

"Yeah, but I don't really want to get into that. I was glad you didn't recognize me."

"I don't get to watch too many sporting events so I wouldn't even know which team plays for which city."

I was standing there thinking how could her mother have known she would grow into such an Angel. She was the kind of woman that could make a man give up all of his bad habits just to spend one day with her. She seemed to be equally intrigued by me and apparently disregarded my attire. Angelica gave me her phone number and asked me to call her this evening, then she turned and left.

I went back to Shawn and David with this blank look on my face. I'd just been close enough to kiss an Angel and now had her phone number. Shawn and David continued their gawking and whistling. I was ready to leave anticipating my eventual conversation with Miss Angelica. After some coaxing, Shawn and David finally agreed to leave the mall as it was starting to get dark outside. My only mission was to get home so I could make my important call.

Getting back home was quick and painless. There was hardly any traffic at all. As soon as we arrived home, I jumped out of the jeep before it came to a complete stop. I didn't want my roommates trying to tie up the phone before I had a chance to use it. I'm sure those young bimbos they talk to would understand I needed to call an angel.

"Hello, may I speak to Angelica?"

"This is Angelica. Who's this?"

"This is Marcus. We met earlier at the mall, and you gave me your number."

"Oh yes, Marcus. How are you? I'm glad you called."

"I'm fine. I'm glad you gave me your number. I was damn near drooling when I saw you."

"My, Marcus, you really know how to make a woman feel good about herself. So what are you doing this evening?"

"Nothing much, I really didn't have any plans. Did you have something in mind?"

"Do you think I could talk you into visiting me tonight? I'd be willing to show you that thing I bought today to spoil myself."

"Tonight?" I couldn't disguise the sound of disbelief in my voice.

"Yes, tonight. Is that a problem Marcus?"

"No, that's not a problem at all, Angelica. Just give me the directions, tell me what time and I'm there."

She gave me the directions to her place and I hung up the phone.

"Yes, I'm the man."

I jumped into the shower, got dressed and put on some of my best cologne and took two rubbers out of my twelve-pack box. I was determined to rock Angelica's world.

I made it to her place in about thirty-five minutes. Her neighborhood was a bit run down, but that didn't matter. I was on my way to see a beautiful butterfly in this cocoon. I found her house and couldn't help noticing a bunch of toys spread across the grass outside. I blew this off and thought they probably belonged to the neighbor's kids who'd been playing in her yard.

I rang the doorbell and wasn't prepared for the surprise waiting for me on the other side of the door.

A small boy answered and said, "What's up, dog?"

I didn't say anything for a minute and he repeated his words.

"I said 'what's up, dog'?"

"First of all, I'm not your dog. Is Angelica home?"

"What you want with my moms?" he said.

"Angelica is your mother?"

"Yeah, why you wanna know?"

"Never mind. Forget I asked." I was about to make a quick about face and get the hell out of there. Just then Angelica came to the door, snatching the little kid out of the way. She was looking as gorgeous as she had when I'd seen her earlier.

"Hello, Marcus. I'm really sorry about my son Kyle. He gets a bit protective at times."

I wanted so much to be mad at her for not telling me she had a child at home, but we never really had time to discuss much of anything.

"That's all right, Angelica, thanks for inviting me over." I was focusing on her beauty as she beckoned for me to come inside. I didn't hear her at first and I caught myself just staring at her.

"Marcus, don't just stand in the doorway, come on in."

"Oh, yeah, I'm sorry." Kyle was standing behind the door as I went inside with his arms folded like a soldier of the Gestapo.

All of a sudden, things became even more interesting as three other children ran into the room. There were two boys and a little girl, none of whom could've been more than five years old. They were yelling and screaming and, apparently, fighting over a toy that the little girl was holding. The two boys were smaller than her and were tugging at her from both sides.

The struggle ended abruptly when Angelica shouted, "Shut the hell up and go to your rooms."

There was perfect quiet and soon the children were out of sight. The living room floor was covered with videotapes, game cartridges and toys. I began maneuvering around the mess, like a GI trying to get around a minefield.

"You have to excuse my kids, sometimes they don't know how to act when someone visits. They are usually well-behaved until company shows up. Would you like something to drink, Marcus?"

"No, thank you. I'm not thirsty."

I felt sorry for her little girl, who was outnumbered by her rough brothers. Angelica told me all of their names, but I wasn't trying to remember anything about those crumb snatchers. I wanted to escape right away. This whole scene was a violation of my own personal commandments. No woman with a child was #1. I was breaking that commandment four times over.

Without much fanfare, Angelica led me to her bedroom, which was surprisingly clean and well kept. She probably never allowed her kids to go into her room. She left me for a moment and I contemplated how I would make my escape from my current situation. Angelica was definitely beautiful, however not enough that I wanted to be around four kids, especially not the kids from hell.

When she returned to the room I realized that the house was all of a sudden very quiet. She must have put the demonic children to bed, or maybe she was in their rooms performing an exorcism. I could see them with their heads spinning around 360 degrees while she prayed over them.

Angelica was wearing a very revealing silk robe with a black teddy underneath. It must have been the one she purchased at the mall. Before I could say anything, she dropped the robe and stepped out of the teddy. This woman had the most beautiful body

I'd ever seen. How could she have had four children? I looked as hard as I could for her stretch marks and there was no evidence of any labor at all on Angelica. She didn't have a mark in sight, and definitely no "I've just had kids" fat.

I reached into my pants and pulled one of the rubbers out. After a few moments of kissing and caressing, I began to make love to Angelica. This was my opportunity to see if she was as smooth and gentle to make love to as she appeared to be. We spent about an hour or so going through several positions and I had guessed right, she was amazing. I was enjoying sex with Angelica so much I caught myself rationalizing being around her and her children. When we finished making love, Angelica just relaxed with her head on my chest. There I was, with the finest woman I'd ever met. I'd just finished making love to her and now I wanted to get as far away from her as I could. She lay there with her head resting on my chest and must have dozed off. I waited a while and slowly eased my way out from under her.

This would definitely be a day to remember. I laughed at the thought of going to the mall with Shawn and David, never buying anything, and then meeting Angelica. I knew I could get a return invitation from Angelica, but sometimes once is enough for a brother. Just knowing she wants you again is usually sufficient for the average brother's ego. I remembered my commandments after I got up out of bed. I stood there over the bed, staring at Angelica's face. There was just enough light from the window to see her. Damn, she was beautiful! I thought about waiting around to see if she was as good looking when she first woke up. But, I knew this would be the last time I ever laid eyes on her. I found my clothes, using the faint light from the window and left the room.

I tried to feel my way back to the front door. I stumbled and fell after tripping on the toys and games on the floor. Just then a small beam of light was smacking me in the face like a slap. I put my hand up to shield my eyes from the light and to see who it was. There on the other side of the room, shining a flashlight down on me, was Kyle. Angelica's oldest demon, he appeared like a hunter pouncing on the wolf caught in his booby trap of toys and shit.

"What's up, dog?" he said.

"I'm trying to go home, and I'm not your dog."

"So, what was you doing banging my momma?"

"That's none of your little smart ass business. When is the last time you got a beating?"

"I don't get whippings. My momma says that I'm her man of the house."

"You are a little boy and you should be taught some manners by a man."

"Well, it ain't going to be you since you ain't my daddy. And since this is my house, you can get the hell out."

"Kyle, you little bastard. I'll leave with pleasure."

I could see myself killing this little boy and burying him in the front yard under all of the toys. They wouldn't find him for months, at least until the other kids decided to play with the toys out there. Damn my foot hurts from tripping over all of those toys and shit on the living room floor.

Angelica's probably the finest woman I've met in a long time, and she may make sweet love, however she'll never have to worry about seeing me again. I broke one of my ultimate commandments, no woman with children. I want to get as far away from Angelica's possessed children as I can. If I ever run into that damn son of hers again, I hope I'm driving a car, little bastard.

TAJ

Brandi is one woman that is pretty cool. I'm always hooking up with her to have drinks or hang out. It's pretty nice having a woman who is smart attractive and you can just hang out together. I've been thinking about her for a while I think I should give her a call.

"Brandi, this is Taj. What's up, girl?"

"Nothing much, Taj, what's up with you?"

"Oh, I was just calling to see how my buddy was doing today."

"How am I doing? As if you really care about how I'm doing."

"Sure I care about how you are doing. I called you didn't I?"

"Yes, you did, but I haven't heard from you in two months. You call that thinking about me?"

"Okay, so I've been a little remiss in calling one of my true friends. What have you been up to anyway?"

"I've just been chilling out trying to find me a decent man."

"What about me, I'm a man?"

"Taj, we've been friends for almost five years why would we start dating now? Besides I already know you're a dog."

"How come every time a woman finds out you are single, uncommitted and just dating that equals being a dog?"

"You tell me, Taj. It's probably because in your quest to remain single or play the field, you wind up dogging out the women you leave behind."

"That may be true, but, it's never something I set out to do, it just happens."

"By the way, Taj, I have a girlfriend I want you to meet. She is just like your ass and maybe you need to hook up with someone with the same attitude you have."

"Don't tell me you want me to do a blind date?"

"Well, what do you want from me, a picture and a resume?"

"You forgot the medical report also."

"Taj, you are so full of yourself, don't you trust your true friend?"

"I trust you, I just know how those blind dates turn out."

"How do they turn out, Taj?"

"Either she is ugly as hell with no personality, or she is fine as frogs' hair and strait-jacket crazy."

"My girlfriend Sharon isn't either one of those, she happens to be a very nice sister. She works as a pharmacist, and owns two houses, a dollar store, and recently sold a pharmacy to a large chain. The girl has a lot going for her."

"Why doesn't she have a man already?"

"Like I said, she has a similar attitude to yours. 'There's nothing a man can do for me that I can't do for myself'."

"If that isn't an attitude, what is?"

"She just says that all the time. I know better than that. When we go out, she's always getting hit on and saying how sweet this one probably is, wouldn't he make a nice husband or I bet he would make some nice babies."

"Babies, you know I don't want no part of that. Don't women know when you mention the word baby, most brothers turn tail and run? Sisters think all they have to do is have your baby, and then they automatically got you.

"We never do anything like family planning, where both people in the relationship are responsible and plan to bring a child into the world together. I really don't think getting child support from two or three different guys is standing by your man."

"Damn, I didn't know you were so set against the baby thing. I'm sorry I mentioned it. So, do you want to meet Sharon or what?"

"Sure I'll meet her, but it has to be at your place, and you'd better have your ass there."

"Good, she's coming over this evening around seven. What time can you be here?"

"You had the whole thing planned out, didn't you? I guess I can be there about quarter 'til seven. Should I bring anything?"

"No, I've got everything under control. Just bring your charming self and leave your attitude home. Okay, Taj?"

"What do you mean by that?"

"I just want you to be nice to Sharon. She's been dogged out so many times. She deserves a nice night with a real man."

"Thanks, Brandi. I'll see you later, and I'll be on my best behavior."

This blind date stuff is taboo. I really hate someone hooking me up. However, I always thought that if I got married someday, it would be someone that one of my close friends hooked me up with.

Sharon had better at least be good looking. I refuse to sit around the whole night staring at a damn monster. Brandi is always trying to hook me up. The last few times, the sisters were pretty nice at first. And then the real person came out after a few drinks. Both of them were some desperate, just-want-to-get-laid-freaks. Of course, I obliged and ignored the messages they would leave on my answering machine. I'll give Ms. Brandi one more chance to redeem herself.

It's that time, so I headed out the door on my way to Brandi's house for my blind date. I get over to Brandi's house about ten minutes to seven and ring the huge doorbell attached to the even larger marble doorway.

Brandi opens the door and she's looking pretty damn fine. I better stop looking at her that way. She set me straight before and told me I didn't have a chance because we've been friends so long.

"Hello, Taj, how are you? You are looking mighty tasty this evening."

She leans over and kisses me on both sides of my face like one of those Italian mobsters in the movies do before ordering a hit on you. That thought made me even more nervous about my blind date.

"Thank you, Brandi. You look very well yourself."

This causes her to do a little spin around to let me get the full view.

"You think so, Taj?"

"Sure. Now where is the beast? I mean your friend?"

"Stop playing, Taj. I told you she is not a beast. As a matter of fact, I'll show you a picture before she gets here."

"I hope you're not going to show me one of her baby pictures and let me figure out how she looks now."

"Please don't be silly, Taj. This picture is only a few weeks old. We went to the beach, some guy took our picture together and we had copies made."

"Damn, you look good, Brandi. How come I've never seen you in a bikini before?"

"Cut it out, Taj. You're supposed to be checking out your blind date before she gets here."

"I know. She's very attractive. I'm glad she isn't one of those monsters the brothers are always trying to hook me up with. I'm sure she'll be sweet. When is she supposed to show up anyway?"

"I talked to her earlier. She's been out of town and should've flown in this afternoon, but I haven't heard from her. I hope she made it in okay."

"What's that I smell, Brandi?"

"That's my famous lasagna complete with garlic bread and salad. I also picked up some new toothbrushes in case you guys want to get close."

"You've got the whole thing planned out, don't you, Brandi?"

"I just want my girl and my friend to hit it off and not have to worry about cooking or cleaning until they're married."

"You can kill that noise. I haven't even met this woman yet and you have us married already."

"I'm just messing with you, Taj. Why don't you take the wine and chill it?"

"You're the one who needs to chill, Brandi."

Brandi and I continued to make small talk. Dinner had been ready for awhile and the salad was starting to wilt. We decided to have a few glasses of wine while waiting for Sharon to arrive and soon the bottle of wine was half finished.

"Don't you think you should call her?" I said.

"I've tried to call her a few times. I just keep leaving messages on her answering machine."

Then the phone rang and it was Sharon.

"Hello? My goodness, Sharon. I was worried sick about you. Are you okay?"

"Yeah, I'm okay, girl."

"Well, what happened? Why don't you have your ass over here? Taj is here eagerly waiting to meet you. I even cooked for you guys. I thought I might go for a drive or go catch a movie after you got here."

"Brandi, I'm still out of town. My plane got delayed. I was stuck on the plane with no way of calling you to let you know I won't be in until tomorrow. The airline is putting us all up in hotels for the night. So, I won't be able to hook up with Taj tonight. Please make apologies for me and see if he will give me a rain check."

"Okay, Sharon. I'll talk to you tomorrow. Good-bye."

"What do you mean, you'll talk to her tomorrow? I know your little friend isn't standing me up."

"No, Taj. Her plane was delayed, and she's stuck out of town. The airline is putting her up in a hotel, so she won't be in until tomorrow. I'm sorry, Taj. I wanted you two to meet so bad."

"That's all right, Brandi. The night isn't a total waste. We still have lasagna and wilted salad. Why don't we just eat?"

"Sounds good to me. I'm starving from cooking all of this food anyway."

We begin to eat and pass the wine until both of us are full and probably a little drunk.

"Brandi, what kind of wine was that? It really tasted good."

"It was one of those new brands of white Zinfandel they sell at the market. I can't remember the name. I'd have to look at the bottle."

"You mind if I break out one of those new toothbrushes you bought? My mouth is starting to feel and taste like a freshly picked garlic clove."

"Sure, Taj, they're in the bathroom on the sink."

The whole time I was brushing my teeth, I was picturing how sexy Brandi looked the entire night. I wondered if she ever looks at me that way. I guess not, she told me to back off a few times. We never spent this kind of time together, just laughing and talking about nothing in general. I figure I don't have much to lose. I decided to see if I could get something started.

When I get out of the bathroom, Brandi is sitting in the chaise lounge in her living room. At first, I thought I was just imagining things but after I rubbed my eyes it was true. Brandi had changed into a sexy black silk robe and I could tell that she was wearing just her birthday suit underneath. She stood there sipping a glass of wine with one leg hanging over the chair.

"Welcome back, Taj. Would you like some more wine?"

Before I could answer, she placed a glass full of wine in my hand.

"What's going on, Brandi? I thought we were going to clean up the kitchen together and maybe watch a movie."

"Don't worry about the kitchen, I'll take care of that later. Judging by that large bulge in the middle of your pants, you like my robe, don't you?"

"I sure do, but I don't understand. I thought I didn't have a chance with you."

"Well, you thought wrong, Taj. This just goes to show you what a little good company, food and wine will get you."

I walked over to Brandi and I could smell the soft scent of her perfume as I got closer. It had an extremely soft smell that made you want to get closer and I did just that. When I got close enough to take a nice long whiff, we kissed, cautiously at first; then it blossomed into the most passionate kiss I'd ever given or received. Before I knew what was happening we were in her bedroom, continuing our kissing and caressing. I never really realized just how firm and muscular Brandi was. The girl was definitely tight.

She dropped her robe and, sure enough, she was naked underneath. I immediately took off my clothes. We began to kiss and touch each other and each movement we made seemed to be pre-calculated and done ever so slowly. It seemed like we were dancing together after years of practice. It seemed like each one of us was thinking the other would say, "stop," and both of us hoping that the other wouldn't. This was very new to me.

Most of the women I've been with just want to get fucked and they want it right away. Brandi is a woman who realizes what she likes and the lady likes it slow and easy.

I came prepared to do her girlfriend, however, Ms. Brandi was an even better entrée. I paused for a moment to find a rubber in my pants.

We began to make love, and she was very tight at first. I could tell by her constant shifting backwards as if to avoid taking me fully inside her. It was as if she was still hesitating about crossing the line from friendship to being lovers. I eased slowly into her warmth, and I could feel her getting wetter. There was nothing between us but my condom and her moisture. She began to start talking to me in my ear. It made me shudder since there was no reason for her to whisper.

"Taj, I want you to make love to me slow, hard and long. Do you understand?"

I almost answered her like I would my fifth grade teacher Mrs. Williams with an obedient "Yes, ma'am." I caught myself, however, and told Brandi that I'd try. She leaned back and let me slowly penetrate her until there was none of me left outside of her.

She groaned just a little, but she took all of me. I began to slowly bring myself in and out of her. I kept this rhythm up for what seemed like an eternity. Brandi began to start talking again. This time her breath was short and her tone was more forceful.

"Right there, Taj, just like that. Don't stop. Keep it up. Please, don't stop."

I had to force myself not to listen to her moans. I knew that might ruin my concentration and ruin this entire evening by my coming too fast. I continued like she asked, and it wasn't long before I heard another outburst.

"Yes, Taj, that's it. That's it. Right there. Oh yes, oh yes. I'm about to come. Yes, I'm coming. Ahhhhhhhhhhh!"

It was about 1/10 of a second after I heard all of this out of her mouth that I let go myself. It snuck up on me so fast, all I could say was, "Oh shit, oh shit!"

It was absolutely awesome. I'd never made love or been made love to like that. Ms. Brandi never looked or felt so good before. We both lay there smiling at each other and for the first time since I've known Brandi, I noticed her eyes. They were round like coins and a nice chocolate brown. We kissed again then wrapped our arms around each other and both of us dozed off to sleep.

We woke up lying next to each other in the morning.

"Good morning, Taj. Did you sleep well?"

"Like a baby. And how about you?"

"I dreamed the whole time and guess what—it actually came true!"

"What was your dream about?"

"I dreamed that I made love to a handsome man last night and for once, he would be next to me when I woke up in the morning."

"Nice dream, it seems real enough."

"It's real all right, and thanks for last night, Taj. It was one of the most intense nights of sexual pleasure I've had in a very long time. So, what's next?"

"I'm not sure I know what you mean, Brandi."

"I mean where do we go from here?"

"You tell me, Brandi. I thought you were saving me for your girlfriend, Sharon."

"I was, but that was before last night."

"Well, Brandi, last night was very special. I enjoyed our night of passion, however I respect our friendship."

"What you're saying, Taj, is you'd rather be friends with me than my lover?"

"All I'm saying, Brandi, is that I don't think that I would change how I am, even if I was your lover."

"So, you think you would still be chasing a bunch of women?"

"Yes, I know I would."

"So, Taj, when do you think that shit will stop?"

"Whenever, I feel that the time has come for me to settle down but, until then, I'm not tying myself to one woman."

"I'm sorry to hear that, Taj. I know I could help you change your mind about having one woman if you'd give me the chance. But I know you won't."

Damn, everything was perfect last night and then I woke up to the Drama. "Where do we go from here?" Brandi had to ask.

If women could wait before they hit a brother with that line, things would go a lot smoother and they might even get a positive response. It never fails. When a brother gets the booty for the first time, and he happens to perform well, the woman wants to know where they are headed. Women never let things evolve. Everything has to be calculated and mapped out. Well, I'm not letting a woman map out my life, not even Brandi.

I had to forget about Brandi. There was no way I could see her again. She was a nice woman, but I'm not letting myself get into that thing called love. I was sure Brandi could find some young punk who would love to be her man. How could I stay with one woman when there are so many out there just waiting for the opportunity to experience me? There is no way I could disappoint them.

MARCUS

I met this young lady today and boy, was she fine. She's about 5'6" with long legs and a sexy body. Her name was Michelle Dwight. Michelle and I met in the music warehouse in one of the malls downtown. I was looking for a new jazz CD that I had heard on the jazz radio station, KYOT.99FM. They always play some serious tunes and after a set of songs they go down the list of artists you've just heard. I keep a pen nearby so I can write down the information. You never know when you may need some new smooth jazz tunes to do some entertaining. Women love jazz and that's all the reason I needed to acquire an appreciation for the fine tunes of a piano, guitar, bass fiddle and God forbid a sexy smooth saxophone. I think God created the saxophone for guys like me to hook up with women. Once you put on some Kenny G, Najee, or David Sanborne, you're in there.

This sister is right next to me also checking out the new jazz artist CDs. She's holding several songs that I'd heard on the radio, so I decided to take advantage of the information I had and go over and say hello.

"Hello, my name is Marcus Turner, and you are?" I asked.

"My name is Michelle, how are you?" she said.

"I'm fine, Michelle, so what's your last name?" I asked.

"I think that is a little too much information to give a perfect stranger, don't you?" she said.

"You're probably right. I was just admiring the CDs you were holding and wanted to say hi and let you know you were making some good choices. Sorry to bother you, have a nice day."

I turned to walk away as if I knew I had blown my only chance to get with this pretty fine thing. This was the perfect move because I didn't get three steps away before she said something.

"Wait, Marcus, wait a second. I'm sorry I was a bit rude but there are a lot of crazy guys who hang out in malls trying to pick up anything they can catch. I usually ignore them and most of the time I'm on the defensive. My name is Michelle Dwight and it's nice to meet you."

"Now was that hard? I just wanted to come over and say hello. Thanks for stopping me. I was just thinking to myself how silly I was to think you would just make small talk with me," I said.

"How could a lady make small talk with you, you're so damn tall?"

"Does my height bother you?"

"No. Should it bother me?"

"I hope not. If it doesn't bother you why don't you have lunch with me tomorrow and we'll discuss some jazz?"

"My, Marcus, you are audacious aren't you?" she said.

"I'm just a brother trying to seize the opportunity to meet a beautiful woman for lunch and discuss beautiful music. Is that so bad?"

"Thank you for the compliment and no, that's not so bad. Sure I'll have lunch with you. Where and when would you like to hook up?"

"I know this nice spot downtown that serves Asian food and usually has some nice jazz playing in the background. The atmosphere is pretty cool too. There are usually a bunch of mature adults hanging out. What time should I pick you up?" I asked.

"How about you tell me exactly where it is and I'll meet you there," she said.

"That will work also. You take the I-10 freeway downtown to L Street and make a right. The restaurant is located on the corner of 15th and L. I'll meet you there about 11:30," I said.

"Ok, I'll be there, nice to meet you, Marcus."

"It was nice to meet you too, Michelle."

I left with my latest addition to my already loaded down jazz collection. I couldn't help but remember that Michelle didn't want me to meet her at her place. That means she either has someone or something to hide. Maybe I'm being paranoid. She is probably one of those throwback women who just like to chill with someone for a while before inviting him or her around to their house. I know some brothers you better keep away from your place unless you want a stalker on your hands.

We met the next day and I was especially careful to be very punctual. She was just as punctual and we almost ran into each other coming around the corner headed towards the restaurant.

"Hello, Marcus."

"Hello, Michelle, how are you doing today?"

"I'm fine and you are looking very handsome."

"Thank you, and you're looking fine yourself, Michelle. Shall we get a table?"

"Sure. This is a nice place, Marcus, how did you come across this spot?"

"A friend of mine owned a restaurant near here and one day we decided to try this place and I fell in love with it."

"So, do you come here quite often?" she asked.

"I come in about once or twice a month."

"What should I order, everything sounds so good? It also smells good."

"I'll tell you what, could you trust me to order for both of us?"

"Sure, Marcus, I can trust you this time"

We ordered our food and made small talk about business matters and the current state of the economy. You can get an awful lot of information about the woman you're with just by making small talk. She will either impress you with her intellect or she will put you in the mood to want to find out if she's better in bed than she is in conversation. We finish our meals and skip dessert.

"That was absolutely delicious, Marcus. Thank you," she said.

"You're welcome, Michelle. I'm glad you decided to come to lunch with me."

Just as I said that, the waitress brought over our check. I reached for it ever so slowly. This was one of my player moves to see if she would offer to cover the meal, her half, or even just the tip. Just as I had the check in my grasp, she spoke up.

"Marcus, why don't you let this lunch be on me? I was very short with you yesterday, and I had such a wonderful time talking with you today."

"I don't think so. The idea to have lunch was mine," I said.

"Yes, however I was the one who accepted your offer," she said.

"Okay, then I'll leave the tip," I said.

I knew the waitress was going to get over today. I was going to leave a sizeable tip so Michelle wouldn't think I was just some cheap bastard. Michelle was all right. I actually felt bad for even trying to get out of paying the check. She was a sweetheart the whole time. She gave me her number, and we said our good-byes. I did the usual brother thing and waited two days to call her back. If you call on the same evening or the very next day you come across as desperate. If you wait longer than two days, she has written you off as a player or an asshole. She picks up the phone on the second ring.

"Hello?" she said.

"Hi, Michelle. This is Marcus. How are you?"

"I'm fine, Marcus. And how are you?"

"I'm fantastic, but I'd be a lot better if I were with you."

"Marcus, you're silly. That has to be one of the oldest lines in the world."

"It's true though. Sometimes the oldest line in the world is exactly what you want to say, and it's the truth. I thought we might hook up and spend the day together."

"That's nice, Marcus, but there is something I wanted to tell you."

"Whatever it is it can wait until later. I'll pick you up in about an hour, if that's okay?"

"That's fine, Marcus, I'll see you in an hour."

We hook up for lunch again and we have a wonderful time. Michelle volunteered to cook me dinner and I was definitely down for that. She's a very attractive lady, smart, and if she can cook that will be another plus.

I'm really getting into her, although Michelle and I can't seem to hook up as often as I would like. It seems she's always busy. So I just wait until we're able to get together since she's so sweet. I'm definitely into this woman. We've been together a few months now, and she's really cool. She is about as fine as they come.

I wonder why she isn't hooked up with someone. She probably just broke up with some crazy ass brother who couldn't handle her being good looking and an intellectual. It sure doesn't bother me. As long as I'm the only one getting the booty, I'm happy. A woman could make more money or have more degrees than I do; it really doesn't matter. I'm about to get dressed and go over to Michelle's house to pick her up.

I hop in my ride and head over to Michelle's place. I decided to take a shortcut that I found when I was out and about last week. The neighborhood she stays in is pretty nice and I wonder what her rent is. It had to be more than $800 a month and that's cheap for the area. A house out here would have about a

$1,500 mortgage. I hit a couple of turns and a short stretch of road and before I knew it, I was almost at Michelle's place. I had knocked at least ten minutes off of the trip. I wound up on the side of Michelle's house and I noticed her in front as I drove up.

She had what looked like a red backpack in her hand and there was a little girl by her side. A brand new white limited edition Jeep Cherokee was parked in front with a brother sitting in the driver's seat. I knew it was a limited edition because I had been pricing those big gas-guzzlers before I got my car. I decided to kick back and watch this little situation. I was early, and she probably hadn't meant for me to see this scene. Michelle was having what appeared to be a heated discussion with the guy in the Cherokee. She was waving her hands and bobbing her head like she was pissed off.

The little girl was standing by Michelle, holding her leg. All I could tell from where I was sitting was that she had a beautiful head of long golden, curly hair. I couldn't exactly tell how old she was, but it looked like she was about four or five from her height. I slid down in my chair, turned the radio down, and cracked the window to get some air. It was a beautiful day in sunny Sacramento. It was impossible to hear anything; they were too far away. Michelle walked around to the other side of the Jeep and placed the little girl in the passenger seat.

When she came back to the front of her house she didn't have the red backpack. The guy drove off and his wheels screeched, making long black tire marks on the street. Michelle turned and went back in the house. I contemplated what I had just witnessed and tried to put it all together. I came to the conclusion that the little girl was Michelle's and this guy in the jeep must have been the father. I guess that's why she wasn't hooked up.

That's the last thing I need is a mother trying to get me to be the father of her child. I've never dated a single parent. I might sleep with them once or twice, but never any long term dating. You have to deal with so many issues. The asshole father of the kids and the stress she deals with because he's late on the child support payment. Before we can go anywhere, we have to get a baby-sitter. I knew Michelle was too good to be true. Now I know why.

Why wasn't she honest about having a child? She probably knew she wouldn't get past first base if she told me she had a kid at home. Most brothers like myself won't date a woman with kids. That's the old just add water and you have an instant family syndrome. The sad part about it is that almost all of the women out there have at least one child. I don't know why, but a lot of brothers have knocked women up and then said goodbye.

Some brothers just get caught up in how many babies they can make by a number of different women. Other brothers slip up, get some woman pregnant, and then high tail it out of town. There are a lot of brothers who have become incarcerated and can't be there for their children. I even know some brothers who had children and then claimed their homosexuality. Isn't that something? The woman comes home to find that her baby's daddy is leaving for another man. That would be enough to make some woman kill her man and his boyfriend.

I decided to get out of my car and ring Michelle's bell and see why she's hiding stuff from me. I walked across the street and rang her bell. Michelle came to the door looking as fine as ever. I almost forgot I was supposed to be mad at her. She invited me in and I followed her into the living room. She turned around and I just let her have it.

"Who the hell was the little girl and the guy you were with out front, Michelle?"

"Were you spying on me Marcus or what? That was my daughter, Ebony, and her father. Why?"

"Don't you think having a child is something you should've brought up earlier, Michelle?"

"I just wanted us to get to know one another better first."

"How much trust do you think we'll have if you start out hiding things from me this early in our relationship? I care a lot about you, Michelle, but you know how I feel about taking care of someone else's child? There will always be this other man in our lives."

"I know how you feel, Marcus, but she's my child also."

"I think we should just cool it for a while."

"Why are you doing this, Marcus? We've enjoyed each other so much these past few months, I have very strong feelings for you."

"Well, just get over it. I'm out of here!"

Michelle just kept looking at me with this shocked and hurt look in her eyes.

"Find someone else to play daddy to your child, Michelle," I said.

"That's where you're wrong, Marcus, I don't need someone to play daddy to my child. She already has a daddy and he's a lying, cheating bastard. I thought you were different, Marcus. Here I am telling you about my feelings for you and all you can think about is my ex-boyfriend being the father of my child.

"I hope you change your mind, Marcus. If you do, I will be right here to show you my love."

"Goodbye, Michelle."

"Goodbye, Marcus."

I go outside and headed for my car. Michelle is a very classy lady. It's too bad she has a kid, otherwise we probably could've kicked it for a while. When I want a baby, I'll settle down and make one of my own.

DÉJÀ VU

<u>CK</u>

My neighbor Theo is this short white guy who teaches at one of the local high schools. His real name is Theodore and he made it quite clear the first time we met that he didn't like being called by his whole name. He's from either North or South Carolina. He has this difficult-to-understand Southern accent. Most of the time I can only get bits and pieces of what he's talking about. He is, however, one of the best neighbors a guy could have. Someone may be hanging around the house or thinking about breaking in and there is old Theo running him or her off. He's better than a home alarm system.

He came over today acting all weird. He was looking around side to side like someone was following him. I asked him if everything was okay.

"Sure, CK, everything is fine, I'm just wanting to talk to you about something.

"You know how people are always talking about black guys being larger than white guys are?"

This makes me look at Theo like he was about to tell me he's gay or something. I thought for a moment that he was going to ask me to expose myself for a comparison. I finally told him I had heard that saying.

"My doctor told me that it's because an average black guy has larger veins than the average white guy. This allows more blood to go to the penis, therefore making the penis larger."

"I can't believe you and your doctor were having a conversation about black penises being superior to white ones," I said.

"I actually went into my doctor because I've been having some problems pleasing my wife."

"You mean you couldn't get it up, Theo?"

"That's right CK, I don't know why but old peter don't want to work sometime."

"What did the doctor say about your little problem?"

"He told me it was natural for men my age to begin having problems with getting or maintaining an erection. I would never have believed that at 43 years old I would start having trouble with my equipment. He gave me a prescription for that new drug Viagra."

"Viagra? I think I've heard of that drug. Isn't that the one some old guys are dying from?"

"Yeah, that's because they didn't follow their doctor's instructions or the warning on the bottle. Those guys were probably taking the Viagra along with heart medication, or high blood pressure medicine. Anything like that will surely kill you."

"So how does this Viagra stuff work, Theo?"

"It helps enlarge the veins in the body and when you get excited it begins filling the love muscle with extra blood. Because that muscle has larger veins it will get more blood, therefore making it larger. It actually increased the size of my penis by about one-third the normal size."

"One-third the normal size! Are you kidding me?" I said.

"At least those old guys are going out in style," Theo said.

"Yeah, they are sort of coming and going at the same time," I quipped.

"I thought you might want one of my pills to experiment on one of the many women you have coming over," Theo said.

"No thanks, Theo. I'll pass. Maybe some other time."

"Are you sure about that, CK? You may have some special woman you want to impress. Pop one of these pills, and you'll scare the panties right off of her."

"Okay, okay, Theo. I'll take a few of them off of your hands. How much do these things cost anyway?"

"My prescription costs about eight dollars a pill. That's probably why I only got six of them. It's not like my little old peter acts up all the time, just on occasion. The old lady and I don't mess around that much anyway. I figure when peter starts acting like he doesn't want to hunt, I'll dash in the bathroom and take one of my Viagra pills and boom, instant hard-on."

"How long do the pills take to work, Theo?"

"They only take about three minutes to work."

"That's great, Theo, thanks for the pills. I'll let you know if an emergency comes up and I get a chance to use Mr. Viagra."

"CK, let me know what you think after you use the pills."

"I will, Theo. Have a good one."

I couldn't get the conversation with Theo off my mind. At first I was bursting out laughing at the fact that some men need a little help getting it up. I can't remember the last time I needed some help. There were a number of times I wished my love muscle would take a chill pill. I might be dancing close with some woman I wanted to get with real bad and sure enough my penis would let the cat out of the bag.

I had to admit, Theo had me pretty curious. I mean what would this Viagra stuff do to a brother that is already hung pretty good and doesn't have any problems getting it up? Theo said it increases the penis size by about one-third. That's scary, one-third larger than I am right now would give me a weapon, not a penis. I'll just put this shit up in the medicine cabinet with the Motrin 800, Tylenol with Codeine, and the cough medicine, just in case I decide to use one.

My medicine cabinet is full of prescriptions and medications that should've been thrown away by now. No one I know ever throws away medicine. When someone decides to stop taking the medicine a doctor prescribes, they should just throw it away. It usually gets tossed up in the mirrored medicine cabinet with all of the other drugs.

I am always curious as to why they make all medicine cabinets with mirrors anyway? It's like someone is playing a sick-ass joke on the entire world. The fact that you keep all of your household drugs behind that mirrored cabinet is sick. You have to face yourself in this mirror before removing anything from the cabinet. There you are face to face with yourself wondering why you're getting another pill instead of sucking it up. Let's not mention the many people that may visit your house, use your bathroom, and go through your medicine cabinet.

I dated a girl once and while using her bathroom I decided to go through her medicine cabinet. Sorry, you can learn a lot about a woman by the drugs she keeps in the medicine cabinet. I found the usual aspirin, alcohol, vitamins and some normal female products. Then I found it! It was on the top shelf behind some other bottles.

A prescription for Prozac with her name written all over it. It sent a strong message to me, simply because the date was pretty recent and the bottle was almost empty. Now I'm standing there thinking should I be alarmed or should I just blow this off. She was a very attractive lady and I was really looking forward to hooking up with her. There was definite cause for concern. It was a simple, spur-of-the-moment judgement call. Now my dilemma was should I confront her, then she'll know that I've been going through her stuff? Or do I hang around and eventually figure out what her problem is and try to help her through it?

My choice was the third option; I got the hell out of the house and didn't speak to her again. She called a few times to find out what happened, but after a while she must have figured I wasn't interested. In this case she was right. I wish women were a little smarter about where they keep their private stash of drugs. If it was cocaine or marijuana where would they hide it? I hope not in the mirrored medicine cabinet!

It wasn't long before I had the opportunity to put the Viagra pills Theo gave me to use. I met this young lady at a seminar on enhancing your management skills. I could hardly manage not to fall asleep. One thing I managed not to miss was this blonde in a revealing halter-top taking some serious notes from this boring ass speaker.

I tried my best to get her attention and it never worked. This must have been her first seminar in her life. I'd been to so many self-improvements seminars it isn't funny, and this one was the most boring. I finally got a chance to say hello to her when the seminar was over. Of course I had to wait for her to ask the speaker about fifteen minutes worth of questions. She walked towards me and looked my way but said nothing. She probably didn't even notice me. I said hello and she replied, "Hello, how are you?"

"I'm fine. My name is CK. What's yours?"

"My name is Debra and I'm kind of in a hurry. But it was nice to meet you. Goodbye, CK."

"Wait, I was just noticing how intense you were in the seminar and I wanted to talk about it with you later."

"Intense, what do you mean by that?" she asked.

"I mean you were so into the information and taking notes the whole time, you looked intense."

"Didn't you get into the information the speaker was sharing about self-improvement?"

"Well I did, but I've been to several of these similar seminars. The information was simply a rehash of what I already knew."

"Like I said, I really need to go now. It was nice talking to you," she said, grabbing up her purse.

"Could I give you my number? Maybe we can have lunch sometime?" I flashed her a smile.

"You are pretty dauntless aren't you?" She raised her eyebrows.

"Not usually, I have just never met such an attractive woman that was interested in a self-improvement seminar. I'm simply intrigued. Is there something wrong with that?"

"No, and I'm sorry I've been so rude. Why don't you give me your number and I'll call you later tonight."

"Thank you, Debra. Why don't we try to do lunch one day this week?" I asked.

"That sounds like a plan, CK. Thank you."

It was about 4 pm and I was just trying to figure out what I could do to pass the time until Debra called. I decided to take a short nap. I set the alarm for two hours. I figured if she called before that I'd hear the phone anyway. It seemed like I was some teenager waiting to get the first phone call of my dating career. Debra called and woke me up exactly two hours later. I shut off the alarm and took the phone into the living room. I wanted to relax on the couch so I wouldn't sound desperate.

"Hello?"

"Hi, CK, this is Debra. How are you?"

"I'm fine. How are you, Debra? I was just chilling out, waiting for your call."

"So, you were actually waiting to talk to me, CK?"

"Sure, I was waiting to talk to you again. I've been trying to figure out what to say to you since we left the seminar."

"What did you come up with?" she asked.

"I thought we might go to lunch tomorrow and talk face to face."

"That sounds good. Where would you like to go to lunch?"

"I know this nice sandwich shop called TOGOs on Sunrise Ave. They have some nice fresh sandwiches, and they have a place to sit, eat and talk. I hope a sandwich isn't too simple for you."

"No, CK, sandwiches aren't too simple, they're actually quite fine with me. How about if we meet for lunch about noon, if that's okay?"

"That will work, I'll see you at noon, Debra."

I was pumped up thinking about the outfit she had on at the seminar and how much I wanted to see what she looked like underneath those clothes.

I woke up today and couldn't wait until noon. That's when I was going to meet Debra. After moping around most of the morning, I met Debra for lunch and we had a very nice conversation. We had such a good time on our date.

Debra was so impressed with our date that she agreed to go out to dinner the next night, which was Friday. She did this on the condition that the meal would be on her since I'd paid for the sandwiches at lunch. I agreed and the date was set.

Debra called me the next day with directions to her place. It didn't take me long to get there, maybe about twenty minutes. She lived in a very nice section of Sunrise, California. It was a very expensive and well-kept apartment complex called "The Ridge." The apartments actually could pass for town houses back in my old neighborhood. I found her parking space number and remembered she told me to park in an uncovered parking spot. People get so annoyed here in California when you park in their covered parking space.

One time while visiting a friend in a not-so-nice neighborhood a guy just blocked my car in front of his parking spot. I had to literally wait until he came out and moved his car from behind mine. The whole time he had this smirk on his face like he had just caught a cat burglar in his house and locked him inside.

I found Debra's apartment and knocked on the door. She came to the door in an emerald green dress with high heel shoes to match.

I notice these things, as all my brothers should. If you notice things like shoes, nails, a new hairdo, or anything that your significant other or potential date has going for her, she will like it and you will definitely get points for noticing. We decided to take Debra's car to lunch which was a nice white Mustang GT convertible. This must be the standard issue car for the average single white woman in California. I've seen at least a dozen of them in the last month.

We took Interstate 50 toward downtown Old Sacramento.

She had chosen a very nice Italian restaurant in Old Sacramento. It was a nice place complete with lots of pictures of Italy and the traditional red and white checkered tablecloths and obese waiters. They gave us so much food I thought I was going to burst. I ordered my old Italian favorite entrée, which was the lasagna, with a cold glass of lemonade. Debra ordered some Fettuccini Alfredo along with some red wine. It looked so good, but I didn't dare ask to share her food.

We finished our meals and Debra suggested a nightcap at her place. I agreed but I couldn't help wondering if she realized that I was just filling up on lemonade while she had her red wine. We went back to her place and I thought this might be a good opportunity to follow up on those ideas I had about getting some of her fine ass body. She went into her kitchen and poured herself a glass of wine and surprisingly brought me a glass of lemonade.

"I thought you could use a nightcap also," she said.

"Debra, are you trying to make fun of the fact that I don't drink?"

"No, not at all. I think that a man who can go around in this day and age and stick to not drinking is alright with me," she said.

"That was sweet of you to say, Debra."

We made small talk and after a few glasses of wine Debra went into her room to get more comfortable. I asked if it was okay to use her bathroom.

"Sure, no problem, it's to the left of the kitchen."

I went into her bathroom and, like most single women's, it was very clean. It was decorated in peach and green. There were green towels with little peach wash cloths.

She had a large mirror trimmed in green, a pink shower curtain, pink toilet cover with matching rugs and green soap dish and toothbrush holder. There was only one toothbrush in the holder, which was a good sign. It led me to believe there wasn't a regular man visiting. I was tempted to go through the medicine cabinet, as I usually do, but I wasn't sure how much time I had before she returned from her room.

I went into the bathroom to take my Viagra pill. I figured if we got into something tonight I would try to see the difference between my usual sexual prowess and after I take this wonder pill for old guys. I figured if it works for someone with a problem getting it up it would do wonders for a guy with no problems at all. I took my pill and sipped some water from the faucet.

I flushed the toilet and let the water run like I was washing my hands. I always wash my hands when I do anything in the bathroom. A lot of guys don't. They just go right from the stall to the door. Women notice if the water ever ran or the soap and towels got used. Don't use any of the above items and you might as well get your coat and hat and head for the front door.

I exited the bathroom and returned to the living room. Debra returned wearing a white terry cloth robe that resembled the ones you are so tempted to steal from those expensive hotels. It actually looked pretty warm and she did look sexy in it.

"You went a little overboard on the getting comfortable, didn't you, Debra?"

"Not really, CK, I'm just used to wearing this old thing around the house."

"I like it."

"No, you don't, you're just being nice."

"If you don't believe me, come over here and let me try it on."

Debra came towards me with this "I dare you" look on her face. I grabbed the belt and untied it from her waist. I was amazed at what I saw. Debra was stark naked under the robe. I was expecting some panties, a brassiere or maybe a nice teddy. I was a bit shocked, but I couldn't let her know it.

"Well, are you going to try the robe on like you said, CK, or what?"

"I don't think I want to put anything on right now."

"I thought you said you liked my robe and you were going to take it off of me and try it on yourself."

"That was before I realized you weren't wearing anything underneath the robe."

"So what do you intend to do now, CK?"

"I thought that I would get undressed and make you feel more comfortable."

"Then why are you still dressed?"

I got undressed in record time. We started kissing and before I knew it we were getting hot and heavy. We somehow scrambled to her bedroom. I paused for a moment to put on a condom. I was about to enter Debra and realized that the rubber was only halfway on me. That's when I noticed that I was much larger than I'm used to being. Theo was right. Here I am looking down at a Government Issue anti-ballistic missile. Debra noticed my largeness also.

"Oh, my goodness. CK, you're huge."

I pretended that the current size of my nature was quite normal. I mounted Debra and enjoyed the grimaces on her face as I entered her moistness. She squirmed and moved like a fish trying to shake loose the hook caught in its mouth. This made me press even harder.

Like most men we enjoy the response a woman has to sex just as much as the sex itself. That's how hookers make so much money on repeat customers. They stroke a man's ego and make them believe they are doing some serious damage during sex. Most of these working girls deserve Oscars for their convincing acts. I can hear them now "Don't stop, don't stop. Hey big daddy, give it to me." Any woman that can verbalize her feelings during sex is going to keep the guy she's with coming back for more and more.

I continued to push deeper and deeper into Debra and realized she was enjoying every minute. The whole thing was so exciting that I let go a little prematurely. What was I going to do? It was my first time using this Viagra pill which made me almost twice as large as normal, and I got too excited too fast. Debra will definitely be disappointed in my performance and never answer another phone call of mine. It was at that point that I realized that I was still rock hard. I had just let go and remained as stiff as a board. Any other time, this happens and I need about an hour nap or a meal to rejuvenate myself. By now, Debra was getting louder and louder. I worried that her neighbors would think I was killing her.

"Yes CK. Right there, right there. Here I come. Uhhhhhhhhhhhh!!! CK, what are you doing to me?"

"Am I hurting you, Debra?"

"No, it just feels so good, and so hard that I don't want to stop. I need to though because my heart is beating a mile a minute," she said.

"I never knew you were so big, CK."

"It's not the size that counts, Debra."

"That's something a woman whose man has a small thing says," she said.

"I guess you're right about that."

"That was the best sex I've had in years, CK. I hope we can do this again."

"I'm sure we can, just say when."

"Well, my heart is beating too fast or I'd say 'when' right now."

I'm going to keep those pills handy. I couldn't stand to use them all of the time, however for those emergencies, or when you have some women talking shit, you can just take one Viagra and she'll be calling you again real soon. I've got to tell Theo how powerful those damn things were.

TAJ

I met Andre just after we both graduated from college. I went to Georgetown University and Andre graduated from nearby Morgan State in Baltimore, Maryland.

We were both business majors and happened to see each other at several job interviews. After seeing each other two or three times, we struck up a conversation and found out we had quite a lot in common. One thing was good taste in women. During one of the interviews, we were both admiring this young lady and decided to bet lunch on who could get her phone number.

I went first and struck out pretty quick and she shot his ass down also. The sister was seriously sexy with plenty of booty and chest displayed. I guess we assumed that meant she was easy. We both wound up buying our own lunch. I was running women just as hard as I could, and Andre seemed to have his share of honeys after him. It turns out that neither one of us got the job. I guess that young lady won that contest also.

Andre and I have been friends ever since. We were real tight, we later found out that both of us even pledged the same fraternity in college, Kappa Alpha Psi. After graduating and entering the job market we never really made much money in the DC area since the competition was very stiff. We were both good students but you had to know someone inside the big companies to get hired and make the big bucks.

After reading an article about Sacramento and its growing business industry we decided to move there. There we were, two brothers on a shoestring budget, packing up our rides and heading out to California. We were acting like the damn Beverly Hillbillies.

The ride from D.C. to Sacramento was real smooth. We stayed on Interstate 5, straight through. Since we were following each other we stopped off about every ten to twelve hours to rest and shower. Each stop we made for food was quick and fast like McDonalds or Burger King. Whenever we would stop for the night, we chose a reputable hotel with a nice restaurant. We weren't totally broke, and these stops were rejuvenating. We made it to Sacramento in three days, and it was raining just a little as we drove into town. We checked into a hotel close to the airport. Even though we didn't fly, the airport hotels seemed to be a little nicer and safer in strange towns. Coming from D.C. we knew exactly how to be cautious.

The next morning was bright and sunny. Andre and I had lost track of the time and the day. We went out to breakfast and picked up the paper. There it was on the front page, "Tuesday May 28, 1998." Now, we at least knew what day it was. That long drive made it seem like we were in a time machine. We also realized that the time was three hours behind D.C. I would have to remember that whenever I called back home.

The paper was "The Sacramento Bee" and it was packed full of so many business jobs we could pick and choose where we wanted to work. This was going to be the place where a brother could finally get ahead. Also, the cost of living here in Sacto was considerably less than in D.C. The newspaper had some crimes in it, but compared to D.C, this was a walk in the park.

It didn't take long before both of us got good paying jobs. We started out making about $30,000 a year each, and after about a year and a half he was making $10,000 more than I. Andre was a much better worker than I and always got raises since he kept his mouth shut and stayed overtime. I always spoke my mind and wasn't afraid to let on to my boss that I wished I could beat his ass and take his position. This was not the kind of attitude that earned a brother a raise. I was just happy to be making decent money.

The same amount of money in D.C. wouldn't have let you afford anything. The brothers back in D.C. had to spend most of that on rent and insurance. Out here, you could make a dollar stretch. I'm stuck in the Corporate American dream. Work this salaried job for thirty years and hopefully retire.

One day, Andre gave me some news that almost ruined my evening. I got home, jumped in the shower, and got dressed. When Andre arrived, he came up and rang the bell. This was strange since he usually honked the horn and waited for me to come downstairs. He claimed there were just too many stairs for him to climb. I answered the door and told him to come in.

"What's up with you, Andre? You never come upstairs when you come over?"

"I have something to tell you, Taj."

"Don't tell me you can't make it to happy hour."

"No, that's not it, Taj. What I have to tell you is very serious. It's time I let you know."

"Sounds serious. Can it wait until after we come back from the club?"

"No, Taj, it can't wait that long."

"Okay, Andre. What is it?"

He stood there looking everywhere except straight at me. Then he let me have it.

"Taj, I'm gay," he said. "There, I've said it. Now we can go out."

"Wait a minute, Andre. Did you just say what I thought you just said?"

"Yes, it's true. I'm gay."

I didn't know what to say. I just stood there with this stupid look on my face. What do you say when your best friend says he's gay? What went wrong? I thought Andre was on the women just like I was. I wondered if he'd gotten a bad piece of pussy or something? Did some woman break his heart? Nothing seemed bad enough to start switching to guys.

I just sat there dumbfounded. Here was my best friend, my running partner, telling me he's gay. I thought about all of the times since we met that he pulled some fine ass woman out of the club and took her home. I couldn't help wondering what he did with them when he got them home. Maybe he cooked for them or played house. I couldn't believe my best friend was gay and I didn't know it.

I broke the silence and told him he was full of shit.

"Andre, this is a sick ass joke and I'm ready to go get my groove on, not bullshit with you."

"It's true, Taj. I'm gay, and I've been that way for a long time."

"Get the fuck out of here, Andre! You expect me to believe that shit? You better cut this shit out or we'll be fighting soon."

"Why does my being gay make you want to kick my ass?"

"Okay, Andre, I'm through talking about you thinking you're gay. What about all of the women you and I have picked up at clubs?"

"Of course, I had to keep up appearances until I could tell you. Now, I won't have a problem just being myself. Look Taj, I just wanted to let my best friend know that I'm gay so you wouldn't hear it from someone else."

"How many people know about your gayness?"

"There are a few guys that I've been seeing and quite a few women."

"You mean you're bi-sexual?"

"No, Taj. I'm gay."

"I'm still not convinced, Andre. How the fuck could my best friend be gay and I not know about it until now? Some of these people who know about you must think my ass is gay, too."

"I'm not trying to convince you, Taj. I'm just tired of keeping this secret to myself."

"Okay, Andre, let's just go hang out like you're straight and forget about you being gay for one night."

I told Andre that as long as he kept his gay life away from me, I would try to remain his best friend. I also didn't want him telling everyone he was gay while he's still hanging around with me. We both agreed that would be how we dealt with this new revelation about Andre's life.

We decided to go out anyway and hit the happy hour scene. We eventually arrive at this club called Deja Vu. This spot has about eight females to one male. Just when you think you saw the finest woman in the place, here comes another twice as fine! I even thought Andre would enjoy himself at a place like this. The whole time I knew he was perpetrating a fraud.

Talking and dancing with all of the women, when he wishes he could take one of the big black brothers in the club home. The thought was making me sick.

He wouldn't dare reveal his femininity in a club like this. He'll probably get his ass beat up. That is until I come into the picture. No one fucks with my boy. Not while I'm around, gay or not. I'd just put one of these 20-inch biceps on them and pow! That's all she wrote.

We've been partying pretty hard the whole night, I think I only missed one song on the dance floor. Every woman I danced with was as beautiful as the first. I'm also getting very, very drunk. I've been switching from screwdrivers, to beer, then wine, and finally sipping cognac with the finest sister I've seen in years, drunk that is.

I begin looking around for my boy Andre and he appears right behind me.

"Taj, what in the world are you doing?" he said.

"What do you think I'm doing? I'm getting my drink on!"

"Well, I'm ready to go, are you?"

"I'm not ready to go, can't you see I'm talking to this beautiful young lady?"

"I can see that, Taj, but I have to get up early tomorrow so I've got to get some sleep."

"Damn Andre, I wish I had known you were going to pull this shit. I would have driven myself."

"How do you think you could drive yourself home in your condition?"

"I can handle myself. Besides, I'm not that drunk anyway." I tried to get up and stumbled. I realized I should give in and call it a night and leave with Andre. I knew my boy would make sure I got home all right.

"Go get the truck, Andre, and I'll see you out front," I said.

Andre drags me to the Range Rover and I fall into a drunken sleep before we turn our first corner.

Somehow or another I wind up in my apartment, awakened by heavy breathing. It seems like I'm in a drugged state, not drunk like I'm used to being. I couldn't help thinking one of those many women in the club must have slipped something in my drink.

I'm glad I went with my boy, Andre. He got my ass home okay.

I can hardly see straight, and I know I'm drunk as a park bench vagabond. I thought the heavy breathing was me but there is someone else with me. It must be one of those women I met at the club. One of them must have followed Andre home so she could be with me. Then I realize that for some reason I'm aroused and my nature is hard as a rock. She was giving me some serious head. This girl was really good, which one was she? I had talked to so many at the club. I'm so drunk I probably couldn't recognize her anyway.

I sat up to see if I could recognize the very talented young lady and I got the shock of my life. It was a man's head going down on me. I could hardly make out who it was, but I think it was Andre. He's all over me and he's going to town. I'm trying to say something, and it seems to come out like gibberish. What's really fucked up is I know what's going on, and I'm so drunk I can't even stop this. It seems like I was drugged or something.

Why in the world is Andre doing this to me? He knows I'm not gay. Is he trying to convince me he's gay? How did I even get excited? My dick must've thought it was one of those women I was at the club with bobbing on me. This shit shouldn't be exciting to me. I guess that's why they call a dick head; it can think on its own. This just isn't right, my best friend is taking advantage of me when I'm fucked up more than I've ever been before.

I felt Andre stop and hoped he had realized how much he had fucked up and that I would kill his ass when I got the chance. Just then Andre was doing something else. I felt him putting something on me, I think it's a rubber. How can I realize what's happening to me and not be able to stop it! It turns out it was a rubber and he began to mount me with his ass right on top of my stiffness. He was bouncing and moving around until he stopped. He must have gotten off. This whole scene is making me sick, only I can't even throw up. I just want this night to end, so I can wake up sober and kill his motherfucking ass. Have your fun now Andre, because I'm going to kill your ass as soon as whatever spell I'm under wears off.

It's about 11:30 in the morning, and I've got the most terrible headache in the world. I feel my way into the kitchen to get a glass of water. I head back to the bathroom to find something to soothe my aching head. I'm smacking bottles of old pills, alcohol and everything else in the medicine cabinet out of the way in search of some Tylenol. I take about four Tylenol and down the glass of water.

I start replaying in my mind the events that led up to my terrible headache. I can remember all of the different drinks that I had and that shit really wasn't smart. I think I was drinking whatever the woman I was talking to was drinking, and that must have been ten different ones. I remember thinking that someone had drugged me. I remember Andre wanting to leave, and I hadn't wanted to since I was having a good time and getting drunk.

I was staring at the mirror in the bathroom and then it hit me. I heard a loud crash and realized that I dropped the glass onto the floor. It made a real mess and cut the top part of my foot. Now to go along with my headache, I was bleeding. I got some tissue and wiped my foot. I had just remembered what Andre did to me last night.

That son of a bitch, I'm going to kill his fucking ass. I thought he was my boy. That faggot motherfucker will never fuck another brother when I'm finished with his ass. I bet his punk ass is sitting at home calling all of his gay buddies bragging about how he got fucked by his straight best friend last night. I may have a headache and a bleeding foot but soon, Andre, your ass will be dead!

I got dressed, grabbed my gun, jumped in my car and drove straight over to his house. I was getting madder by the fucking minute. My best friend took advantage of me last night, and he'll be feeling some hot lead real soon.

I make it to Andre's house in record time and I saw his Range Rover parked outside. I knew that I would soon be in jail for killing this faggot ass motherfucker. I wonder if the judge would understand what I was going through and let my ass off. Fuck the judge, I'll kill his ass too if he doesn't agree with what I'm going to do to Andre's punk ass. Andre happened to look out of his window and saw me downstairs with my pistol in hand. When Andre saw me look up at him, he ducked back inside. He could probably tell I was breathing fire.

Don't hide now, you motherfucker, your ass wasn't bashful last night. I could still feel my head pounding like a drum and my sock felt wet like my foot hadn't stopped bleeding. My only concern now was to see Andre bleeding.

I didn't even wait to get inside his house, I started shooting at his fucking ass from the street. I could see people ducking out of the way and screaming "call the police." I didn't care, I was standing there firing my 9mm automatic like some gunslinger in a western movie. I remember shooting the tires on his Range Rover out, then the windshield, and when I got to the front door I shot a hole in that, too.

I began searching the whole house for his punk ass. I knew he was hiding and I was going to find and kill his ass. I kept searching and shooting at everything in sight. I shot a floor lamp and some clothes hanging on a door that looked like a person.

I found Andre hiding in a closet, shaking like a fucking leaf.

"Come out of the fucking closet, Andre," I shouted. He was yelling and screaming like a bitch.

"Please, Taj, please, Taj, don't kill me."

"Your ass wasn't in the closet when you decided to take some dick last night."

"I'm sorry, Taj. I just got carried away."

"Your ass is going to be carried away in a fucking body bag today."

"Please God, don't let him kill me, please God," he said.

"God can't help your sorry gay ass, but I'll make sure you get to meet him."

I didn't want to hear shit else from Andre. I looked at his sorry ass and pulled the fucking trigger but nothing happened. I pulled the trigger again and nothing happened. Was my gun jammed or what? I checked the barrel and the clip. It was empty and I didn't bring a spare clip. My dumb ass had shot up all 15 rounds and Andre was still alive. I know he was thinking that God had heard, and answered his prayers.

I turned the gun around and started pistol whipping his ass into a bloody mess. I was even madder now since I had to beat his ass to death instead of just shooting him like I had planned. The whole time I was hitting his ass with the gun I started feeling better and better. The funny thing is his faggot ass wasn't dying fast enough for me. He just kept hollering and screaming for me to stop, and begging me not to kill him.

I remember two cops busting in on me beating his ass and yelling, "freeze."

I just kept on beating Andre's ass with the butt of the gun. The cops grabbed me, slammed my head into the ground while they handcuffed me, dragged my ass downstairs, and placed me into the squad car. I was covered in Andre's blood. I hoped he didn't have AIDS.

That didn't matter to me right now. If they let me loose, I'd go upstairs and finish Andre's ass off. I was on my way to jail and there was no way I was going to tell anyone why I was beating the shit out of Andre. I could see the brothers in jail now wondering if I really liked it with Andre and if I wanted a boyfriend during my stay. One thing is for sure, I'm not gay, and I still love women.

I've been out of jail on bail for about a week. It's fucking ironic that I later found out that Andre is the one who bailed me out. He never even pressed charges and the district attorney dropped all of their charges. They probably wrote the report up like a domestic dispute. I couldn't believe I was chilling at the club on Friday and cooling off in jail on Saturday.

What am I going to do about Andre? He's still my boy but I can't get past that foul shit he did to me. I thought we respected each other and I know I never led him to believe that I was even slightly gay. He's probably thinking I got my gun back and I've reloaded. I can't shoot his ass now. The judge warned me not to ever show my face in his courtroom again and he made me pay for everything I shot up. He promised that if he ever laid eyes on me again, I would go to jail for sure.

I hate thinking about that night. I was a rape victim, and I can't get that shit out of my mind. I was violated like some helpless child. Here I am a grown man with a gay experience on my conscience. Andre really has my head all fucked up now.

PERPLEXITY

<u>JOE</u>

It's been over a year since Trina and I decided to get married. Now the wedding is in a few weeks. Trina's been stressing out a lot lately. Everything must be exactly perfect or she hits the roof.

She's knocked the shit out of me quite a few times lately. I feel like I'm being smothered more than I've ever been with her before. I'm starting to have second thoughts about getting married at all. I know if I stand this woman up and don't go through with what she considers "the most important day in her entire life," I'll be dead. She'll hunt me down like that vicious dog, Kujo, only he'll seem like Lassie after she finishes with me.

The only thing I have to look forward to is my bachelor weekend. CK, Marcus, and Taj are going in together to make this one hell of a weekend to remember. If I know those brothers, we're going to be getting busy the whole weekend. I can't wait, I wish we were leaving tomorrow.

My bachelor weekend could not have come at a better time. I'm supposed to be getting married in two weeks and I'm stressing out something bad. Work is a bitch, and so is my fiancée. That seems like a pretty sorry ass way to describe the woman that will be carrying around my last name. She's been driving me crazy, and I don't know how I can stand another moment around her ass, let alone the rest of my life.

The brothers are coming to the rescue. Tonight we leave for Lake Tahoe for a fun filled weekend of dancing and romancing. Trina is going to be going crazy trying to figure out what we're up to. She thinks we are just going up to do some gambling and drinking. I know she wouldn't want us driving back down to Sacramento after partying the night away.

Little does she know that her soon-to-be husband will be crowned big dog player of the year after this trip.

"Joe, what in the hell are you smiling so hard about?"

"Oh, Trina, I was just smiling because soon I'll be your husband."

"Joe, that is the sweetest thing you've said to me in weeks."

"You know you're my sweetheart, and I love you, Trina."

"I hope you aren't going to Lake Tahoe to have too much fun with your brothers."

"You know my brothers are just hanging with me for one last weekend before I get married. They realize that all of my hanging out will stop when I get married."

"That's why I'm marrying your sweet butterscotch ass, Joe. I love you so much."

"I'm sure I'll just be doing a little hanging out, some gambling, but most of all missing you."

"So what time are they supposed to be picking you up?"

"About eight o'clock, why?"

"I just thought we had a little time on our hands and hmmm."

"Hmmm, what, Trina?"

"You know what I mean by that hmmm, Joe."

"Yeah, I know what you mean, so come on over here and give me some sugar."

"I'm right here baby. Just take me, Joe. I'm yours, take me!"

Well, I guess it's only fair that I start my weekend of fucking around on my fiancée with fucking my fiancée. I started right there on the floor. The brothers wouldn't arrive for another three hours, so I had plenty of time to bang Trina real good and then pack. Then, I'll be off to Lake Tahoe for some serious messing around.

<u>CK</u>

The road to Lake Tahoe is about as curvy as the women in the centerfold of a nude magazine. It just keeps turning and turning. The slightest bit of over-compensation at the wheel could have you on the wrong side of one of the 150-foot cliffs. The climb to Lake Tahoe is nearly 7,000 feet above sea level. It almost makes my ears pop thinking about the height.

We decide to take my car since I have the smoothest vehicle. My Lexus 400 really hugs the road. They couldn't feel any bumps nor did they realize they were going over 85mph even in the curves, until Marcus spoke up.

"What the hell are you going so fast for, CK? We all want to get there, but we want to get there in one piece,"

"Shut the hell up, Marcus. When we drive that piece of shit Honda of yours, you can go as fast or as slow as you want," CK said.

"Piece of shit? At least my ride is paid for and my insurance isn't as much as another car note."

"That may be true, Marcus, but I can afford to pay for this car and the insurance on it. Thank you."

"Why don't we change the subject and talk about how I'm going to be kicking you brothers' behinds when we get to Lake Tahoe?" Joe said. "That's right, all of you will be owing me a favor, just wait and see."

"You're always tripping, Joe, nobody is scared of a little women competition, especially against a whipped man like yourself," Marcus said.

"Whipped, who the fuck is whipped? I am not whipped, I've just found the woman I want to marry," Joe said.

"Sure Joe, everybody except Trina knows you're a sex crazed dog," CK said.

"Yeah Joe, you'll probably get some strange pussy on your honeymoon," Taj said.

"I know that's right. You'll never be monogamous, Joe, never," Marcus said.

"Hell no, I'm going to be faithful to my sweetheart. This is the last weekend I'm going to be fucking around on Trina.".

"You believe that shit, CK and Taj?" Marcus asked sarcastically.

"No, I don't think Joe knows the meaning of faithful," CK said.

"He probably thinks it's a full glass of church wine," Marcus added, laughing hysterically.

"Keep on laughing. I'll have the last laugh after this weekend, just wait and see," Joe said.

"You all can stop tripping. I'm the one that's going to win the contest. After all I am the smoothest brother in this ride," Taj said.

We arrived in Lake Tahoe and checked into the Harrah's Hotel casino. It is richly decorated with wall-to-wall royal blue carpeting and expensive looking pictures on the walls. I'm sure many tourists have donated their savings to provide all of the luxurious decorations.

People crowded around the tables and slot machines. There were blackjack tables, crap tables, Caribbean Poker, "Let it Ride," and every kind of slot machine imaginable. Three cherries to win, four sevens, three bars and the huge mega-bucks machines. These were the largest slot machines you ever seen. The jackpot on these was about 10 million dollars.

119

People were winning and screaming all over the place. The air was filled with winning. Bells, whistles and people hollering at the top of their lungs after winning a mere 300 quarters on the slot machines, or hit for $20 on the blackjack table. This type of atmosphere just gets you all pumped up to gamble.

We all realize that we aren't here for gambling, just to win the Joe's Mack Daddy contest. We had it all planned. Everyone was to get separate rooms. The attendant at the counter inquired why we wouldn't double up and save about $200 off of our hotel costs for the weekend. We just told her that Joe snores, CK has a foot odor problem, Taj sleep walks, and Marcus is an insomniac. This made her laugh. Little does she know that the reason we were in separate rooms was to ensure each one of us had the privacy to pull as many women, as often as we could, this weekend.

Joe wasted no time, he was at the end of the counter talking to some fine-ass sister working the registration desk at the hotel. I'm sure she told him that they were strictly forbidden to mess around with the guests. That didn't stop Joe one bit. She was smiling ear to ear and clinging to Joe's words like a little schoolgirl, listening to the words of her favorite teacher. I wanted to go over and warn the poor girl, however the weekend was a game of challenge and I was not about to player hate.

We all got our electronic room keys, climbed into the elevators, and went up to the eighth floor. Our rooms were lined up, two on one side of the hallway and two directly across the hallway. Joe and Marcus got the even numbers, 824 and 826, me and Taj got 823 and 825.

This would work out perfectly, all of us would be able to do a little spying on each other. The spying would be to ensure everything was on the up and up. Everyone retreated to their rooms and began to unpack. I had packed very light and finished the task in less than ten minutes.

I decided to go down to the lobby and see what was lurking about. There were a bunch of beautiful women in the lobby, and then I decided to cross over to the casino area. There were waitresses wearing royal-blue short shorts with matching push-up-type bras that made even the smallest set of breasts look like they should be working at a Hooters restaurant. All I could see was nice breasts and shapely butts all over the place. The unfortunate thing was most of the best looking women were already hooked up with a man. There were a few women hanging out together, probably girlfriends. They were mostly white women, which seemed to make me feel like I had an edge on the brothers. It seems like the odds are very much in my favor. That's right, it's definitely CK's playground and the brothers didn't even know it.

All the brothers know that CK loves some vanilla in his diet. Marcus once told me at a club that I had something on my forehead that only the white girls in the club could see. He thought it might be an infrared dot. These white women would be coming up to both of us, but only say hello to me. They would do shit like pinch my ass or blow kisses from across the room. This shit would drive Marcus crazy. He would call me a white woman magnet. Marcus wasn't the only one tripping at the white women. The sisters in the club would always get pissed also. I remember one sister I didn't even know came up to me and said what the hell did this white bitch I was with have that she didn't have. I politely replied "me"! That sent her ass off steaming.

I ended up talking to this sexy, slender woman who happened to be up gambling with her sister, whom she couldn't find at the time. She was about 5'8" and had a round ass similar to some sisters I know. She had dark hair and it was done up like that famous gold-medal skater Dorothy Hamill. She was really cute. We exchanged pleasantries and I couldn't remember her name even after she told me. We made small talk and soon she was up in my room taking me in her mouth like she had some kind of lollipop. I couldn't believe how easy her ass was. I found a rubber and we assumed the missionary position for about thirty minutes. I stopped, still hard, and told her I had to meet my brothers in a few minutes. We agreed to hook up later and I pretended to be enthused by this. It turns out that sex with her was about as exciting as watching paint dry. I still took her panties and she didn't even mention them as she left. This little contest of Joe's is going to be won by yours truly. I've only been here about two hours and I got my first set of pink thong panties, size 6.

JOE

Donna is the newest trainee at the hotel check-in counter. I've been giving her some of my best rap. The brothers told me I was wasting my time trying to pick up a worker in the hotel. They were definitely shocked when they saw her ass sneaking into my room on her break. She didn't waste much time taking her clothes off, underneath was the smoothest, sexiest black skin I've ever seen. She was wearing a pair of emerald green panties and bra to match. They reminded me of the kind a preppy princess might wear. She ruined the moment when she spoke.

"I only get thirty minutes for my break, Joe, what do you want to do?"

This was one of the dumbest questions a woman standing in her panties and bra could ever ask. I simply replied, "We are going to fuck for twenty-nine of your thirty-minute break." With that I removed her underwear and was inside of her in a matter of moments. She didn't even make me put a rubber on. If a woman doesn't say anything I won't wear one. Them damn rubbers don't feel natural, are always busting, and if I'm going to catch something I'll catch it anyway.

I couldn't help thinking the whole time I'm fucking Donna that I'll be married in a week and this is the kind of shit I was giving up. Imagine all of the lonely women in the world just working day to day, waiting for a brother like me to come along and give them just what they want, some good old stiff loving.

I'm tossing little Donna around like a freshly prepared salad complete with my own specially prepared dressing.

When we finished she could hardly talk. She put her clothes back on, minus the panties of course. She protested the fact that I wouldn't give her the panties back, but I already had them and I wasn't giving them back. She started out of the room, headed back downstairs to work, mad and pantyless. My whole mission in Lake Tahoe is to win the contest and show the other brothers up. As soon as Donna went back to work, so did I.

I went back down to the casino to find my next victim. I decided to pass some time playing black jack. I started out with twenty dollars and before I knew it I had about $150. It was at that moment that this sister sat right next to me. I didn't even bother to look over at her at first. I was still concentrating on winning. When I looked up I saw her face, and then I leaned back to get a look at her ass. She had a nice round ass that I could've just reached over and grabbed. I think she caught me, because she was smiling at me when my eyes returned to hers. I smiled back, and said "Hello, my name is Joe, what's yours?"

"Hello, Joe, my name is Uman."

Uman was a very attractive sister with large strands of braids in her hair with some kind of weird hairpiece holding them together at the top of her head. Her complexion was as brown as an island girl after basking in the summer sun. Her makeup was done perfectly just like a model awaiting a photo shoot. I was very impressed, the sister looked like she had it going on.

She had a really strong foreign accent that was difficult to understand at first. She seemed like she was from West India or some island like Jamaica or Guyana. Whenever I hear someone talk with a hard accent and they are black, I always assume they are from West India, never Africa. I don't know why that is. We call each other African Americans, however none of us could tell you what African people talk or look like. The only way I know what they look like is because I watch the Discovery Channel.

"Where are you from, Uman?" I asked with a very sarcastic look on my face.

"I'm from San Francisco," she said.

"No, I mean where were you born?"

"I was born in the Dominican Republic. Where are you from, Joe?"

"I'm from Detroit, the motor city, have you ever been there?"

"I can't say I have. Is it nice?"

"Of course I'm biased, but I think it is the bomb! What brings a beautiful woman like yourself to Lake Tahoe?"

"Blackjack, gambling, and having fun."

"Don't they have blackjack in San Francisco?"

"Sure, but those are the small Indian reservations and they only have video blackjack."

"So, Uman, what else do you have planned?"

"That depends, Joe, did you have something in mind?"

"As a matter of fact I did. I thought we might go up to my room, order some dinner and get to know one another. How does that sound, Uman?"

"You move pretty fast, don't you?"

"Not all the time, only when I meet a beautiful woman from the Dominican Republic by way of San Francisco."

"I trust you haven't met too many women like that," she said.

"No, not at all, this must be my lucky day."

"In that case I'll go to your room if you include some wine with that food."

"You got it, Uman, you got it."

We get upstairs and a couple of the brothers were in the hallway, probably comparing the one set of panties they acquired. (I wondered if they were even trying to get hooked up since they were always in the damn hallway.) I could see their mouths drop from checking out Uman. She was looking so thick and juicy and I could hardly believe she followed me to my room so fast. I love

125

how these island women are so free spirited and well built. I think one would say they were built "like a brick shithouse." I was hoping to get a chance to test her tough frame out.

Surprisingly my room was clean, the maid even picked up my clothes and hung everything up. I hope she didn't go through my shit. I didn't think she would, this is one of the best hotels in Lake Tahoe and they wouldn't put up with thieving workers. I invited Uman to sit down. It was convenient for me that there was only room on the bed for her to sit. I purposely moved the table and chairs out of the way. She would've had to move stuff around to sit anywhere else. We made small talk and tried to figure out what we wanted to order from room service.

We figured out that Italian was what we wanted to eat with some red wine, which would complement the meal. Can you imagine an African American and a Dominican Republican each agreeing on Italian food without much discussion? I decided to seize the opportunity and make myself more comfortable. I went into the bathroom, out of respect. Normally I would just take all my clothes off right there in front of most women, but she seemed classy. I come out in a pair of silk boxer shorts with a robe to match.

"My, aren't we comfortable?" she said.

I played it off and said, "Is this too much for you? I just like to be comfortable when I eat with a beautiful woman."

"I'm glad we didn't choose the restaurant, it would be a little chilly for you in that robe," she said.

"That's very funny, Uman."

"I'm just teasing you, Joe, I wish I could get just as comfortable, but all of my stuff is in my room."

"I only brought one robe with me," I said.

"I could be convinced to put on a nice long-sleeved dress shirt if you have one, Joe?"

I must have whipped the shirt off the hanger and out of the closet in record time. She took the shirt I gave her and retreated to the bathroom. She returned after a few moments wearing the shirt and nothing else. I thought about rushing into the bathroom where she left her clothes to find and hide the contest pair of panties. I just chilled and complimented her on how much better she looked in that shirt than me.

"Thank you, Joe," she said. I love a woman in a man's dress shirt. Something about that look that really gives me an extra hard erection. I don't even know how I came to realize that I liked seeing a woman like that. I often wonder how brothers figure out what they like to see or when they realize how to make love to a woman. I don't always fuck, sometimes I make love to a woman. I make love to Trina, that's why her ass is marrying me. I never learned a damn thing about pleasing a woman from my father.

Most black families treat sexuality like it is taboo. I guess my parents were like most. My mother used to walk around like the Gestapo, ensuring we never missed a church gathering. Making sure my sisters wore skirts down to their knees and never pants. We always wore robes around the house and never ever were seen in our birthday suits. My father gallivanted around the neighborhood like an adult teenager. He was commonly known as the Mack daddy of the little public housing project where we grew up on the south side of Detroit.

Even when my parents decided to make love, fuck, or whatever they called it, it was always hush, hush. They would put their large mirrored dresser in front of the bedroom door, providing a Fort Knox type barrier between them and us (we couldn't even peep through the keyhole). This was the exact moment me and my brothers and sisters always wanted something, however we knew not to knock or try to gain access. As soon as they finished we would trickle in to ask questions and the room would smell like a recently-filled-to-capacity gym or sauna. The smell was what I later found out to be the distinctive smell of fresh sex.

Why didn't daddy pull my brothers and me to the side and give us a lesson in stroking, caressing, making love, or even how to fuck a woman? I found out all of that shit on my own, by trial and a whole lot of error. Most brothers start out jumping a woman and humping to see just how many times they can stick it in and out of her before their nature goes soft. Some never learn how to really make love to a woman.

All women are different, however, they are all the same when it comes to being loved. They may like it different ways, but they still like it. They desire attention, caressing, kissing, good conversation, and finally the actual act of sex. I found my best skills while dating this one sister in college. We were both rookies when it came to making love, having sex, or giving each other pleasure. I mean she had some basic skills and so did I, however it was really pretty boring and ritualistic. One day we decided to do some experimenting and read books on the subject of sex. Eventually we became better and better at our sexual exploitations.

I remember times when we were able to even please one another without any penetration. Let me tell you when you can make a woman reach an orgasm without giving her head or using your lower head, you have arrived.

The first time it happened to me I remember smiling myself to sleep, while my sweetheart kissed and hugged me. The other thing brothers need to learn is it is necessary to give a woman some afterplay. The foreplay is all good, the actual play is good also, but good loving deserves good afterloving. I like to think of it as a complete workout. First you stretch, then you warm up. This is to prepare yourself and your lover, then the actual lovemaking takes place. Once that is done, just like a complete workout, you need a cool-down period. A period of time to just hold and caress her like she's the sweetest, most gentle thing you could hold. (Also since she just made you feel so good inside).

I've noticed some brothers hit the gym, still cold from outside, and jump right into their workout. As soon as their last set or game is done they make a mad dash for the car, no warm-up, stretch, or cool-down. I can't help but wonder if their love lives are getting the same kind of rush. I bet it is. I hope the ladies do their homework and follow their next mate to the gym just to see how he does it. If he isn't going to the gym or working out somehow, don't wonder why the love isn't happening, he probably just doesn't know what a complete workout is.

I hear a knock on the door and it's a guy from room service with the wine and our food. I tip him quickly and send him on his way. I turn to see Uman has made herself comfortable on the bed in my shirt, and is just waiting for me. I bring the tray of food to the bed and begin serving my Dominican acquaintance.

She sits there like a spoiled child being served by her protective father. I break open the wine and we begin to dine. I've dropped the robe by now and keep only my boxers and watch on. She has unbuttoned the shirt to where I can see how curvy and firm her breasts are. It is a little chilly in the room, because I can see her nipples protruding through the shirt. They remind me of the large M&Ms with peanuts. I'm anxious to see if they would in fact melt in my mouth, *or* my hands. Uman noticed me staring at her breasts and broke the silence:

"Do you like what you see, Joe?"

"Of course I do. You're sexy as hell, Uman."

"Would you like to see more, Joe?"

"Hell, yes!"

Before I could get the last syllable of yes out of my mouth she was undressed. I realized at that moment why men go so crazy over some foreign women. She seemed so uninhibited and comfortable with her sexuality. She had a slight thickness about her, which actually made her sexier. Not fat or what I would classify as a woman in shape. She had a very nice body of a woman that spent a lot of her earlier days working out. It did appear that the last few years had allowed some excess pounds to seep onto her already long and tall frame. I just stood there admiring this girl's body.

"So what do you think we should do now?" she asked.

"Let's just be quiet and show each other what we should do."

We began to kiss passionately which evolved into making love. It was so intense I felt my heart pounding and had an extreme shortness of breath. She knew exactly how to please a man and showed me what pleased her. This was definitely a woman a man would fall in love with on the very first date. After we made love for what seemed like over an hour, I was so tingly inside. I felt like one of those sensitive-type men women always talk about wanting.

We kissed goodbye without any conversation or promises of seeing each other again. The one thing I forgot to get was the prized pair of panties. I later realized she wasn't wearing any. I didn't even care about them. I actually didn't think of her as a conquest to win the contest. It was very ironic that she didn't have any underwear for me to keep. I couldn't help thinking if I would see her again. I knew I wouldn't forget her. I laughed when I said her name to myself, Uman. I would remember it by saying to myself, "you are the man."

MARCUS

Man, none of these women seem to be by themselves. I've been spitting out some of my best material on these single bimbos. I can't understand what's going wrong. I better get me some panties soon. All I get is "it's nice to meet you, Marcus, but I'm married" or "I'm here with someone." One young lady had the nerve to give me her e-mail address so we could hook up back in Sacramento. I needed their underwear here in Lake Tahoe not when I get back home. The brothers are going to laugh my ass all the way back home if I don't get a few pairs of panties.

Just as I was going into self-pity overdrive I saw the finest sister I've seen in a long time and she was walking alone. This was my chance to hook up with some prime booty. I walked around the casino so I could head her off and appear to run into her. I was pushing and bumping into strangers in my attempt to meet a perfect stranger. She was coming towards me now and I took a moment to catch my breath. As she walked closer to me she began to smile at me and said "hello."

"Hi, my name is Marcus, what's yours?"

"My name is Elizabeth, but you can call me Liz for short."

"It's nice to meet you, Liz."

"Likewise, Marcus, and what brings you to Lake Tahoe?"

"One of my best friends is getting married and we are just hanging out for the weekend."

"So is this the 'bachelors' weekend together?"

"Something like that, we are just trying to have a little fun before the big day."

"Are you and your friends going to tempt your buddy into having some wild strip party with booze and plenty of wild sex?"

"No, however, I'm sure you and I could come up with a private show of our own."

"You think you could handle that, Marcus?"

"I'll put my best foot forward, Liz."

I could not believe my ears. Moments ago I was trying to figure out how to get myself a pair of panties and then I run into this beautiful sexy, woman. After talking to her for a few moments she winds up being the freak of the year. We make our way to the elevators and up to my room. I couldn't help looking at her very slender, lovely ass. It reminded me of that movie where this hooker whipped her pussy on this guy so good he called his wife and told her he was never coming home again. They called her Sunshine. I could sure use some Sunshine right now, and a pair of Sunshine's panties. I don't have a wife to call, but I'd gladly dial the operator and tell her.

We got to my room and I was pissed that none of the brothers were around in the hallway to see big Marcus bring home a fine sister. Liz didn't waste much time once we got into the room. I was getting head right by the door. We were knocking furniture around and bumping into everything trying to get to the bedroom. We made it to the bedroom and did it on the floor right next to the beautiful bed recently made up by the maid. It was intense, and I had thought this was going to be one of those lame weekends. She was so animated the whole time I was doing her. She kept yelling for me to do it harder or yes right there. It was very nice to hear a woman let go.

She wasn't like a lot of women I know, afraid to let their man know just what they like and exactly where they like it. She must have had at least two orgasms that I could tell. We finished and I got up off of her feeling pretty good about my performance.

She showered and asked me if I had seen her panties. Of course I denied knowing where they were. We both did some superficial looking around and decided that the room was in such a mess that they could be anywhere. She finally thought about how many pairs she had and told me I could keep them when I found them.

She got dressed and then came towards me with this sinister look on her face.

"That will be $100, Mr. Marcus," she said.

"What do you mean $100, for what?"

"What do you think? The $100 is for the fuck I just gave you. You don't really think you charmed me with your wit and lured me into your hotel room so fast to make love to you for free, do you?"

"I thought you just wanted to get busy with me just as much as I wanted to with you."

"No, Marcus, I am a working girl and I just finished my job so I would like to get paid."

"You mean you're a whore?"

"That word is a bit out-dated, don't you think? I prefer working or call girl."

"Out-dated, my ass, it still applies to what you do, doesn't it? I'm not paying you shit. You can just get the fuck out! I'll just call hotel security and tell them you are soliciting in their hotel. I'm sure they have some vice agents that would love to take your ass to jail."

"I'm not leaving until you pay me. Call them. As soon as they get here I'll rip my clothes myself and tell them you raped me. I'll be even more convincing than I was when you were sticking your little nature in me. Besides no one knows me around here, I come up here about once a month and take guys like you to the cleaners simply because you think with the wrong head. I want my money and I want it now!"

I contemplate the situation and I realize that I should pay the woman and avoid any undue attention, especially rape charges. That is one thing that you never get away from. Once someone accuses you of rape even if you didn't do it everyone seems to think you are guilty even after you are proven innocent.

I paid her the $100 and told her to "get the fuck out of my room."

"Don't be upset, Marcus, you got what you wanted and I got what I wanted. Isn't that unusual when a man and a woman get together? The woman is usually the one who gets cheated. When you find my panties keep them as a souvenir to remember our time together," she said sarcastically.

"I'll probably burn them to remind me of the place you came from, hell!"

I slammed the door on her and realized that a professional had just taken me. I thought I was cashing in on my first pair of panties to win the contest and they turn out to be the most expensive pair of panties I've ever bought. Forget this stupid contest, I'm just going to chill out for the rest of the weekend. Besides now I'm damn near broke.

TAJ

I can't win this stupid contest of Joe's. I've been here two days and the only underwear I've gotten are boxers and briefs. I guess I'm holding my own little contest. This is some sick shit I'm going through. I'm a confused heterosexual, who is probably bisexual, however I must be homosexual since I haven't been with a woman since the incident with Andre. It's been about two weeks since I got out of jail and I haven't seen or talked to him, but I can't get him out of my mind. He's also left me with this intense desire to be with other men. Here I am in Lake Tahoe trying to win a heterosexual contest with my over sexed brothers and I'm slowly turning into a hard-core homosexual. I have to get some panties one way or another.

I know the brothers will be laughing their asses off when I show up without one single pair of panties. Maybe I could find some woman and buy them off of her. I'm so confused because I agreed to this stupid contest with the intentions of getting some pussy and getting my ass back on track with women.

I've been with three men in two days. It's like I've got some newfound magnetism for butt buddies. How in the world did I become gay? I'm also starting to get targeted by guys who seem to know I'm willing to swing that way.

The first guy I met was in the hotel gift shop. I was just picking out a sweatshirt to take back to Andre. My plan was to

135

give him a call when I returned to Sacramento and remind him how fucked up what he did to me was.

This very well-dressed, nice-looking guy comes into the shop. We catch each other's eyes and he smiles. I look away, appearing to be disinterested. When I looked up again he was only inches from me still looking and still smiling.

"Hello, my name is Paul," he said.

"I'm Taj, it's nice to meet you," I said in my deepest voice and still appearing disinterested. We shook hands and I remember trying to squeeze his hand to show him that I was all man, but his grip was even stronger than mine. I was a little embarrassed.

Did I have a big mark on my forehead that said, "over here, I just became gay?" Some people say gay men can tell when another man is gay. I always thought you could tell this because he would be bouncing around acting like a damn woman. I definitely don't fit that description. Why was this guy in my face like he knew a secret that I was hiding?

Paul was 6'2", a clean-cut white guy with dark hair. He looked like he could be a model. I knew he worked out because he had the nicest arms and shoulders. I couldn't even figure out why I was thinking about stuff like that. I would notice guys before but never thought twice about how built they were. Before I could say anything to deny my recent gay curiosity, he made a motion with his head like I was to follow him. I quickly purchased the sweater for Andre so that I wouldn't feel totally guilty later. I was turned on by Andre and now was about to start having casual sex with other men just like I did with so many women. I was "dating" men now. This was definitely a scary thought.

I followed Paul up to the elevators and prayed that none of the brothers saw me. I don't know why I was afraid for them to see me, I wasn't actually doing anything that would make me appear to be gay. We entered the elevator and I waited for the doors to close and we were alone.

I stood slightly in front of Paul and on the other side of the elevator. I couldn't believe I was actually afraid. His hand brushed by me and I began to get excited. He was reaching to push a button for the floor we were headed to. He pushed the ninth floor and I could feel my heart beating in my chest. The silence was excruciating and I couldn't help wondering what the hell Paul was doing behind me. He probably was just waiting for me to turn around so I could see that silly smirk on his face again.

I just watched the elevator take forever to get to the ninth floor. It was strange that the elevator never stopped to pick anyone up. The elevator stopped at the ninth floor and Paul brushed by me and got off. I almost let the door close between us but my hand slipped into the door and it opened up again. There was Paul with that same smile on his face.

He didn't say anything since telling me his name. It's like he knew that I'd recently been converted to being gay and still had certain impressions to maintain. I was about to have another gay experience and Paul was the experienced one in this situation.

I'm used to running the show when I'm after some prissy little woman who thinks her shit don't stink. When I put the burners on in hot pursuit, she would soon be submitting to me and then I would just dump her ass. It did wonders for her disposition, however it was hell on her self-concept. Now here is a perfectly strange gay guy picking me up. My, how times have changed.

We walked down the long hotel hallway headed to Paul's room, and I remember maneuvering around a maid's cart. I was thinking that hotel maids probably saw more wild shit than you could put in a book. I was moving fast now, I didn't want some cleaning woman to see me going into Paul's room. We got to his room and he unlocked the door. I remember it was room 932. It was an even number and there were two odd-balls about to enter. Once safely in his room Paul took charge. I was just standing there by the door with my hands at my side. I stood there like a scared little puppy. I was clearly taller and about thirty pounds heavier than Paul was. I knew that if he started anything I didn't agree with that I could kick his ass.

He didn't waste any time. I let him undress me from head to toe and I actually stepped out of my slacks for him. Paul took me in his mouth and I closed my eyes and caught myself picturing Andre. I thought this was crazy. Anytime I was with some woman who wasn't that attractive but maybe had a nice body I always pictured someone famous.

I would picture Jada Pinkett, Vanessa Williams or Janet Jackson. These were some of the finest women in the world and I would fantasize about them. I even had my line all set if I ever met any one of them. I would say, "Who would believe me if I told them I slept with you anyway?" While they contemplated this obvious question I would eventually wind up knee deep in some Hollywood booty. I was really scaring myself, that I was thinking about Andre instead.

Paul interrupted my thoughts when he stopped. He led me by the hand into his bedroom and actually pushed me down onto the bed. It was a little late for me to get defensive now. He placed a rubber on himself and then took the time to unroll one inch by inch on me. I never uttered one word. I just lay there like so many women I'd taken advantage of.

I knew I would object soon, since I saw him put a rubber on himself. Andre never got me to the receiving part. My ass still had a sign on it that said, "exit only." Only shit came out and nothing was going in. I was clearly from a football standpoint a tight end, not a wide receiver.

Paul placed his tight, lubricated ass right on top of me and started grimacing and groaning while jerking off. He did this until he came right into the rubber he was wearing. The whole thing was so clean it was funny.

I got up and got dressed and left Paul lying there without any words. The next two guys I slept with were just a result of my becoming a bolder faggot. I mean homosexual or whatever is the most politically correct description of my closet antics.

Each guy realized that I was a new recruit. I guess it was the way I looked or acted. I don't know what it is but I've had three men pick me up and have sex with me in one weekend. I can't remember having three women pick me up like that. I guess it's because usually I'm the one doing the picking up.

Joe's little panty challenge is about to end and I need to get my hands on some woman's panties. I contemplated how I would be able to do this and I thought about the hotel concierge. They get paid big bucks to remain discreet and they know everything. I found him standing by the desk with his name written on a large gold placard. His name was Donald and he must have been about twenty-two. I approached him and asked him if he could help me with a small problem and if he could remain discreet. I explained the contest we were having and that I needed the panties to be used. I handed him a $50 bill and he dashed off. About twenty minutes went by and Donald was on his way back towards me. He handed me a small bag from the hotel gift shop. I thought I explained to him that they couldn't be new. The guys would smell the newness on them and jump in my shit for trying to cheat. I looked in the bag and inside were three pairs of used women's panties, each a different size.

This was perfect. I asked Donald how did he get them so quickly. He laughed at first, then he told me not to say anything when the women working out in the hotel gym complained of someone stealing their panties. The hotel will simply buy them a new pair of their choice from the hotel clothing shop. I was finally breathing easy, I could show the brothers that I did my share of trying to win the contest, and Taj would still be the man, in their eyes anyway. The ironic thing about getting three pairs of women's panties is that I actually slept with three guys.

JOE

I got back to my room and had a pair of panties slide under my door with a note that read: *A little something to remember me by, signed Uman*. How did she know about the pair of panties? I couldn't believe she actually came back and left me her panties. I sure would've liked to get some more of that Dominican ass. Oh well that makes two pairs of panties for yours truly. The brothers would never find out that my third pair of panties came from Donna, the little clerk from the hotel registration counter.

They would probably call it cheating but she was on my tip so hard I had to hit it again. To think this girl would risk losing her job twice just to get some dick. She came up to my room after calling me to see if she could have an encore of our first encounter. I roughed her up as usual and put her out of my room, once again protesting about my keeping her panties. Donna was wearing thongs this time and I was actually proud to have taken them from her. She probably thought I had some kind of panty fetish. I didn't give a shit. I'm just a brother trying to win a contest. I want all of my brothers owing me a favor and I want to be crowned "Big Player" before I get married. I could care less what she thinks anyway. We'll probably never meet again, and if we do I wouldn't even speak to her especially if I was with Trina. I even gave her a bogus number to call me whenever she was in Sacramento. I don't know what number I gave her. I just wrote down some numbers and handed it to her.

Sisters should always have a brother repeat his number to them even if he writes it down. If he can't repeat what he just gave them, he is definitely full of shit, just like me.

I went back down to the lobby to see if I could find out how well the other brothers were doing with the contest. I spotted Donna talking to this other sister at the hotel registration desk. She was a lot taller and even finer than Donna. She was a lot healthier also, I figured she wore a nice loose 9/10 dress.

Most men don't even know what size their women are or how to tell about what size a woman is. I make it a point to be real attentive to what size women wear, from their clothes to their shoes, and especially waist and wrist size. All of this information will come in handy when you are looking for the perfect gift when trying to make a good impression or if you've just fucked up.

I'm just standing there, checking out Donna on her day off giving me some pussy and not to mention another pair of panties. I casually walk up to the counter. Donna says hello as if she didn't really know me. Then she decides to introduce me to her co-worker. Her thicker girlfriend's name was Stephanie. Stephanie had a nice large ass. It made dear old Donna's ass look like a small grape standing next to an extra ripe and juicy grapefruit. I couldn't help watching her butt as she reached for keys and handled her business at the counter while Donna was looking through some papers.

"So how long are you and your buddies going to be staying in Lake Tahoe?" Stephanie asked.

"We only have one more night left, we leave tomorrow evening."

I could tell that Donna had been running her mouth. How else would she know about me and the brothers checking in the other day? I told Stephanie it was nice to meet her and waved good bye to Donna. I headed for the elevator and went back up to my room to take me a nice needed nap.

I think I went to sleep before my head hit the pillow. Why was I so tired? Donna wasn't much of a challenge this time. She squirmed and groaned for almost an hour while I wore her ass out. It must be the fact that I was probably winning my own contest and it was wearing me down.

The phone awakened me, and I knew it was one of the brothers calling me to see what or who I was up to. To my surprise it was Stephanie, the other clerk at the hotel. At first I thought she was calling me for Donna who wasn't on duty today. I knew something was strange though, because she was actually whispering on the phone like someone was listening to her. It was like she didn't want anyone to know she was calling me. I played stupid for a moment.

"Can I help you with something, Stephanie?" I asked suspiciously.

"Um, I was just down here thinking about what you said earlier, that you and your friends were only here for one more night."

"Yes, that's true. I was just taking a nap so I could go out partying tonight."

"Where were you all going to go?"

"I'm not sure, do you know of any spots up here that we can check out?"

"There are a couple of nice clubs but they are usually filled with college kids."

"Well, what else is there to do?" I had her ass then because she got real quiet. It seemed like the silence lasted for nearly a minute.

"I did have something in mind."

"What's that, Stephanie?"

"Well, I get off at 8:30 and even though I could get into a lot of trouble I could swing by your room and hang out with you on your last night."

"That sounds like a plan. But what about your friend Donna?"

"She's a co-worker and I really don't consider her a friend. I thought she was a friend of yours, Joe?"

"We just met this weekend so she's definitely not a friend of mine."

"So I guess I'll see you a little after 8:30," she said.

"Okay, I'll see you then. I'll just leave the door unlocked. You can come straight in."

"Should I bring anything?" she said.

"No, just you would be fine enough."

I hung up the phone and yelled out, "I'm the mother fucking man!"

I should have told her to make sure she brings her panties, since she won't be leaving with any.

Donna must have told Stephanie how I wore her ass out. I could hear her now "girl, that man put something on my ass I will never forget. He had me in so many positions and I must have come four or five different times."

Women always tell on a brother. If he did well it gets told; if he strikes out it also gets told. I call it referral pussy. When I get some pussy as a result of a woman telling another woman it's "referral pussy."

Women need to realize that they can't tell their girlfriends everything. It goes along with that old saying about keeping your friends close and your enemies even closer. When women start revealing the intimate details of their relationships with a man, they should be prepared to share that man with the woman they gave all of the information to.

The reason some women act on the information provided is simple. There are entirely too many brothers out there not representing. They're mistreating their women either physically or emotionally and then not even taking the time to make the sex good. They go around bragging about their sexual prowess and the women involved are singing a totally different tune. When a woman finds out about a brother who is laying the pipe down right they are immediately intrigued. No matter how they found out about the brother.

The woman giving up the information should not assume that the female she's talking to is getting the same thing at home. She may be getting the two-minute limp dick surprise at home and you come along and tell her about the hour of power. Eventually the woman starts to wonder if what you say is true or if his shit will work on her as well as it worked on you. Once curious the rest is history.

I heard the door squeak and I knew it was Stephanie. She must have rushed up here since it was only 8:35 and she got off work at 8:30. I was in the bedroom stark naked, straddled across the bed with my dick standing hard and tall like a flagpole with no flag. I heard Stephanie calling me.

"Joe, it's me, Stephanie, where are you?"

"I'm in the bedroom." She walked into the bedroom and I saw her mouth drop when she saw that I was in my original birthday suit.

"Oh my God, Joe." she said, fumbling her words. She was dumbfounded. Just then she started getting undressed.

It works every time. Just be naked when a woman invites herself over to your place and you know she wants some dick. The pressure of being the only one in the room with their clothes on will get to her eventually and soon she'll be undressed also.

We didn't waste much time getting our groove on either.

I couldn't help noticing Stephanie's panties before she took them off. They were kind of sexy, however they looked too small for a woman with such a big ass. I uncharacteristically placed a rubber on this time, and laid her down on the bed beside me. She seemed to me like a very confident woman who was getting cheated out of exploring her sexuality.

She was nervous and I remember telling her to relax. She was wet before I even had a chance to penetrate her. I entered Stephanie and she let out a very sexy groan while grabbing my shoulders real tight. This made me smile and begin concentrating on the mission at hand.

I knew Donna had given her a real good report, why else would she go to the trouble to hook up with me? I had to make sure I held up to my end of the bargain. I started getting into my rhythm and thinking about different things to keep my mind off of how good she felt so I could remain hard. I was thinking about this being my last weekend of messing around on Trina. I had to make every moment count.

Stephanie was quiet at first and then the ghetto started coming out of her.

"Yeah, mother fucker, yeah, Joe, you mother fucker."
"Hit that shit, Joe, hit that shit."

At first she was nervous and quiet and now she was yelling the whole time. I was getting a little scared because I thought someone might think I was beating her ass and call security. I have to admit her obscenities and screaming really had me excited.

Now any brother will tell you that there are a lot of women out there afraid of exploring their sexuality. When we find one that isn't afraid to talk, laugh, or scream out during sex, it is a beautiful thing. This kind of thing really pumps a brother up and makes him want to do more and more to make her yell louder and louder. Stephanie was yelling and letting me know she was about to orgasm. She must have had about ten years of build up. I never knew a woman could enjoy sex so much. I think she had about four orgasms in a row. I couldn't keep up with all of them, she was just too damn loud. When we finished she just lay there on the bed like a towel dropped after a shower. I was so pumped up trying to get her off, and I was still hard as a rock. I got up, made sure I hid my prize winning pair of panties, and took me a cold shower.

When I got out of the shower Stephanie was asleep. She was sleeping like a baby and I couldn't believe how peaceful she looked. She was like a child sleeping on Christmas night after a full day of gifts and excitement.

I didn't want to bother her so I went into the next room and cut on the television to see what was on. I caught an episode of Cops and was laughing at all of the brothers hiding from the cameras to avoid being seen on the news. Some brothers are a trip.

Have a news crew show up in any city neighborhood and just watch all of the brothers that try to give their version of what happened. Soon as they get caught robbing or shooting someone they throw a jacket over their head and avoid the cameras, the shit is really funny. I was having a good time when the phone rang. I answered it and it was Donna.

"Hi, Joe. It's Donna. What are you up to?"

"I was just watching some TV."

"I was wondering if you wanted some company on your last night here."

"I don't think so, me and the brothers are going to hang out later on."

"Well I guess that means I won't get to see you before you leave?"

"I'm sure you'll see me before I leave, I'll stop and say goodbye before I check out."

"You know what I mean, Joe, I mean actually see you up close and personal."

"Maybe we can hook up in Sacramento when you get the time?"

"I imagine that's all I can look forward to. I'll see you tomorrow, good night, Joe."

Man, that was close. I should have invited Donna over and watch the sparks fly when she saw her co-worker lying in my bed. In fact, why am I so concerned about her anyway? I'm getting married in a week and I really don't care what happens between these two bitches. Neither one of them can cause too much confusion because they'll both lose their jobs.

I was feeling pretty sinister. I guess it was from watching Cops or I needed some more excitement my last weekend as a bachelor. I called Donna back and told her that I changed my mind and I to get her ass over here as soon as possible. She gave me her cellular number earlier and could tell she was in her car, probably nearby.

"I'm only a few minutes from the hotel so I'll see you in a few," she said.

"I'll leave the door unlocked, so let yourself in."

I waited a few moments and then went into the bedroom and sure enough Stephanie was still sleeping. I decided that I would begin round two with Stephanie and be banging her when Donna came in. I started feeling on Stephanie and kissing her on her butt and on the insides of her thighs. She started getting wet again and before you know it she was taking me in her mouth and the girl had some skills.

Stephanie was going down on me with the intensity of a high priced hooker. Just then I heard the door close. Stephanie must not have heard it because she kept on sucking and tugging on me like no tomorrow.

Donna came in and she must have been watching us for a few moments from the doorway.

"Joe, what the fuck is going on?" she said. "You invited me over to watch some other bitch suck on you?"

Just then Stephanie jumped up and turned around toward Donna and said, "Who are you calling a bitch?"

"Stephanie, what the fuck are you doing here?"

"What does it look like I'm doing her? I'm giving Joe some head!"

"Why can't you find your own man? You need to go behind me and get sloppy seconds?"

"Where do you get off thinking that you can lay claim to someone just because you had them first? You should've kept your mouth shut about him anyway. I found out he is just as good as you said he would be, only I think he fits me better. Don't you think so, Joe?"

"Well it sure felt good to me," I said smartly.

"Joe, you said the same thing to me," Donna said. "You are a son of a bitch. Why would you do this to me?"

"I haven't done anything to you, you did this to yourself. Why did you tell your friend about us anyway?"

"I was just sharing an exciting adventure with someone I thought was a friend," Donna said, while looking at Stephanie.

"Friends? Why do you think we are such good friends, Donna? Have we ever done anything together outside of work? Do we talk to each other on the phone? Have you ever been to my place or invited me to yours? The answer is no, so where do you get off talking this friends bullshit!"

"I guess you're right, I just thought that if I told you I was messing around with a man you would respect that."

"I respected that and waited until you weren't around to get a piece of him myself."

"Well I think one of us should leave and it's not going to be me," Donna said.

"I'm not going anywhere, Donna, you'd better get a grip. I intend to finish what I started," Stephanie said.

I couldn't believe my eyes. Stephanie started sucking on me again even harder this time. She was slurping and making these extra noises to accentuate her act for Donna.

Then things got real freaky. Donna started taking her clothes off and my eyes got wide as two doughnuts. Donna climbed onto the bed and began kissing on me and rubbing my head. This was some wild shit, I thought I was in some X-rated movie. Stephanie moved up and started kissing on my chest and sucking on my nipples, almost moving Donna out of the way. This whole scene was really turning me on. Donna picked up where Stephanie left off and started sucking on me like it was a contest. I was ready to start banging someone. I wasn't sure which one I should start with.

Maybe Donna, since I met her first, or maybe Stephanie, since she was here first tonight. I wasn't sure. Just then I got the shock of my life. Donna was no longer sucking on me, but Stephanie was kissing me. Stephanie abruptly stopped kissing me and all of a sudden she slammed her head back onto the pillow like she was being pulled from behind. It scared me for a moment.

I looked down and there was Donna with her face buried in Stephanie's crotch. I couldn't believe my eyes, they were about to fight only moments ago and now she was going down on her. I got myself together and seized the opportunity to take Donna from behind. She was making Stephanie moan and groan and soon I was stroking her doggie style.

After several moments like this everything swapped. Now Stephanie had her face buried in Donna's crotch and I was inside of Stephanie. They were both enjoying this little menage-a-trois and I was having the time of my life. Who would have thought I would have two freaks in my room at the same time one week before my wedding? Who needs bachelor parties? This was the ultimate closure to a sex-filled single life. This whole scene went on for about forty minutes but it seemed like hours. I wondered how women come to realize that they are freaks. When we were done we all got into the shower together and washed each other.

Why was I giving up shit like this to get married? I must need some psychological counseling or something. At least I'll have some real good memories when things aren't going too well with Trina. She was even tripping when I left to come up here this weekend.

Heaven knows I couldn't marry one of these women here in the shower with me. I'd probably come home one day and find another woman in my bed. That wouldn't bother me unless my shit was packed and I was being replaced. That is the price you pay for messing around with a woman who has experienced being with another woman and liked it.

We all got dressed and Donna started again.

"Where the fuck are my panties, Joe?"

Of course I claimed my innocence. "I can't find mine either, Joe," Stephanie said.

They both looked at each other and laughed. Neither one of them was leaving with their panties. When I closed the door I replayed the whole night in my mind. A brother couldn't ask for a more pleasurable fun-filled weekend of fucking as I had just experienced.

I was up to five pairs of panties and thought that would be enough to win the contest. Even if I didn't win the contest I had validated myself as "The Player" this weekend. Now I could cut up my players' card and get married with a clean slate.

I'm sure my daddy would be proud of me. I bet when he was my age he was a sweet lady-killer just like me. My mother always talked about how whorish he was and I guess I grew up to be just like him.

One thing is different about dear old dad and me, I will not cheat on my wife or leave my family. Besides Trina would kill my ass if she ever caught me cheating or trying to leave her. Tomorrow we head back to Sacramento and I'm going to walk right up to Trina and tell her I want to spend the rest of my life with her. That would be straight from the heart, since I'll have this weekend of sex behind me. I'm convinced this weekend is the last escapade of promiscuity I'll ever have.

CK

I continue my quest to find the next pair of panties to win this contest. It seems like a vanilla ice cream convention, vanilla being the flavor of women I prefer anyway. Most of the women here are married or with someone. I knew, given the right circumstances, even some of the married ones are willing to mess around. The wife is usually with some high roller husband. He visits Lake Tahoe and spends ten to twelve hours in a high stakes poker game.

You can usually spot the wife a mile away. She would be overdressed, wearing an evening gown in the middle of the day. She'll have plenty of makeup on, tons of jewelry, and expensive perfume. She can be found sitting in the lounge or seeing a show by herself or maybe in the cafeteria nursing a cup of coffee with "I'm lonely" written all over her face. I actually noticed someone who fit that description perfectly.

She was an older white woman about fifty or sixty years old. The gray hair was the only thing that gave her years away. She was very refined and one could tell she took very good care of herself. The money dear old hubby had was being spent on manicures, pedicures and facials. She was actually kind of cute. I can't remember looking at a woman that much older than me and wondering what it would be like to sleep with her. I took a chance and went over to say hello to her.

"Hello, my name is CK, what's yours?"

"My name is Mona, and I'm expecting my husband to join me at any moment."

"Is that a fact?"

"Yes that is a fact, and I would appreciate it if you would leave."

I would've left right away under normal circumstances, but she was smiling and winking at me while telling me to leave. It was some sort of mixed signal, verbally blowing me off, but interested in me at the same time. She convinced me to walk away, however I made sure she saw exactly where I was headed. I chose a nice hidden row of nickel slot machines no one seemed to be playing. I sat in front of this machine with a bunch of different ways to win. The best combination was three sevens. I pulled a twenty-dollar bill out, put it in the machine, and began to play.

I figured I would mess around with this machine until Mona decided to come over. I was pulling the large handle of this one-armed bandit. Someone sure coined a perfect phrase for slot machines since they rob more people than they pay off. I'm trying to appear inconspicuous, however I can't help looking around to see if Mona has made her way over to me. I finally noticed what appeared to be Mona coming towards me and I got excited. Here I was like a little child playing this stupid machine trying to look inconspicuous while I waited for this sexy old lady to approach me. It was silly but it was a very nice feeling. I pretend to be into this machine until she gets right up next to me. I turn to say hello as I pulled the handle on the machine again.

I was standing there smiling about to say something to her when the damn machine started ringing, whistling and lighting up. It startled me at first, then all I could think about was shutting the machine up. It was drawing too much attention to Mrs. Mona and I. The machine was spitting out nickels so fast I couldn't even figure out how much I had won. I glanced up at the screen and there were three sevens in a row, like a perfect hit on fourteen in blackjack. Mona interrupted all of the noise, "It looks like you hit a jackpot!" "And I also won some money," I said.

"So, Mona, tell me, why the mixed signals earlier?"

"My girlfriend, who happens to be married to my husband's best friend, was watching me. I just wanted her to think I was blowing you off, but I was very intrigued by the fact that you came over and said hello to me in the first place. She makes it a point to be in my business whenever she can."

"So why were you sitting by yourself?"

"I was just relaxing and I was tired of gambling. I wasn't expecting my husband. He's probably in the poker room having the time of his life with a bunch of cigar-smoking, card-playing low lifes."

"Mona, calm down, it can't be all that bad."

"It is actually. I can't remember the last time he paid me any attention."

"How often do you come up to Lake Tahoe?" I asked.

"We fly up once or twice a month. We own a cabin right off of the south lake. It's a real nice cabin, but we don't stay there that often. Most of the time we check into one of the hotel casinos. That way my husband can drink, play poker until the wee hours of the morning, and then stumble up to our room, before crashing to sleep. Once we came up on a three-day weekend and he played poker for two days straight. He slept the entire third day, so you can imagine how much fun that was."

"What do you do for fun while he's playing poker for days?"

"I usually play a few nickel and dime slots, some roulette, or watch a show, I'm not much of a gambler. It gets very boring sometimes."

"Mona, I may have an idea to spice up your vacation."

"What's that, CK?"

"I thought you and I should have lunch together."

"I couldn't, CK, someone might see us together, especially my nosy girlfriend."

"Not if we had lunch up in my room."

"That's awful bold of you, CK, do you realize that I'm probably twice your age plus?"

"I realize you're an older woman but I thought you were attractive the moment I saw you sitting by yourself."

I could tell that she was very much intrigued at this point and I knew I had her.

"I'll have to think about lunch in your room, CK. Why don't you give me your room number and I'll let you know if I can show up."

"If you decide to show up, I'll be expecting you around 12 p.m."

I said goodbye to Mona and turned to find the attendant had finally shut the machine off and was preparing some paperwork for me to sign. The IRS had to get their part of my little jackpot. When I was finished I had won almost $1,200 in nickels. I signed the paperwork, put the cash in my pocket and headed up to my room to await Mona's possible arrival. All I could think about was another pair of contest winning panties. They'd probably be from Neiman Marcus or Nordstroms, very nice and very expensive.

It seemed like I was in my room for only a half-hour when I heard a knock at the door. I took my time waiting for her to knock again and wonder if I was there. I went to the door and opened it. There was Mona, looking totally different than I had seen her before. She had this very nice black silk dress that was clearly too much for the occasion, however that seemed to be Mona's thing. She looked even more attractive than earlier. I could now see her almond colored eyes, which were brought out by the contrasting lipstick and the foundation she was wearing.

Mona was a petite woman with a body that looked like she had been a dancer or cheerleader years ago. She reminded me of one of those sexy, seductive women on the soap operas that have all of the men on the show waiting for their turn to be manipulated by her beauty. I invited her in and asked her if she wanted some wine. The hotel actually had a couple of complimentary bottles of Californian White Zinfandel chilled in the fridge. Mona was happy to have some wine. I had a little, even though I really don't drink.

I asked her about herself and it turns out she came from pretty humble beginnings. Mona grew up in a small town in Hastings, Nebraska, 56 years ago. She was a kind of a throwback to the old chaperone era. Where you have to take someone on a date with you to ensure nothing promiscuous happens. I could tell she was nervous, being this older white woman alone in a hotel room with a brother. I hoped the wine would take the edge off of her anxiety. I placed my hands on both of her shoulders from behind and it seemed to make her breathe easier and relax.

"That feels good, CK. I haven't had a man touch me like that in years," she said.

"Mona, are you really hungry?"

"Not really, CK, I had a big breakfast, why do you ask?"

"I thought we might make lunch the two of us."

"CK, was this lunch meeting a plot to get me in your room by myself so you could take advantage of an older woman?"

"Yes, Mona, it was."

I realized she was ready for whatever I wanted us to do. She was smiling the whole time she was talking to me.

I grabbed her by the hand and led her straight over to the bedroom. I had a fresh twelve pack of rubbers for this vacation. I grabbed the sleeves of Mona's dress and slid it down to the floor. Mona stepped out of the dress and there she was wearing the nicest pair of bra and panties that I've seen in a long time. They were pearl colored and probably made of some kind of expensive silk. The brothers should give me ten extra points just for showing them this pair of panties.

The years had been very good to this woman. She was almost sixty years old and still had slightly tight skin with a small potbelly that actually made her look even sexier. I could tell she was getting embarrassed standing there in her underwear. I told her to lie on the bed. While she lay on the bed I began to take off my clothes. I had on my favorite pair of Jockey bikini briefs.

Like most brothers I did about fifty push-ups before she arrived to make my arms look bigger and feel harder. A lot of brothers either do push-ups or pump iron before going to the club or having sex. It gets your body ready for whatever is going to happen. A fight could break out in the club or some sex might result from going to the club. I caught Mona admiring my body, especially my tight midsection or "six-pack."

"My, CK, you have a very nice body."

"I was thinking the same thing about you, Mona."

I eased onto the bed next to Mona and we both lay there in our underwear. We began kissing and now I knew why older is better. She was patient and passionate with her kiss. I noticed how soft her lips were and her sweet perfume was starting to have a rising affect on me.

"CK, you know I can't stay too long."

"What's not too long?"

"I probably only have about two hours."

"That's plenty of time, Mona. I'll just set the alarm for an hour and 45 minutes so you won't get into trouble and we don't have to watch the clock."

I undressed Mona the rest of the way and was very careful to caress her at the same time. I stuffed her panties between the mattresses. I didn't want to forget about my contest points. Mona had her eyes closed with this little smirk on her face. At this point I was kissing on her face, eyes, and cheeks. I was very slow and methodical about where I placed each kiss. I continued my soft pecks all over her body. I spent a few moments taking each kneecap into my mouth like I was sucking on half a juicy orange.

I kissed around her thighs, moving her from side to side so that I could kiss each one from front to back. When I skipped up to her navel I could feel her getting wet on the insides of her thighs just above her knee. Her nature was sweet smelling and well groomed.

I continued back up until I had her right breast in my mouth. I started with the right side and worked my way to the left. I could hear Mona's heart pounding like a drum. She was beginning to moan and groan pleasurably, which made me want to do more and more. Women should realize that men enjoy the response of the partner almost as much as the feel of the sex itself. I paused to place a rubber on. I began to enter Mona and I noticed her hold her breath for a moment. It must have been a while for her. She was soaking wet, yet it was difficult for me to get inside of her. After some maneuvering I was finally inside of her.

I'm not bragging but I know I've been blessed with a decent sized penis. It's not so small that you would get embarrassed to show it in the locker room at the gym, and it's definitely not so large that I could do porno videos for extra cash. Once snuggly inside of Mona her groans got louder and louder.

One thing about a woman that has been around for a while and knows her body, she's not afraid to let you know what she likes. Mona was grabbing my ass and telling me exactly how good it felt. This was actually making me harder. I got into a nice Mandigo Warrior groove and only ten or fifteen minutes from the time we started kissing I can hear Mona about to come. As she pulled me tighter and groaned louder I could feel her fingernails pressing against my butt. Mona had this very distinctive way of letting you know she was coming. She was arching her back, while squeezing my butt, and blowing her hair out of her face until she just held her breath for what seemed like a minute. I thought she was going to suffocate. She let out this very loud and pleasurable groan that sounded like something between a saxophone and a high-pitched flute. It was kind of funny, but cute.

She was sweating profusely and clearly ready to go home or get some oxygen. I was not going to let her off that easy. I raised my body up almost to where my chest was on her forehead.

This gets women every time. I read about this position in one of those ladies magazines like Cosmopolitan. It's called the CAT technique.

I don't even remember what CAT stands for. What happens is while penetrating a woman a guy raises his torso so that it is directly on top of her clitoris. The woman remains still until the man is in the right position. I usually wait until they come the first time, since that causes most women to remain still while they wait to see what happens next. The man then starts moving up and down with his weight resting on his arms and all of the concentration is on moving his torso. The woman should be able to pick up on his rhythm and began pushing towards him when he is pushing down and vise versa. This position only takes about five minutes to master and once you do it only depends on how many times the woman you're with wants to come. I did it with this nineteen-year-old once and she must have let go about eight or nine times. Mona was up to about her fourth orgasm and she begged me to stop.

I finally had to stop because she thought she was having a heart attack. I could tell Mona was not used to this, especially with her unique style of coming. I really didn't want to overdo it and kill her in my hotel room.

I came down off of my position, excused myself and went into the bathroom. I turned on some water to muffle the sound of me jerking off. I think I was envisioning one of my favorite movie actresses and it didn't take long for me to get off.

Mona was lying there dripping wet from both our sweat. She wasn't saying anything, I was hoping she wasn't dead. She broke my thoughts with her words.

"Thank you, CK, I haven't had someone make love to me like that in a very long time. I can't even remember the last time I came so many times. I do know I wasn't married."

"I just like to take my time and please a woman."

"You sure have the pleasing part down pretty well. I feel like I'm twenty years younger. I wonder if you would let me please you in my own little way?" she said.

"What did you have in mind, Mona?"

"Not just yet, CK. Let me get dressed and I'll tell you what I have in mind. Where are my panties? All I see is my brassiere."

"I'm sure they're around here somewhere. All we have to do is look real hard."

"Don't bother, I have plenty in my room, besides I'm sure my husband wouldn't even notice if I walked in with no panties on."

"I'm sure they will turn up and I'll save them for you, Mona."

"I have an idea, CK. I want you to wait an hour and then go down to the front desk and pick up an envelope."

"What's in the envelope, Mona?"

"Don't worry about that, CK, just be there to pick it up in one hour."

Mona left pretty quickly and I couldn't help trying to imagine what in the world she was going to have waiting for me in an envelope. I hoped it wasn't one of those long love letters. Brothers don't usually read past the first or second line. We would just as soon get some physical affection if at all possible. It can't be cash, she wouldn't try and compensate me for my sexual prowess, or would she?

I decided to take a nice long hot shower and kill some time relaxing on the bed. When I finished my shower I must have dozed off. I was awakened by the alarm clock and it scared the daylights out of me. I suddenly remembered that I had set the clock so that Mona could get back before two hours. Between my shower and dozing off I figured I had about thirty minutes before I had to pick up my envelope from Mona.

I got up, dressed, and walked down the hall and got into the elevator and headed down to the lobby. When I arrived downstairs the lobby was pretty quiet. I approached the hotel desk and there was a peculiar looking, older white guy with a big pair of spectacles hanging from the bridge of his nose. He appeared to be reading something because he didn't notice me approach the desk.

I was really wondering where the young lady that Joe had been with the other day. She must have the day off, or she may even be in his room. If I know Joe he probably has her coming over several times a day with a new set of panties on so he can keep them for the contest. I cleared my throat and the guy behind the desk immediately jumped up to assist me.

"Yes, sir, may I help you?"

"Sure, my name is CK and I'm supposed to have an envelope here for me."

"Oh, yes, sir, I have it right here."

Sure enough he handed me a large yellow envelope with my initials in large black letters. I thanked the clerk and went over to this bench near an artificial plant to be inconspicuous. I must have thought I was in some spy movie, I was hiding and opening my secret envelope. I opened the envelope with the anticipation of a child on Christmas Day. Inside the envelope I found a note written on the hotel stationary with the fanciest penmanship I've seen in a long time. It read:

Dear CK,

I had such a wonderful time with you this afternoon. I wanted to say thank you. Please allow me to thank you in my own way and I'll feel I did what I could to make you feel as special as you made me feel today. I'll remember this day for years to come. We will probably not be able to see one another again while you're still here in Lake Tahoe. However if our paths ever cross again you can be sure my heart will be beating just as hard as when you saw me last. I want you to go outside the front of the hotel and find the driver of a black limousine. He will take care of everything from there. Don't worry about tipping him, he has been handsomely compensated for his services.

Yours Truly,
MONA

I walked outside to find the only black limousine waiting. I went up to the driver and told him my name. He called me "Sir" and told me he had been waiting for me. He opened one of the doors to the extremely long limousine and told me to get in. I got into the limo and couldn't believe how large and roomy it was. It was about as big as some apartments. It had more stuff in it than my apartment. There was a TV/VCR, a small refrigerator, a completely stocked bar, a microwave, and a stereo with CD player. There was a rack adjacent to the stereo with a collection of CDs. There was everything from Jazz, Rap, to Country and Western. The seats in the limo were gray leather and smelled like fresh strawberries mixed with leather. The seats were so long I remember lying across one side and neither my feet nor my head touched either end of the limo and I'm six feet tall.

This was great! I opened the tiny refrigerator and to my surprise there was a six-pack of my favorite pop. I popped open a can and began fumbling through the CDs. I found an old Kenny G CD, cut the stereo on and placed the CD inside. I cranked it up and kicked back with both feet up on the seat. I wondered how she knew I liked this kind of music and soda. I was rolling in style and no one could tell me anything. I suddenly realized that I had no idea where the driver was taking me. I turned down the CD player and tapped on the little window separating the driver and me. The driver lowered the window and I asked him where we were going.

"I'm afraid I'm not supposed to say sir," he said.

"What do you mean you aren't supposed to say?"

"The lady gave me specific instructions and one was not to say one word about where we were headed. I was not to ruin her surprise."

"Okay, I'll go along with this for a while but this better not be some weird, freaky shit!"

"I can assure you sir, it's nothing of the sort."

Moments later the limo comes to a stop. I realized the power windows weren't working. The driver must have the window locks on like there's a mischievous child in the back seat.

The door opened and the driver was standing there beckoning for me to exit. We stopped in front of what appeared to be some sort of high-fashioned shopping mall. There were only a few stores, maybe six or seven, each accessed from the outside. It wasn't the normal mall I was used to where you could get to different stores from inside other stores. I followed the driver and noticed we were headed toward a large Men's Warehouse clothing store. I've never shopped there, however I loved their commercials and saw a lot of nice suits some friends of mine had purchased from there.

The driver escorted me right to the front entrance of the Men's Warehouse. He went over and had a few words with this very distinguished looking, well dressed, older white guy. The guy came straight over to me and with a snap of his fingers two other guys joined him. If they weren't wearing suits I would've thought they were going to jump me.

The distinguished looking guy said hello to me and asked me to step up on this large square block and extend both of my arms. I obliged and then one of the two other guys pulled out a pad and pen and the other a tape measure. They proceeded to take my measurements from head to toe. I was then taken to a dressing room. There were several suits, sport jackets, slacks, and shirts handed to me to try on. I liked almost all of them but I couldn't help thinking I would eventually have to choose one or two outfits. I must have tried on six or seven different complete outfits.

I was then led over to the shoe department of the store. There were all sorts of expensive Johnson and Murphy, Kenneth Cole, and Stacy Adams shoes. I picked out a pair to match each outfit and wished I could keep them all. Each pair fit like a glove and seemed to make me float as I walked through the store with them on. I finished this exercise of trying on clothes and shoes and got dressed in my own clothes. I was exhausted from all of the changing. I felt like I had just finished a light workout. The bill for all of the outfits and shoes must have been over three thousand dollars. I was trying to debate on which ones I would eventually have to choose.

Just then the distinguished looking gentleman came up to me and asked if I was satisfied with how everything fit? I responded with a very hesitant "yes."

He then invited me over to this small lounge where there was plenty of coffee and doughnuts free of charge. I had a doughnut and some water and took a seat.

I noticed the driver walk back into the store and then walk back out with a few garment bags and shoeboxes. That's when I realized Mrs. Mona was picking up the tab for some of the clothes I picked up and the driver was her confidant. I attempted to go up and help the driver, but he wouldn't let me or the clerks in the store lift a finger to help.

This must have been another one of his instructions given to him by Mona. When he returned for the last time I realized that Mona had picked up the entire tab for every single outfit and pair of shoes I picked out, even the ones I didn't like that much. The driver returned and asked me if I was ready to go. I said yes and thanked all of the clerks and shook the distinguished gentleman's hand. His name was Dave. I don't know why it hadn't come up earlier, however he was very helpful and nice. I would definitely recommend that clothing store to all of the brothers.

I wondered if they would get the royal treatment that I got. Probably not, since Mona wasn't picking up the tab.

I climb back into the limo and we head back to the hotel. We get downstairs and I notice Joe, Marcus and Taj were all standing in the lobby like they were about to check in again. There were a few young ladies hanging around them and I couldn't help smiling when the driver came up behind me and asked if I wanted him to have the bell-man deliver my items to my room. I said sure and the brothers were all over me with questions. I told them the story about Mona and what had just happened and they couldn't believe it. Joe started right in on me.

"You must have put a serious beat down on that ass for her to buy you all of that shit I just seen them hauling up to your room."

"Shut up, Joe, she was a lady, not a piece of ass," I said.

"Yeah, CK, what did you do, eat that old stuff?" Taj said.

"I'm not like you, Taj, I don't lick it before I stick it."

"Man, you're crazy, I don't lick anything before I stick it," Taj said.

Marcus just stood by saying nothing like he was mad about something.

"What's up with you, Marcus?" I asked.

" Nothing, CK, I'm just ready to leave this fucking place."

"He's just pissed because he can't win the contest," Joe said.

"Fuck your dumb ass contest, Joe, and you too," Marcus said.

"Chill out, Marcus," Taj said. "I'm not worried about that contest either, brother."

I suddenly realized that it was late Saturday and we were in fact leaving in the morning. The contest was ending today and I couldn't tell if I was ahead of the other brothers or not. I only had two pairs of panties and I was sure that was hardly enough to win the contest. Joe probably had about twenty pairs. It's funny you can't get a bunch of pairs of panties when you are trying to get them. Either way I hit a Jackpot and met Mona. I damn near got a complete new wardrobe at her expense, all for a little good loving. I'm definitely the man whether I win the contest or not.

We all went up to Joe's room to officially conclude the contest and announce the winner. As we went up in the elevator everyone was joking around except for Marcus. He looked mad as hell. We all retreated to our rooms to get the evidence of each conquest this weekend.

Everyone met in Joe's room and it was a mess. It looked like he had thrown a wild sex party. The furniture was rearranged, and it looked like the maid had refused to enter the premises. We huddled around what used to be the couch and everyone began to pull out his collection of panties. Marcus only had one pair, smooth ass Taj had three pairs, that was one more than me. I just dropped my two pairs on the table. Joe dropped what seemed like four or five pairs on the table. He counted them out loud and actually had five pairs of genuine used panties. Some of them were a little on the worn side.

It was clear that the man about to be married had upstaged us all and won his own contest. Joe was having a good time laughing at all of us, especially Marcus.

"What's up, Marcus, you couldn't get your groove on in Lake Tahoe? You have to have some familiar pussy to get a pair of panties? You should be the one getting married. You apparently have lost your touch!"

"Fuck you, Joe, I'm ready to go back home and forget about this damn stupid ass contest."

It was official. Joe was the winner, Taj was second, I came in a close third, and Marcus was last. The contest was over and each one of us owed Joe a favor to be cashed in at his leisure. The thought of owing Joe a favor was the last thing I wanted.

We each retreated to our rooms to pack. The next morning came as fast as the night went away. We all met downstairs to check out of the hotel, and it seems Joe was hiding from someone. He was rushing around trying his best to avoid the registration desk. I guess he didn't want the girl he met to see he had put his engagement ring back on. She wasn't there and Joe was clearly relieved. He was the first one in the car. We packed up my car and headed back down to Sacramento. It took us less time to get back than it did to get up to Lake Tahoe. I was driving like a bat out of hell and we made an hour and a half trip in 70 minutes.

SURREPTITIOUS

MARCUS

Working at the airport is the greatest job in the whole city to pick up women. There are so many women that come through this airport on business or vacation and they can never resist a good-looking, tall, African American stud. I'm just the one to satisfy their yearning. Some of them are married and are seeking a nice rendezvous with a discreet brother. I usually try to run my "I'm a basketball player" role on the woman, however, I can't do that when I'm sitting here with this stupid skycap uniform on. I usually wind up helping women with their bags and eventually I'm helping them take their clothes off. It is a beautiful thing being young, single and black in America.

Today I met this sister named Davina. She's an executive vice president at one of the major banks like Bank of America or Wells Fargo. She was flying into town on business. I can always spot the women that have plenty of money or are the executive types. They usually travel light and have very expensive luggage. They're the easiest to hook up with since they are so focused on their careers they seldom have time for a relationship. They're usually beautiful strong women and need to be occasionally reassured of their femininity.

A weekend of business and pleasure with a brother is just the solution for what ails them. Davina was pretty short, about 5'4", however she was fine as frog's hair. She had nice long jet-black hair and very athletic legs. She stepped into the baggage claim area and I could see several guys' heads turn as she walked by them. I noticed all of this and made my move on all of the other skycaps. They were still drooling when I approached her and asked if she needed any help.

"What kind of help are you offering?"

"Well, I was going to help with your bags, unless there is some other assistance you need?" She had such a nice mischievous smile when she asked me what type of help I was offering. I smiled back and I could tell this sister was definitely interested. She was even better looking as I stood there beside her. Now I could tell she had the nicest light brown eyes that seemed to be accentuated by the light brown shirt she wore. It was very hard to keep my composure in the presence of such a lovely sister. She seemed so confident and sexy at the same time. I introduced myself.

"By the way my name is Marcus, what's yours?"

"My name is Davina and it's nice to meet you, Marcus."

"Are you here for business or pleasure, Davina?"

"Do you always get so inquisitive with your customers, Marcus?"

"No, actually I don't, only the extremely attractive ones."

"How many of them do you encounter?"

"You're the first."

"Good answer, Marcus. I'm here on business. I'm attending a seminar this week at the Hyatt Regency downtown. Here's my cellular phone number. Give me a call and we'll do lunch tomorrow on me."

"Thank you, Davina, and it was very nice meeting you."

"You also, Marcus, and don't forget to use that number."

"I won't." She dropped the digits so fast I could hardly keep from smiling ear to ear. I kept saying to myself that I was the man. All of the other skycaps wanted to get the scoop on Davina when I came back from helping her with her bags. I simply let them know of our plans for lunch and the fact that she insisted that it be on her.

I thought about how independent some of the professional women are today. It's a beautiful thing to see a woman who knows what she wants and goes after it. I met Davina the next day at the restaurant inside the hotel she was staying in. I thought this was a little too convenient, but she set everything up. I went along with the program even though this was some new shit to me.

Most of the time I have some woman on a hook and I'm the one trying to wine and dine her just to get into her panties. Once I hit that ass I'm usually at a loss for words for her after that point. Davina had her shit together she was definitely hooking a brother up. I arrived at her hotel and it was breathtaking. I had never seen such high ceilings and large windows. Everything in the hotel was huge. The lobby was immaculately clean and the décor looked very expensive. All of the employees attended to everything. There was a double elevator with glass doors in the lobby, taking people up to the floors above. I caught myself standing there with my mouth open.

The concierge came over and asked if he could help me. At first I thought this was one of those classic cases of "make sure the brother isn't trying to steal anything." I told him I was meeting a friend and I didn't need any help. He informed me that it was his intention to help me find my friend. He wanted to know my friends' name and if he or she was a guest in the hotel. I told him she was a guest in the hotel and her name is Davina. He brought a note from his jacket pocket and handed it to me.

"What is this, some kind of joke or something?"

"It's no joke, the note does have your name on it, doesn't it, sir?" The note did have my name written on the outside.

"It sure does, how did you get my name?"

"I was instructed by Ms. Davina to locate a very tall black gentleman looking for a friend."

"Thank you very much." I opened the note and it, was nicely typed and it smelled like Davina's perfume. The note also had a pair of lips on the top like she had kissed it. The note was short and sweet:

Dear Marcus,

I'm glad you were able to make our date. The reason for this letter is that I got scheduled for a meeting that I could not miss. Meet me in the piano bar. I have a tab set up under Davina, and they are expecting a very tall man to walk in and order some refreshments while he waits for me. I'll join you in about 30 to 45 minutes and I promise I'll make up for the inconvenience

Yours truly,
Davina

I couldn't help wondering if this was actually happening to me. This beautiful woman arranges for me to meet her in this fabulous hotel, she's late, and then makes arrangements for someone to find me and hand me a note explaining what happened.

She goes one step further and sets a brother up with a tab at the piano bar. What in the world is a piano bar anyway? Does this hotel have so many bars they have names for each one? I wasn't about to ask and make myself look like a fool or embarrass Davina. I went into the bar and sure enough there was this extremely large cream colored Baby Grand piano. It was so big everyone that walked in had to notice it. The bar was tastefully decorated and looked just as expensive as the rest of the hotel. The bar itself had to be some kind of cherry wood or mahogany. It circled around like a half moon, separating the bartender from the vast amount of people trying to get an afternoon drink in. I'm sure during an average night they could have six bartenders back there and still not keep up with the crowd.

I mentioned Davina's name, and the bartender just started pouring drinks for me, this was great. I started with the expensive stuff, just in case there was a limit to my tab. If I had to pay for my own drinks I could switch back to the more economical brews. When I finished my second glass of top-shelf cognac, I asked the bartender just how large was that tab of mine. He simply told me that I had an unlimited dollar amount on all drinks and refreshments while I waited on Ms. Davina. I decided it was time to move up to the A'lize and see how fast I can reach that unlimited tab. I only had a chance to sip my first A'lize when someone tapped me on the shoulder.

"Hello, Marcus, I hope you weren't waiting too long for me."

"Hi, Davina, no I wasn't waiting that long and you look extravagant." She had on this tight-fitting brown mohair sweater with a sport coat and skirt to match. The outfit had classy and sexy written all over it. I bet the guys in her meeting couldn't concentrate at all for looking at Davina's very curvy figure. She had the most perfect set of breasts. I bet most people would immediately start debating if they were purchased or real. I didn't really care. As far as I am concerned any woman that has a nice set of breasts, they are hers as long as she keeps her receipt.

"Thank you, Marcus, so are you hungry?"

"I sure am, what did you have in mind to eat?"

"I thought we would go to the little restaurant here in the hotel and order whatever you want. My company is picking up the tab for this trip so I should make the best of it."

"So which company do you work for? Also what do you do for them anyway? You never mentioned which bank you work for or what you do. Is it some top-secret stuff?"

"No, Marcus, it's not top secret. I just spend such a lot of time working at my job and talking about it with my co-workers that I don't like talking about it after work is over. I'm just an executive vice president of a major bank."

"That's cool, I really didn't mean to pry. Let's get some grub."

We enter the restaurant and it looks just as expensive as everything else. I was really curious how much one of the rooms in this hotel cost for one night. I bet it cost over three hundred dollars. I wouldn't dare ask Davina, she would really think I'm ghetto.

The menu at the restaurant had everything from swordfish to T-bone steaks. I caught myself looking for the fried chicken. I couldn't order fried chicken in a place like this. Davina would probably just get up and walk out on me. I ordered the swordfish just to seem sophisticated. Davina had the T-bone, medium well, and a baked potato. I can tell a lot about a woman by how she likes her steaks.

Davina was a take charge and in control sister who made her own decisions about everything. Once she sets her sights on something it is a done deal. If she doesn't get her way, somehow she rationalizes that she really didn't want it anyway. Yes, she is definitely a medium well lady.

I know a few medium rare women. They're indecisive, ordering their steak like that so that if it wasn't done enough they could send it back until it was cooked to their satisfaction. She wants to see a little red in the middle, thinking that this would ensure the steak had more nutrients at this stage (a misconception).

"How's your fish, Marcus?"

"It's delicious, Davina, how about your steak?"

"It's fine. What are you in such deep thought about anyway?"

"Nothing, I just want to pinch myself."

"Pinch yourself? What do you want to pinch yourself for?"

"It must be my lucky day. I'm sitting inside a very expensive restaurant, having lunch with a very beautiful lady, in a very expensive hotel. I would say that is lucky."

"Don't worry about it, Marcus, there is more to come."

"What do you mean more to come?"

"Finish your food and you'll find out."

I thought she meant we were going to try some fancy dessert or something like that. She really had me curious about her "more to come" statement.

We finished our meals, passed on dessert, and the waiter brought over the bill. I made the usual brother feeble attempt to reach for the bill. I hope none of my brothers try this unless they are sure the sister they are with is absolutely loaded. It worked out. Davina grabbed the check and said, "Remember, this is all on me."

She signed her name on the check and before I could say anything Davina grabbed my hand and led me towards the glass elevators. We got in and she pushed twelve. That was a good number, I could feel it. We arrived on the twelfth floor and went down a long hallway to room 1234. I was writing this number down in my head. I would be playing it in the big four lotto drawing, boxed for the rest of the week.

Davina was fumbling around trying to find her key to open the door. I took the moment to notice her beautifully round athletic behind. The thought of possibly seeing it in the buff had me pumped up.

She opened the door and we stepped into her room. Davina switched on the lights and with the same switch music began to fill the room. It was a jazzy tune that I knew was the group Fourplay. How appropriate since I was hoping to get some foreplay in myself.

The hotel had someone go through a lot of pains to give this room an African motif. There were expensive-looking African game throw rugs on the floor. Delicate, hand carved, African tribal masks lined the walls. Kente cloth was used as wallpaper, and it added an unusual yet tasteful touch to the entire room.

The bookcase had several books on Africa and the African American struggle. I noticed the autobiography of Malcolm X, and right alongside it in politically correct forum was the autobiography of Dr. Martin Luther King Jr. All of the other books were about African American poetry, history, songs, and culture. It was all done very tastefully.

Sometimes people attempt to put a room like this together and it comes across gaudy. Like visiting an antique shop that hasn't sold a piece in months, but stuff keeps coming in. As I passed the master bedroom I noticed the oversized bed made of bamboo. It made me look twice. It was made up with an African animal print comforter that would bring out the animal in the most tamed brother.

I noticed that Davina had disappeared while I was checking the place out. She returned from one of the rooms in this massive apartment-style hotel room, wearing a leopard skin print camisole that took my breath away. She stood there looking as delectable as the meal we'd just eaten. She noticed the shock on my face and put me at ease right away.

"Don't be shocked, Marcus. I made up my mind when we met in the airport that I was going to have you."

"I'm not shocked, just thoroughly impressed with the whole afternoon. Davina, you're definitely a very sexy lady."

"You haven't seen anything yet, Marcus."

Davina came over and grabbed my hand and led me to the massive room with the oversized bamboo bed with the leopard-skin print comforter. I felt my palms sweating and I know she noticed. I felt like a little boy who was being led by the school nurse to get whatever medicine she wanted him to take. It's a feeling that you never forget, and it never ever hurts. Davina placed me across the bed and began taking my clothes off. She then took what was left of her clothes off and I'll spare the explicit details. She even handed me a rubber. I just saved the ones I always travel with. Davina finished with me and got into the shower. It seemed like we were in that room for about four hours. The whole place was hot and smelled like a tribal ritual dance had taken place for hours just moments ago. I decided to get into the shower with Davina and she welcomed this gesture.

We went at it again in the shower until the water ran cold. We then took very quick, very cold showers. We both got dressed with little conversation. Davina walked me to the door and asked for my number. I gave it to her and headed down the glass elevators to the lobby. I headed to the front door and noticed the concierge giving me the thumbs up like he knew exactly what I had been up to the entire afternoon. I responded with a nice smile and went out to the street. I didn't drive here since I wasn't sure where this hotel was or what type of parking was available.

It usually costs you an arm and a leg to park for a few hours. It's good I didn't drive, this little episode with Davina would have cost me a fortune in parking. I would gladly pay the price, because that was the best afternoon I've had in my entire life. I hailed a cab and decided to stop off and play Davina's room number in the lotto. 1234, I would remember that number for a long time.

ENRAPTURED

JOE

Today I'm finally getting married and it really feels strange that in less than an hour I'll be a married man. To think I'm finally settling down with one woman. The one woman I want to spend the rest of my life with.

The rest of my life, every time I say "the rest of my life" it sounds so long. Most of my single brothers have some words for the married life. They call it locked down, shackled, whipped, fenced in, clocked, hen pecked, trapped and any other non-freedom word. I'm surprised none of them said slave. I don't care what they say, Trina is definitely the one. Why else would I get rid of all of the women that I could have, just to spend my life with one? It's too late to back out now, even though I've got some serious second thoughts.

I'm standing here in the church and I must say there are some fine ass women coming into the church to see me say I do. I don't even know any of these women. They're probably some type of wedding freaks. Show up at a brother's wedding with a centerfold, aerobic, muscular body wearing next to no clothes, just to show you what you're missing out on. Soon as you decide to take a look, she catches you and smiles. They give you that look like "I know you're thirsty and I've got some sweet lemonade."

This whole wedding scene is making me nervous. To hell with all of these freaks, in about 30 minutes I'll see my beautiful new bride and forget about all of these ½ naked women. Trina's been so excited the last few weeks I could hardly stand it. I haven't seen her since yesterday, she didn't want me to see her the day before our wedding. I was to see my fiancée as she walked down the aisle to become my wife.

The only one I've been able to see a lot of is that damn expensive wedding planner. I was afraid to see the final bill from her. Everything was billable to her. It was like hiring a lawyer for your murder trial and in walks Johnny Cochran. You know you will probably get off but you'd wind up poor or homeless in the end. The wedding planner acted like she was the one I was marrying. She was going around giving everyone orders, including me. I told her that I'm paying for a part of this wedding and she had better back off. The one thing I'll give the lady, she has her stuff together. She ensured the photographer was on time, in place, set up, had plenty of film and a backup camera. She had the groom's party and bridesmaids rehearse their roles two hours before the actual ceremony. My brothers were standing there looking pissed off. There was Marcus, CK and my cousin Paul, who stood in for Taj who couldn't make it. It turns out someone in his family got sick at the last minute. He's been acting kind of strange every since the bachelor weekend.

Everything was jumping around to the tune of the wedding planner. The soloist had to do a special rendition of our song, "Ribbon in the Sky," a Stevie Wonder original, just for her. She even made him do it for her a cappella, since the sound check had been done before he arrived. She ensured the pastor had his Bible bookmarked to the right spot. The lady didn't miss one little detail of planning our wedding. Every one was hopping and jumping to this expensive ass wedding planner drill sergeant.

All of the flowers and the decorations were tastefully placed around the entire church. As I looked around I caught myself complimenting the expensive old bag. It was approaching time for everyone to take their places. She directed me to take my place in the front of the church. The wedding planner was standing by the door with a clipboard only minutes before the music was about to begin. I wondered if she was going to drop her clipboard and come on down the aisle just to ensure everyone knew how to look at the bride to be. She disappeared into the crowd just moments before the organist started playing the music for the grooms' party and bridesmaids to begin their march down the aisle. It was a familiar tune, kind of Blues and Jazzy rendition of Luther Vandross' "A House Is Not a Home." It was real sweet, you could tell everyone caught the tune. Everywhere I looked someone else was lip-synching the words to the song.

I watched the brothers in my grooms' party take the arms of each bridesmaid and walk her down the aisle, placing them on my soon-to-be bride's side of the church. It was at this moment that I realized the kind of division that goes on during a wedding. My family took their places on my side of the church, and Trina's very fat-ass family took their places on her side of the church. Her family was the typical huge high-blood-pressure-having black folks.

How could Trina be so fit and trim and all of her relatives were big as houses? The whole sight scared me. I sure hope she doesn't grow into one of those cows parked on her side of the church. Every one was divided, even our friends were sitting on the proper side of allegiance. Looking at this made me realize that all of this is just a symbol of the separation prior to a wedding.

The two individuals about to be married are like a bridge for both sides to cross over and become one. I would hate to be the bridge that some of her family used, it would probably break from all of the fried-chicken-and-pound-cake-eating weight they were carrying. Trina and I were the bridges that would take two strange families and give them a common bond by which to become one larger family. The analogy actually made me smile.

The organist began playing the wedding march and it interrupted my moment of intellectual observation. I heard the music and looked toward the door, but I couldn't see Trina. The large double doors of the church opened up, letting in a bouquet of sunshine. Trina appeared through the sunshine like I've never seen her before. She wore a silver jeweled tiara on her head and it had a white veil which was laced with the tiniest pearls covering her face. The pearls seemed to make her silhouette sparkle through the light. Her long luxurious white wedding gown was laid with beautiful white chiffon with a satin underlay, then overlaid with soft delicate white lace. It had a long train that must have been down the street while she stood in the doorway. Her shoes completed her angelic gown and reminded me of Cinderella's at the ball. This vision of beauty standing in the doorway, about to make her approach down the aisle, was about to become my wife.

Each step she made towards me made little knots materialize in my stomach. I reached into my right inside tuxedo pocket and pulled out my silk handkerchief and wiped a tear from my eye. Trina finally arrived by my side, with her father holding her arm. I could see her fighting back her tears of joy. I'm sure she didn't want to ruin her delicate makeup. I was on top of the world. I began to stare at her with the largest grin on my face and it seemed to hurt. The hurt was so, so good.

The pastor was the illustrious Bishop Raymond Walker Jr. He was the pastor of this large church in Sacramento called Rock of Ages Holiness Church. He was also Trina's Godfather and he loved her dearly. He had baptized her years ago and now his little Goddaughter was getting married. Bishop Walker began his part of the ceremony with a word of prayer. He asked God to bless both families and friends present for the ceremony. He also asked God to bless our union with a special kind of love that no man or woman would ever want to separate from.

The pastor made it seem like he was actually talking to God face to face. His voice was deep, firm and resounding. I'm sure every one in the church was hinged on every word he uttered. He stood in between us and asked who was there to give away the bride and Trina's dad spoke up.

"Her father, Charles Emanuel Higgins the Third." He said. He sounded just like the pompous asshole I knew him to be.

He left Trina and returned to his seat looking like a father who had just lost his only child. The pastor continued by telling everyone they were present to bear witness to the joining in matrimony of Trina Elizabeth Higgins and Joseph Ronald Williams.

The pastor asked us to face one another and join hands.

He started by asking Trina Elizabeth Higgins, "Do you take this man to be your loving husband? Do you take this man of your own free will and without reservation?"

"I do," she said.

"Do you take Joseph for your husband, for richer or poorer; in sickness or in health, and until death do you part?"

"I do."

"Place the ring on Joseph's finger and repeat after me."

Trina and I repeated each word of our vows and paused after each statement to stare at one another.

My words seemed to come out of my mouth like I had a speech problem. These were simple words that you've heard a thousand times. They aren't the same when you are standing there making this mutual commitment with the woman you want to spend the rest of your life with. Both of my eyes were watering now. The pastor completed the ceremony with these words:

"What God has joined together let no man put asunder. I now pronounce you husband and wife. You may now kiss your bride."

I took Trina's veil off of her face and her beauty just glowed from beneath it. I paused for a moment just to look into her eyes. I told her that I loved her and then I kissed my beautiful new wife. The kiss lasted only a few seconds, but it was the most passionate kiss we ever gave one another.

The pastor announced to the crowd, "Ladies and gentleman please rise to receive Mr. and Mrs. Williams." This made my chest stick out. I'm holding Trina's arm and we begin our rise back up the aisle together. It was that same aisle that only moments ago we came down separately. Pictures were being taken from everywhere. I could hardly see from all of the flashes going off at the same time. I saw the wedding planner out of the corner of my eye. She was directing people out of the aisle so we could get out of the church. We exited the church to a shower of rice and people cheering on both sides of us.

We took more pictures at the direction of the planner, then climbed into the long white stretch limousines. Trina's train seemed to take up half of the limousine by itself. We headed off to what I knew would be an exquisitely expensive reception prepared at one of the fanciest local hotels. This was the first time alone with my bride in a day and a half. We seized the moment and just kissed.

We finally arrive at the Hilton hotel in downtown Sacramento. The place was absolutely beautiful and especially expensive. We get to the lobby where who else greets us but Ms. Wedding planner herself. She shows us the ballroom she booked for us about six months ago. I was thinking of a quiet little room for my bride and me to check into.

I was anxious to get this honeymoon thing started as quickly as possible. The room was decorated in a 70s kind of funky disco motif. It was real neat and I couldn't help but wonder how the wedding planner would allow such a thing. I was curious how all of the people at the wedding dressed in their finery would respond to such a scene.

Just as I was thinking about this, the doors swung open and in walked the entire group from the church. A strobe light was affixed to the top of the ceiling, just like the many discos I'd been to. The music began like it was cued to start as soon as a crowd arrived. The DJ started with my all-time favorite 70s song, "Flashlight," by Parliament.

The music was loud, so loud it made you go out on the dance floor and get your boogie on. Trina and I took this chance to have our first dance as husband and wife. One thing I sure like about Trina, the girl can really shake her groove thing. We were bumping and dancing around on the floor until I felt myself breaking a sweat. The second dance of the night went to Trina and her father, with me dancing with her mother. This seemed really weird, since I haven't been close enough to touch Trina's mother since we met. Before you could say "go for it" everyone was on the dance floor. The DJ had worked his way up to some LakeSide (Fantastic Voyage). Anyone that wasn't dancing was standing around reciting every word to the song.

There was so much food on the buffet. There was fried chicken, which I know wouldn't be around much longer as soon as Trina's fat-ass family got a whiff of it. There was plenty of bread, salads, desserts, and an open bar, which made my side of the family very happy. It seems that alcoholism runs pretty deep in the old Williams family. Half of my aunts, uncles and cousins were locking up the bar with all kinds of different drinks in front of them. I just started laughing at the sight of them.

Trina's family at the buffet table and my family at the bar, how could they ever attempt to come together as a larger family? We partied for almost 45 minutes before the wedding planner motioned us over to cut the cake, throw the garter, and toss the bouquet.

Once we obeyed her orders, we partied for about another hour then climbed back into the limousine and headed to the airport for our honeymoon in Cancun. I couldn't wait. My wife, beautiful white sand beaches, and blue still water was just what I needed about now. The best thing was we would be finally rid of that damn wedding planner, until we get her bill.

Cancun was absolutely breathtaking. We landed and checked into our hotel to find a bouquet of roses and champagne waiting for us, with a note from none other than the wedding planner. This lady doesn't miss a beat. She definitely covered every angle from start to finish. I would actually recommend her old expensive, cantankerous ass to any of our friends that were getting married.

Trina put her bathing suit on and immediately went down to the beach. I of course put on my swimming trunks and went with her, since I knew there would be a ton of guys checking out my sweet, sexy new bride. I can't have that shit. I'll just be standing guard until my baby gets done swimming, since I can't swim.

While Trina was in the ocean swimming I noticed all of the beautiful women scattered around the beach. It was like someone whispered in my ear to wake up and look around. Each one was finer than the next. Oh shit, this is the first opportunity for temptation as Trina's husband. I wanted to turn around and run back upstairs. I could hide in the room until Trina and I finished our honeymoon. What was I going to do around all of these women while we were here? I'm okay. I can handle myself. I just need to focus on my beautiful new bride and ignore all of these beautiful half-naked women on the beach.

What the hell possess me to spend my honeymoon in Cancun? This should have been the site of the bachelor weekend. Man, I'd probably have 100 pairs of panties by the weekend. All of that is behind me. The king of the contest is married now. Come on Trina get out of the water so we can go back to the room. I was feeling very content with my ability to resist the temptation of the women on the beach until this sister caught my eye.

This sister walked past me in an orange two-piece bathing suite. Her bathing suite looked like it was at least a size too small, however it exposed everything so well. I looked to see if I could see Trina and she must have been way out in the water. I then turned to get a good look at this sister. She noticed me looking and just smiled. She stopped only a few feet from where I was sitting. She laid her towel down, set up her umbrella and bent all the way over so I could damn near see her heart beat. This shit was too much. I was damn near drooling when she turned around again and caught me staring. Again she smiled, but this time she waved. I waved back and turned around like a little boy that just got caught peeping in the ladies room. I wanted Trina to hurry up for real now. I needed to get away from the beach and in her arms. Why was I being tempted like this on my honeymoon? I couldn't resist the temptation to look back one more time. This would be the look that ruined everything.

The woman was beckoning me to come over to her. What was I going to do? Trina could come out of the water at any moment and it would be some shit on the beach. My ass would get kicked and Ms. Orange bathing suite would probably get her long hair pulled. My dumb ass went over to her thinking I was just going to make small talk. If Trina caught me I would just say I thought I knew her, or lie and say we went to college together.

I was intending on making whatever conversation we had short and sweet. I was not prepared for what was about to happen. I went over and she never said a word. She handed me a small piece of paper. It had her room number with a note that simply said if you're really so curious come see me.

I took the note and almost ran back to the spot where I was waiting for Trina. What the hell was I doing talking to another woman on this special occasion. Just then Trina appeared almost out of nowhere. I was so glad to see her and I hugged her as soon as she got close to me.

"Damn, Joe, what's gotten into you? You never grabbed me like that before."

"I know, Sweetheart. I just couldn't see you in the water and thought you might have drowned or something. Anyway I'm glad you're okay."

"I'm fine, Joe, I want to go back to the room and take a shower."

"Sure, honey, that sounds like a good idea."

I held Trina's hand and walked on the other side of her so I wouldn't have to look at the woman in the orange bathing suit. I could feel her watching us the whole time, however I didn't dare get caught looking back at her.

Trina took her shower and I watched some TV while contemplating how I would survive the temptations of the women here in Cancun. We still had four days left in this sunny paradise and I knew it would be hell resisting the temptation of women like the one I saw earlier. I still had the note with her room number on it. Why was I even keeping it? I'm a married man now I just need to suck-it-up. I just need to concentrate on my future with my wife. Trina and I ordered room service and stayed in our room the whole night, which was cool with me.

Trina woke up the next morning and I think she must have eaten something last night that didn't agree with her. She spent about an hour in the bathroom throwing up. When she finally got to where she could relax I sat next to her on the bed rubbing her head with a cold towel. She eventually dozed off and I just sat there staring at her. I got up and read the newspaper. I wanted to watch TV however, I didn't want to wake Trina. I decided to go for a walk. I wandered around the resort headed no where in particular. I just stuck my hands in my pockets and walked. I then realized that I still had the note that I got from the woman in orange. I pulled it out and read it again. What in the hell was I doing? Here I am with a beautiful, sick wife and I'm contemplating visiting this woman. I couldn't help myself and found her room. I knocked and it was like she was waiting for me. She answered the door and this time she was wearing a spandex top and bottom. This was probably the most clothes she had ever worn on the island. She invited me in and I walked by her like a lost puppy being taken in by a friendly neighbor. This was crazy! I spent about an hour in her room and once again I gave into the temptations of a beautiful woman. I don't deserve to be married to Trina. Why can't I just spend the rest of my life refusing to be tempted because I know how much I love Trina? If I keep this shit up I know God is going to punish my ass.

I got back to our room and Trina was still asleep. She probably never noticed that I had even left the room. I just got on my knees right next to Trina and began to pray. I was praying that God would forgive me for my indiscretions and also help me to resist the temptations of my flesh. Trina woke up and saw me praying.

"Joe, I've never seen you pray. What's the matter?"

"Nothing, Sweetheart. I was just praying that you were okay."

"I'm fine now. I must have thrown everything up that I had in me. Also that nap I took helped a lot."

"I'm glad you're okay, Sweetheart. I was also praying that God would let me spend the rest of my life trying to make you happy."

"I'm already the happiest woman in the world, Joe."

"So am I, Trina. So am I."

I was determined to be the husband I should be to Trina and now that I involved God I'd better keep up my end of the bargain.

We spent the remaining two and a half days in Cancun and it was wonderful. On the trip back home Trina and I just held hands without saying a word. We got back to our apartment and realized how much of a dream wedding and honeymoon we had. Reality set in when Trina started opening the mail. There were a ton of bills just waiting in the mailbox for us. I went through the stack of mail and on the bottom of the entire stack of about 40 envelopes was the wedding planner's bill. I knew Trina and I only had to cover a small portion of the bill. Her father was picking up the largest portion. The planner sent us a courtesy copy of the detailed listing of the charges made in conjunction with our wedding. The bottom line was a whopping $15,598.69. Imagine spending your entire single life in preparation for a lifetime together with your new bride and starting out minus $15,598.69.

I was outraged at the price, however there was no turning back now. Trina and I had just experienced the most perfect wedding. To be honest the whole experience was worth twice what we were being charged. I'm sure Trina's father will come up with the entire bill if dear old Trina just asks. The bottom line is I have a beautiful new bride and I will be spending the rest of my life in love with her.

EXHILARATION

TAJ

I haven't talked to Andre since I came back from Lake Tahoe. I had to leave town to visit my sister in the hospital and I missed whorish Joe's wedding and thank God for that. I'm feeling pretty weird about calling Andre. I've been with three other men since he turned me out that night. It's pretty strange that I actually did something like that. I actually wanted it to happen. I knew I would be miles away from Sacramento and no one would find out about my gay activities so it was a perfect situation.

Now that I'm back in town where I know so many people I have to keep up certain appearances. I guess there is no time like the present, I'm going to call his ass up right now! I dialed his number and hoped he wasn't there so I could leave a message and appear to make the first move. That backfired, he picked up on the second ring.

"Andre?"

"Yes, this is Andre."

"This is Taj."

"I know your voice, Taj, I'm just wondering why you're calling me?"

"You've got a lot of nerve, Andre, asking me why I'm calling you? I'm calling you to schedule an appointment to beat the shit out of you some more, bitch!"

"Well, Taj, I'm still recovering from the bruises you gave me, and I'm sorry about what happened that night. I saw an opportunity to make love to the man I've been in love with for years, and I took it."

"You're in love with me, Andre? What kind of sick joke do you think you are playing, Andre?"

"It's no joke, Taj, I'm in love with you and nothing you can say will change that."

"Why me? I thought we were boys. I know you told me that you rolled that way and I respected that. Why couldn't you respect the fact that I don't swing that way?"

"I really don't know why. Was there ever a woman that you fucked that you actually loved?"

"What the hell does that have to do with what you did?"

"It's no different than my being in love with you and not being able to have you."

"Don't go pulling that psychoanalytical shit with me, Andre."

"I just wanted to know if you gave any of your many women an explanation or reason why you continued to sleep with them and weren't in love with them? The point is, Taj, I love you and I really don't know when I realized it for sure, but I've been sure a few years now."

"You're making me sick, Andre, you know I'm not gay. Why did you fuck with my head like that?"

"I told you, Taj, it's because I'm in love with you and couldn't resist the temptation of making love to you regardless of the consequences."

"Well, you realize this puts an end to our friendship? I don't want you to call, or come around me ever again. Is that understood?"

"Yes, Taj, I'll stay away from you, however, you still need to hear it one last time. 'I love you!'"

"Look, Andre, you can keep that shit to yourself. Oh I almost forgot. I brought you something back from Lake Tahoe. I was going to bring it over, but I think I'll just mail it to you."

"Thanks for thinking about me while you were there, Taj. Good-bye."

Andre is full of shit. In love with me, my ass. He knows I'm not one of those butt buddies he has around him. Something inside me still wants to kill him. I just don't want to spend the rest of my life in jail for murder. I'm not gay, but I've had four different gay encounters.

My ass is still virgin and that's what counts the most. I can't go to the cops and say he raped me. That will make the morning papers and by the afternoon I wouldn't have one woman to call. I'm sure my phone would be ringing off the hook with unsuspecting men wanting to comfort the rape victim. What the hell am I thinking about? Andre has my head all messed up.

I just want to put this entire episode behind me and get some rest, I just can't seem to get Andre off of my mind. It's like my mind is playing tricks on me. I'm contemplating calling back and apologizing to him. What the hell am I going to apologize to him for? He is the one who decided to have his way with me while I was drunk and I still think he drugged my ass. How could I trust him around me again? I'd always be so paranoid. Look at me, I'm sounding like a woman. I'm just going to call him again.

"Hello, Andre? It's me again."

"Hello, Taj, I thought you weren't going to communicate with me again."

"I know what I said earlier. I decided to bring the gift I got for you in Lake Tahoe over and talk things out with you. Is that okay?"

"Sure, that's okay, Taj, as long as you don't come over here acting like the most recent recruit for 'Gay Bashers of America.'"

"Look don't push it, Andre, I'm making the first move at reconciling our friendship."

"I'm sorry, Taj, I didn't realize you were having a change of heart. What brought this on?"

"Well, we've been friends so long that I guess I've grown accustomed to having you around, gay or not."

"What about what happened that night?"

"I'm so confused about myself right now, I don't even want to discuss it. Let's just forget it ever happened. You also have to promise to never mention it again either, Andre."

"I can't promise to forget about making love to the man I love. You know I would never say anything about us to anyone else in the whole world, Taj."

"Why can't you forget that night ever happened, Andre, is it just to torture me?"

"No, to remind you of what I told you before, that I love you."

"Andre, please don't go there with me. I have no intentions on salvaging our friendship to become your lover."

"I'm sure you don't, Taj, not yet."

I show up at Andre's place and I can still see several of the bullet holes that I made when I was trying to kill his ass. He never covered them up. I was hoping no one in the neighborhood recognized me. If they did I'm sure they would be ducking out of the way thinking this was round two.

Andre answered the door with this sick puppy look on his face that made me want to slap him. I restrained myself and went inside. I gave him the sweatshirt that I had brought for him just prior to slipping away with Paul. This gay shit was really sick and I was right in the middle of it. I knew it would only be a matter of time before my newfound, gay boldness landed me right in bed with Andre, by choice.

Andre and I decided to go out like old times and check out the sexy women that were lurking about. I just felt like a good piece of poontang was all that I needed to bounce back from my recent gayness.

We decided to go to this club that just opened. I heard there are usually a ton of fine women just waiting for some fine brothers to arrive. I just hope I don't have gay written all over my forehead.

We get to the club and sure enough there are plenty of sexy women all over the place, however I'm not having as much fun. The music is too loud, and I've only danced once. All of the women I see around here are fine as hell, but it just doesn't matter to me. I'm just sitting by the bar leaning on one of the fanciest, most comfortable bar stools ever made. I'm also getting very drunk. This whole scene is depressing me, and I'm ready to leave.

Where in the hell is Andre? I found his ass on the dance floor with this sister getting his groove on.

"Andre! Yo, man, I'm ready to go."

"Damn, Taj, we've only been here for a couple of hours."

"I know how long we've been here and I'm still ready to go."

"I'm having fun, Taj, can't you wait another hour?"

"I'm not waiting another minute, Andre, let's leave now!"

This bimbo he was dancing with decides to enter into the conversation.

"Yeah, Taj, or whatever your name is, can't you wait?"

"Who the fuck asked you anything, bitch?"

"Who the hell are you calling a bitch? You're the one acting like you're Andre's bitch"

"I'm nobody's bitch, so mind your fucking business. Andre, I'm leaving now. You can always take your ass home with this bimbo!" I said.

"You see a bimbo, you slap her," she said.

"No problem," Wapow! I slapped her ass like a pimp who just got short-changed by his best money-making hoe.

"My God, he just slapped me. I'm going to kill you, motherfucker!" she said.

By this time the club security comes over and I'm wrestling with two three hundred-pound bouncers. Well I'm not a small brother myself and we mix it up pretty good, just the two of them against me.

Andre steps in and punches one of the guys. He starts to work some weird ass karate/kick-boxer shit on these boys. I was lying on the floor at this point, wondering how Andre learned the shit he was using on these two big-ass bouncers. He took both of them out, grabbed me, and pulls me away from the crowd starting to circle around. In no time we're in Andre's Range Rover on the way home.

"Taj, I'm proud of how you came and rescued me from that woman, ha! ha!"

"That's very funny, Andre. How about you saving my ass from those two big ass bouncers? What was that shit you were using anyway?"

"Never mind what that was, Taj. If you didn't have a gun the last time you wanted to kick my ass, I would have used it on you."

"Thanks for saving my ass, Andre, I owe you one."

"Andre, I wasn't rescuing you from that bitch. I was simply tired and she opened her mouth at the wrong time. So I decided to shut her up."

"You should not have hit her, Taj, she was only dancing with me. If I didn't know any better I would say you were jealous."

"I'm not jealous."

"You sure acted like it, Taj."

"I'm just tired, Andre, and a little high."

"Anyway, Andre, you seemed a little protective when those bouncers were kicking my ass."

"I figured if anyone messes with your ass it will be me!"

"Don't go there, Andre, we already settled that."

"We never settled anything, Taj, we just agreed not to say anything to anyone else. I fully intend to remind you that I love you every chance I get."

We get to my apartment and go inside. I have a few more drinks and so does Andre. After about an hour we are both lying in bed naked and about to make love. The strange thing about this night is I initiated everything. Fuck it, I just did it. Whatever happens next I just have to deal with.

We wake up the next morning in bed alongside one another.

"What's up, Taj, how do you feel this morning?"

"I'm not really sure, Andre, how are you?"

"Wonderful! So what do we do now, Taj?"

"I don't know, Andre. You tell me. What does a man do when he first makes love to a man, by choice?"

"You continue your life just like always."

"What do you mean just like always? I've always had a woman lying beside me or on standby for me to hook up with."

"Well, now you have me, Taj. I may not be a woman, but I can be just as fulfilling as any woman and still be your best male friend."

"All that sounds nice, Andre, but what do I tell all of the women I've been sleeping with?"

"Tell them that you are no longer interested in them."

"Should I tell them the reason is I'm gay."

"It's up to you, Taj. You can lie to them like you've been doing all of these years. You could also tell them the truth and stop living with lies."

"What is the truth, Andre?"

"The truth is you love me, just as much as I love you."

"You're making me sick, Andre."

"You weren't sick last night Taj, now were you?"

"Whatever, Andre, I think I need to go to some 'I just found out I'm gay, what should I do support group.'"

"You just need to be your newfound self, Taj, you'll be fine."

"Maybe we should move to San Francisco or Atlanta. That's were all the gays are living these days isn't it, Andre?"

"What would that accomplish, Taj?"

"At least I'd blend in with all of the other queers in the world."

"The first thing you need to do, Taj, is lose those stereotypical connotations."

"You're right, Andre, this is something I've thought about for a while. I'm also the one who chose to become this different breed of brother. I also was the one who initiated our recent encounter. I'm just going to have to get used to being gay. After all, it's supposed to mean happy, isn't it, Andre?"

"I know I am, Taj, I know I am."

MARCUS

Davina is something special, I really don't know how I lucked out. I've dogged so many women and I wind up with this amazingly special sister who is secure with herself, financially well off, and totally into me. What more could I ask for? It's almost too good to be true. It's been almost six months and I think I'm starting to fall pretty hard for Davina. She's the best thing that's happened to me in a long time. I'm going to wait a few more months and then I'm going to ask her to move to Sacramento and stay with me. I've been running women for too long. I'm not getting any younger and I need to start thinking about settling down.

Listen to me, Davina has got my ass ready to turn in my player's card and settle down. You know that's some good loving when you're ready to be with just one woman. I think about her all the time. When I'm at work, just walking around or hanging out. I don't even look at other women like I used to. Hell, before I met Davina, anything in a skirt would at least get a glance. If I thought they were willing I was definitely able to hook them up. That was then but now I'm focusing on one woman. It's only been a short while, but I think I'm in love with Davina.

I better not tell her that since she'd know she has my ass. Once they get you to say those words on your own, you're at their mercy. It's not the same if women say "do you love me" or say "I love you." When you respond to those questions with a "sure I do," or "me too" it really doesn't count in the players' book as an actual unsolicited I LOVE YOU! I guess I have to deal with my feelings for Davina. She seems to be into me also. I'll let her know my feelings when the time is right.

DAVINA

First-class is the only way to fly. I remember all the years that I was forced by my lack of money to ride in coach. All cramped up and inconvenienced by all of the rude or overly friendly riders on the flight. There was always someone traveling with screaming uncontrollable kids. Those wimpy parents trying to patronize them rather than beat their ass and shut them up. They would run all over the plane chasing one another and harassing other passengers. Parents should realize that some people don't like kids. Do you think the parents even considered that? The first passenger that slaps the shit out of one of the little pests would probably be in a class action lawsuit along with the airline.

Some passengers would take their shoes off and pretend their feet don't smell. There were drunks who didn't know how to keep their hands to themselves and the drunker they got the more physical they got. The flight attendants would never move you unless the person next to you was a hijacker brandishing a weapon. First class allows you to escape all of that and have plenty of room to relax and unwind.

No rude passengers, and parents who can afford first class seats have the most well-mannered kids in the world. Everything is better in first-class. The food is better and I do believe they put the best flight attendants in first class. It must be a seniority thing or something. God knows I've seen my share of the "I'm just starting out" flight attendants in coach. I've been flying in and out of Sacramento to visit Marcus once a week for about six months now. Here I go again. It's a long weekend since Monday is Labor Day. Most people are at amusement parks or cookouts, but I'm on a mission and I won't stop until it is complete.

Marcus is so smooth, tall and good-looking that I couldn't resist making him my target. I've been picking up the tab to wine and dine his ass the whole time. I know he's been bragging to his friends like he's the man. He is the man. The man I picked to have my baby. I've got a nice career, a beautiful home, and now I just want a baby. The only thing I don't need is the man that goes with it. I'm just using Mr. Marcus as a little experiment. He's my prototype man that will get me pregnant and never see me again.

He's so sure of himself it's funny. I can even tell in his voice when we talk that he is falling for me. I make it a point to ensure he thinks the feelings are reciprocated. I have it all planned out. I've been the one providing the condoms for each and every rendezvous we've had. Each one of them complete with three to four nice needle holes in the center to allow my future son to seep through. The condoms are always lubricated, but never with nonoxynl-9.

Most men don't even know that nonoxynl-9 is the lubricant used on some condoms to kill off sperm cells. The last thing I wanted to do was kill the little cells that would eventually wind up as my son or daughter. It really didn't matter to me what it was as long as it was healthy. If my baby is a girl she will grow up to be just like her mother, successful and financially stable, all without any assistance of a man.

If it's a boy he will be totally different than any man I've ever dated or spent time with. He will be raised to respect women, treat them right, and most of all he will be taught how to love a woman. His lessons will come from none other than the woman that had him, his mother! My son will not grow up trying to emulate some dumb-ass jock either. He will be a well-educated, well-dressed, eloquent gentleman. When a woman does meet my son she will definitely need to have her shit together. I'll make sure he can smell a no-good bitch from a mile away. He will never know who his father is, even if I have to tell him his daddy died.

Marcus won't ruin my son's life with that long lost daddy routine. I can see him now trying to ruin all of the years of training and education my son has with one reunion.

I'm scheduled to see Marcus this weekend and he knows that I'm not on business this time. I'm just here to see him. Even though I have made seeing him my business at least until he knocks me up. I don't know why it's taking so long, there may be something wrong with his sperm or something. Maybe he's impotent and that would explain why I haven't been successful in getting pregnant. I'll give his ass a little while longer and then I may have to dump him and find a new prospect.

I check into my hotel and call Marcus. He takes forever to answer the phone.

"Hello, Marcus, what took you so long to answer the phone? Don't break my heart and tell me you've got another woman with you." That wouldn't break my heart, but it would explain why I couldn't get pregnant, he's wasting my child's sperm cells on some bimbo.

"I was just taking a shower so that I would be nice and clean when you got into town."

"I'm sorry, sweetheart, I was just getting a little jealous."

"You have no reason to be jealous, Davina. For the first time in my life I realize that I only need one woman. You are that woman and I can't imagine any other woman making me feel the way you do."

"That's so sweet Marcus so what are we going to do this weekend?"

"I thought we might go over to Magic Mountain or Universal Studios and get on some of those scary rides."

"I'd love to do that, Marcus, but you know I'm afraid of heights and roller coasters scare me." I'm not telling Marcus but the truth is I really love roller coasters and theme parks, but I'm trying to have a baby and I definitely don't want to shake up my chance of having one.

"So, Davina, did you have something else in mind?"

"I thought we might go out to dinner, rent some movies that neither one of us have seen and come back to my hotel and watch them."

"Davina, we always spend your visits in your hotel, it makes our relationship seem so professional."

"Don't be silly, Marcus, our relationship isn't professional. I just feel comfortable paying my own way at least until we become closer."

"It's been months and you've never even been to my house, Davina, you don't find that strange?"

"No, that's not strange, honey, that's just the unique part of our relationship. You can allow me to maintain my individuality by staying with me in my hotel, and when I feel comfortable enough about us I'll start staying at your place when I visit."

"Okay, Davina, it really doesn't matter where I spend time with you as long as I'm spending time with you."

"Thank you, honey, that is exactly what I want to hear. So when are you coming to pick me up to go eat?"

"I'll be there in about a half-hour."

"That's all I need to get ready for my man. See you in a few, Marcus. And Marcus?"

"Yes, Davina?"

"I miss you, honey."

"I miss you too, Davina."

JOE

Trina and I have only been married for about six months and it's been a real high-speed roller coaster ride. We've been going at it like two Energizer Bunny rabbits. We do a lot of crazy things to keep our marriage interesting.

We've made arrangements to meet at different happy hours and pretend we're picking each other up. We would pick a club to meet at, and when I arrived she would come over to me and blatantly start flirting with me. One time the shit almost backfired. This sister was on me so hard I couldn't breathe. When Trina came in I thought she was going to beat the shit out of this woman trying to pick me up. She was actually real cool about the whole thing. She just pretended like it was a contest and this lady was none the wiser.

Trina flirted and danced with me and when she took my hand and led me out of the club I could see the other woman with her mouth wide open. Even the other brothers in the place were amazed. My wife is the bomb and nobody can hold a candle to her ass. Whenever we got back home we would have such a big laugh at what we just did. It was one way of keeping things fresh. This was just another reason for us to love each even more.

Trina came home today all pumped up, and smiling like she had a secret. I asked her what's up?

"What do you mean, 'what's up?'"

"You know what I mean. Why are you so happy?"

"No reason, Joe, maybe its because I'm married to you."

"That's sweet, but you're sure you're not hiding anything?"

"Honey, would I hide anything from you?"

"All right, so what's for dinner tonight?"

"I thought we would go out to eat tonight."

"Trina, sooner or later one of us is going to have to cook a meal at home. We always eat out or order take-out."

"Joe, we will have plenty of time for full course balanced meals from all food groups. Right now I want us to go out and celebrate."

"Celebrate, what Trina?"

"I meant to say go out and have a nice meal at a nice restaurant and celebrate our love."

"You are hiding something from me, aren't you?" I asked. She then begins to rub my head. The only times she rubs my head is when she wants to make love, wants money, or has something huge to tell me. The last time we went through this she got a $2,000 a month raise at her job and it cost me money for her new wardrobe.

"No, honey, I'm not hiding anything at all," she said.

"Okay, Trina, I'll go along with your little charade. I'll be showered and dressed in about 30 minutes."

The entire time I'm getting showered and dressed I'm trying to figure out what the surprise is that my wife won't admit to.

A wise man once told me that when you get married and your wife has a surprise it's usually expensive or traumatizing. I wasn't sure which category Trina's surprise fit into.

We both get dressed and get into Trina's car and head out of the door.

She hardly ever rode in my vet, which was cool with me. I could leave shit in my car and it was safer than in the house. I wasn't messing around on my wife anymore, but I was still in touch with a few old flames. A lot of brothers make the mistake of telling their wives they are still friends with an ex-girlfriend. That is a terrible mistake.

The first time she finds a number, or anything placing you with this other woman, you're dead. I wouldn't dare tell Trina I was still in touch with an old flame. There was one in particular I would never mention. Her name is Brenda and Trina turns into a damn monster whenever she hears that name. She hates the ground that woman walks on and I make it a point not to even work with anyone named Brenda.

We take interstate 50 going towards town. Trina is so quiet during the trip, never letting on where we are going. We make a right turn onto interstate 5 headed towards Redding, California, which is also the direction towards Sacramento Metropolitan Airport.

"Are we going out of town to this restaurant?" No sooner have I said this then Trina made a right turn towards this restaurant called the Rusty Pelican. I had heard about this spot when I used to hang out, however, I never got the chance to hang out on this side of town. The place was exquisite. The décor was plush, purple crushed velvet with soft gold trim. The furniture and bar were all gold plated and everything looked real expensive. All of the workers were dressed in purple slacks and custom made vests with small initials "RP" underneath a gold embroidered Pelican. Everything about the place said very, very classy. I looked over at Trina and smiled.

"You picked a very nice place, sweetheart. I wonder if the food is as good as the restaurant looks?"

"Thanks, Joe, I knew you would approve, I heard the food is excellent."

The Hostess sat us in a nice window section that gave us a view of a man made pond full of pink and white pelicans. It was absolutely gorgeous.

We took our time and went through the menu. All entrées were deliciously described, from the roast duck in a special hollandaise sauce served on a bed of wild rice to the Ribeye steaks in honey and Italian dressing. I stopped right there. I am definitely a steak man. I ordered my steak medium, which is slightly pink inside just like my lovely bride. It came with a salad with plenty of ranch dressing and a baked potato loaded with lots of butter.

Trina ordered crab legs, of course. It seems that she ordered crab legs every where we went to eat. If they didn't serve crab legs, we never went there again. I swear her ass is going to turn into a crab leg. Maybe she enjoys breaking those shells and dipping her meat in butter sauce. The whole meal makes a mess all over the place. The whole time I'm trying to enjoy my steak she is over there cracking and smacking her little heart away. We both finished our meals and looked equally pleased with the ambiance, the food and the service. Trina's eyes were popping out and she looked as stuffed as a Thanksgiving turkey.

"How was your food, honey?"

"Fine, Joe, but I can hardly move now."

"Thanks for bringing me to such a fine place, Trina, we'll definitely have to come back here. This was really a pleasant surprise."

"Joe, this isn't the surprise I had for you. This is just the place I picked to show you my surprise."

"I knew you were hiding something. Did you get another pay raise?"

"No, but I do have some good news to tell you."

"Well, what is it, Trina?" The whole time I couldn't help thinking of what that old guy told me about wives and their surprises. We are already married so she wasn't going to propose. She probably bought something really expensive. I hope her daddy gave her the money. He's always telling me that she will always be his baby. We just got our joint checking accounts and credit cards. She must have maxed out one of the accounts to get this surprise of hers. If she's starting out like this we'll be in the poor house quicker than we could say "broke."

We might even wind up moving in with her parents. I would take the poor house over her parents any day. Trina interrupts my deep thought by shouting my name.

"Joe! Don't you hear me calling you?"

"I'm sorry sweetheart, I guess I was just trying to figure out what the surprise was."

"You don't have to figure anymore. Here is the surprise I have for you."

Trina hands me a case that you would put a new bracelet, gold chain or watch into. Now I was positive that old guy was right. This was a gift and it had to be very expensive. Why did she bring me to this nice expensive restaurant, fill me up, and then lay this high-priced gift in my hand?

"Trina, I thought we decided that we would not buy each other expensive gifts until after we finish paying for the wedding and the honeymoon."

"Joe, would you please shut up and open the case?"

"I'll shut up but I hope your daddy is ready to bail us out of debt already."

"My daddy doesn't have anything to do with this, just open the damn case, Joe, okay?"

I shut up and open the case slowly. I was expecting to see the glitter of a Rolex watch or 14K gold chain. To my surprise it was a long piece of plastic. I thought Trina was playing some kind of joke. This was like when you give a loved one a gift and wrap it in a certain box, or put in a bag from their favorite store, and the gift has nothing to do with the wrapping or the bag. I felt just like that.

"Is this a joke, Trina?"

"No, Joe, this is not a joke."

"Then what the hell is this, Trina?"

"Take it out and see, Joe."

I took this long plastic item from the case and examined it. All I could see was the initials EPT etched into the top part of the thing. On the other end was a little window-looking area with a plus sign in it. I thought I might know what this was but I was afraid to guess wrong and ruin Trina's surprise. The worst thing a man could do is go out on a limb when his wife or significant other is trying to surprise him and guess wrong. I chose the safe approach. I decided to ask a rhetorical question.

"This isn't what I think it is, is it?" She took the bait. I didn't have to answer the question, she told me exactly what the surprise plastic thing meant.

"It sure is, honey. You're going to be a daddy."

I was happy and relieved at the same time. Her news was not going to cost me any money, well maybe not right away. This little plastic thing she gave me was an early pregnancy test and the results were positive. I was about to be a father. My sweetheart was pregnant.

The news hit me slowly, however, in a few moments I was smiling from ear to ear. I got up from the table and began jumping around. I paused for a moment. Then I hugged Trina and gave her a big wet kiss on the mouth. I remembered seeing a case in the front of the restaurant that had cigars in them. I laid my new Visa card down and purchased a box of them. I should have asked the price, since I found out later that they were a total of fifty bucks. I started passing them out to every guy in the place. I was hopping around shouting, "I'm a daddy, I'm a daddy."

I ran out of men and started handing cigars to the women in the restaurant. Trina was probably embarrassed as hell watching her husband make a complete fool of himself. I couldn't help myself, for the first time in my life I was going to be a daddy. I was wondering what to name him or her. What should I be buying for my kid right now? I was so excited it was killing me. Trina had to drag me from the restaurant, however by the time we left , the whole restaurant was applauding me. I was so drained by all of the excitement that I fell asleep on the drive back home.

When I woke up we were in the driveway. I jumped out of the car, ran over to neighbors and gave them cigars with my good news. Trina and I went into the house and made love, very carefully since I didn't want to hurt my new baby or ruin her chances of having a healthy child. I had one more reason to love this woman I married. She was about to have a child of mine. My first child, the thought sent chills all down my body. Would it be a girl? If so I was going to purchase a gun the day after she was born. I know some doggie dog brother was going to break my little girl's heart just like I did so many women? I would take care of his ass.

I know the game and I would try to hip my baby to every trick in the book. What if it is a boy? I'd hip him to every game in the book, however, some other father would be facing me for what my little dog son did to his daughter. I would just say, "that's my boy." I just want a nice healthy child to raise the right way.

I really don't want my son to grow up dogging women or become a thug. Whatever the child turns out to be it will be loved dearly. What would we name the boy or girl? This is a whole other dilemma. I would never give my son a name that ends in Jr., but it would be nice to have a Joe Jr. or Joe the II. If it were a girl I would want her to have her mother's name. I just don't want us to name her after some freak I'd dated in the past. I bet that would be about 100 names that were out of the running. I'm sure Trina and I will spend some long hours thinking of names.

I've been trying to be the best new father I can be. I spent about $100 on baby books, Lamaze books and classes with Trina. This baby had better arrive soon or I'll go crazy. I'm already on edge and so is Trina. We don't get any sleep and I swear when she gets a cramp or contraction I feel it first. She's all belly, I never knew a woman's skin can stretch so much. It was like watching an episode of the Elastic Man.

We did find out it's a boy. I just hope he doesn't grow up to be as big a dog as his father was. I'm glad I gave up all that whoring around. I'm sure that sooner or later I would've caught something. Thank God He spared me. I could have given Trina a sexually transmitted disease and prevented her from having a baby or have the baby born deformed or something. That would just crush her. I'm just praying that she has a healthy child. We talked about names and Trina insisted that his name be Joseph Jr. I tried to talk her out of it, however she wasn't budging.

I knew he would have a tough time in school being a Jr. I know I used to mess with a bunch of kids because they were named after their daddy. All of that will come back to haunt my son. I think Trina wanted our first son to be named after me because she loves me so much.

I thought she was going to have the baby the other day. I woke up to Trina's moaning and groaning. I asked her if she was okay and all I could see was her breathing hard and heavy. I immediately ran for the bag that we had pre packed to go to the hospital. I'm glad it was a false alarm since she was about three weeks early. I can't wait for the time to come.

I've been a prisoner in this house for the last two months. The brothers keep calling me to see if I can hang out. I would like to go out once in a while, but Trina would be here all by herself. I could see it now, as soon as I go and hang out she'll be at the hospital and by the time I get there she would have had my son already and I'd never hear the end of it. It would be the family story: Your daddy was hanging out with the brothers so he couldn't be with your mother while she was having you.

The brothers will have to understand this time. I intend to try and keep my family intact. I can't start that hanging out shit. Soon as I get a whiff of the club scene or some old flame catches up with me I'm in trouble. I sure could use some regular old tight-ass pussy about now. Trina is so big it's like climbing Mount Everest. She's always horny these days, which makes me try and hide or look busy. I don't want to be going at it and hurt my son. It's funny she couldn't give me enough ass before she got pregnant and now I'm hiding. Isn't that ironic?

DAVINA

I'm sitting here with 6 different early-pregnancy test kits. The look on the store clerk's face when I sat all of them on the counter was pretty funny. I know she wanted to say how pregnant do you think you are? One of these damn things had better be accurate. I tried the first one and couldn't wait long enough to see if it was positive or negative before I opened another package.

I opened the one with the plus or minus sign and tested myself again. I waited and checked the window and couldn't believe it, the thing had a plus sign. I reached over and looked at the first one I tried and it was also positive. I was getting too excited. I tried the other four and it was true, an actual six for six positives, yes! I was finally pregnant.

It's been almost seven months that I've been putting up with visiting Marcus, trying to get pregnant. Now I could finally get rid of his tired ass. I can't wait to tell him that the roller coaster ride is over and he has to get off.

The last part of my plan is complete. I'll finally have my own little child that I can raise and provide for by myself without the help of some man.

It's Tuesday and I think I'm going to fly down to Sacramento and see Marcus and then dump his ass. Wait a minute, he has no idea what I'm planning to tell him and it might be too much of a shock. I know he has feelings for me. He will probably overreact and try to kick my ass or become a part of my baby's life. I'm not flying down there anymore, I'll do the typical man shit and lower the boom on his ass over the phone.

He doesn't even know my last name and he thinks I work for some bank. In actuality I had a very bad accident a few years ago that left me hospitalized and out of work for a year. The settlement some lawyer I found in the yellow pages got me, along with my own shrewd investments, has left me quite comfortable. I won't ever have to work again and neither will my child. There's no time like the present to take care of things. I'll just call Mr. Marcus up right now and tell him. I dialed his number and waited to hear his lost puppy voice on the other end.

"Hello, Marcus?"

"Davina, I was just talking about you to one of my friends on the other line."

"So, what were you telling your friend about me?'

"That's why I'm glad you called. You must be psychic or something because I was going to call you when I got off of the phone. Let me just clear the line so we can talk."

"Okay, Davina, I'm back."

"Marcus, I have something to tell you."

"Let me go first, Davina, I don't think I can hold my thoughts any longer."

"Go ahead, Marcus, say what's on your mind.'

"Well, you know we've been together almost seven months and you've been flying in and out of Sacramento to visit me. Every time you leave I miss you and can't wait for you to return. When you're here my feelings grow deeper and deeper for you. I really think I'm falling in love with you and I want you to move to Sacramento and stay with me. I know that is a big move but I think I'm ready to start doing things for you like you've been doing for me. Davina are you still there?"

"Yes, I'm still here, Marcus. I was just a bit overwhelmed with all the things you just said."

"You said there was something you wanted to say to me also?"

"I do have something I need to tell you." I should have told Marcus before he dumped all of this "I'm in love shit" on me. Why am I feeling sorry for him? He told me himself that he has dogged several women out. Shit men have been pulling this type shit on women for years and getting away with it. It's time some woman turns the table and send some shit their way.

"So what do you have to tell me, Davina?"

"Well, Marcus, I do have feelings for you but I don't share the same love you do for me. I also have some other news for you, I'm pregnant with your child and I intend on having it."

"You're pregnant, how did that happen? We were always careful and I wore a rubber every time we were together."

"To be honest with you, Marcus, each time we made love it was special but remember I provided the rubbers for you. You never had to do anything but supply me with your body. I took care of everything and now I've finally got what I want. I wanted a baby and thought you made the perfect prototype man to give me one. I poked holes in the rubbers and I've been taking fertility pills to help me get pregnant. I don't want anything from you, Marcus, and I also don't want you to be a part of my baby's life."

"What the fuck do you mean your baby's life? The child is mine too, Davina."

"I knew you would react like this, that's why I purposely didn't allow you to know too much about me. I know this is a low down underhanded thing to do but what's done is done."

"It's underhanded and I wish I had my hands on your neck right now."

"Don't worry, Marcus, there's no way that you'll ever find me."

"That's what you think, Davina. I'll find you if it kills me. You will not deny me being a part of my child's life. No matter how long it takes, Davina, I'll find you."

"Whatever, Marcus. I'll hang up now so you can begin your search. You don't even have a picture of me, just a first name. Good luck on your investigation, Marcus, good-bye."

MARCUS

"Wait, Davina, don't hang up, I love you." She hung up the phone and while I listened to the dial tone I couldn't help thinking I fell in love with this woman and she played my ass hard. I tried that *69 call back and her number was blocked. I also tried to call the operator in hopes that she could give me the number that Davina had called from. The operator thought I was playing games and told me unless it was some kind of police investigation or emergency I couldn't get that information. I sat there contemplating the thought that I would probably never see her again.

She was pregnant with my child and there was nothing I could do. Was Davina even her real name? Did she actually work for one of those large banks?

I'm sure I've broken some hearts in my day but I've never done anything like this to a woman. I could kill her ass right now. I've at least got to try and find her. I don't even know where she was visiting me from. I'll try and use some pull at the airport and hope I get some information on Ms. Davina. One thing's true, if I do find her I'll do whatever it takes to be a part of my child's life. I know a lot of brothers out there aren't taking care of their kids. I want to take care of mine and I won't be able to.

"Davina, you bitch, I hope I catch up with your ass."

The one thing that bothers me the most is that I've spent my whole life vowing not to bring a fatherless child into the world. My father did that to me and now this bitch Davina is setting me up to crush that promise I made to myself. I've never knowingly dated women with kids for any length of time. I think it's because I didn't have my father growing up. I never wanted to raise someone else's child. Now all of that is a damn joke. In one swoop this woman has made all I've stood for a joke.

I've been thinking about Michelle a lot lately. I walked out on her and she really cared about me. I've always been looking for "the one." A lot of single brothers like myself are searching for that supposed special lady. We never realize that we've come into contact with several women that could have been "the one." All we needed to do was take the time required to get to know them and be willing to grow with them. I'm sure if I took the time to get to know Michelle and her daughter that I would have found "the one" in her.

I decided to give Michelle a call and apologize for how I acted when I found out she had a child. It took my getting tricked by Davina to realize that it isn't about what you want to happen in a relationship, it's about working together. I never gave Michelle the opportunity to be honest with me. My whole conversation was about me selfishly wanting a woman without what I termed "excess baggage," otherwise known as children. I had my mind so set about not wanting to raise someone else's child that I would ruin my chances to have a really good woman.

I remember sitting around thinking about how special Michelle makes me feel and how much fun we had together. To think she was keeping the fact she had a child from me just so she could convince me that she was special in her own right.

After going through this madness with Davina, my plans of finding someone that didn't have kids only to start a new family with them has backfired on me. I owe Michelle the chance to show me that her child can be mine without having my DNA. I was going to call her but I thought it would be too easy for her to hang up on me. I decided to go over to her place unannounced and make her slam the door in my face.

I drove over to her place and on my way the radio station just happened to be playing one of my old favorite songs "The Second Time Around," by the group Shalamar. The lead singer had this high-pitched voice that made you feel the song in your body. It was very appropriate. I was on my way over to Michelle's house in an attempt to get me a second chance. I arrived at Michelle's house and just sat with the car off, quietly waiting. I don't know exactly what I was waiting for, but I knew I had to think about what I was going to say. I didn't have much practice going back to a woman and asking for forgiveness. Most of the times I would just say the hell with her ass and move on to my next conquest.

Michelle was a real woman and she was definitely worth a little extra work to get back in. I got out of the car and went up to her door and rang the bell. I could hear her little girl yelling for Michelle to answer the door. Michelle came to the door and she seemed to pause for a moment like she couldn't believe it was me. Thank God she opened the door.

"Hello, Marcus, what brings you by here?"

"I wanted to talk to you."

"It's been a long time since you walked out on me and you just show up on my doorstep wanting to talk. I'm sorry, I have my child here and we were just playing a game. I'm sure the fact that she is here will scare you away."

"That wasn't fair, however I can see why you would say that. I want to first apologize for the insensitive way in which I responded to you having a child. That's why I'm here. I wanted to explain to you why I've always been so adamant about not dating women with children."

"There's no need for you to explain anything to me, Marcus."

"I know but if you'll let me I would like to explain myself. You can kick me out after I say what I have to say and I'll leave you alone."

"Okay, Marcus, I'll give you a few moments to explain why you made me feel like a complete ass. Also I've had so many problems with men that I date having a problem with the fact that I have a daughter. The clock is ticking, you better start talking and fast."

Michelle had this look of disgust on her face that was similar to a policeman waiting for you to explain you're reason for speeding right after he caught you on radar going thirty over the speed limit. I began by telling the story of my mother and father. I told her that my mother never let any other men into my life after my father and it made me resentful. I love kids but I never wanted to take care of any one else's kids because no one hooked up with my mom to take care of me.

It left me with a feeling of emptiness that I really didn't want to experience with a mother and her child. I always thought that every single mother had a monster like my father waiting around the corner for the boyfriend to show up.

"The day I was supposed to pick you up, and I saw that guy in the Jeep, I was so jealous and mad at the same time and I really don't know why. The only thing I was focusing on was that you had a child. I never thought about the way you make me feel and how much I really liked you. The fact that you have a child didn't change any of my feelings for you, Michelle. I want the chance to spend time with you and your daughter together like the family I never had."

Michelle was standing there with her hands folded crying. Her daughter came up and wanted to know who I was.

"Mommy, who is this and why are you crying?" She was gorgeous. She had the prettiest long hair. I remembered I could tell this from my car when I first saw her. She had Michelle's eyes, only you couldn't tell that right now because Michelle's were watering.

"This is Mr. Marcus, a friend of mommy's."

"Is he going to come in and play with us?"

"I don't know, why don't you ask him," Michelle said.

"Mister Marcus, are you going to stay and play with us?"

"Sure I'll stay and play with you, your name is Ebony, right?"

"It sure is and now we can go play." I never had a chance to hug Michelle, Ebony took me by the hand and led me into the living room where her and Michelle were playing. They were in the early stages of a game of Uno. I remembered playing this game in school and I wasn't too bad at it. I realized that the worst thing I could do was beat Ebony at Uno. Michelle, Ebony and I sat there playing Uno, and for the first time in my life I felt like I was complete. Michelle sat there watching me throw the wrong cards out and Ebony correct me every time. She was such a well-mannered child, just like I said mine would be.

This was the family I yearned for and I almost let it get away. Life has a strange way of giving you what you think you want, only to make you realize it wasn't what you needed. I still wondered about Davina and my child she was carrying, but God must have wanted me to be here for Michelle and Ebony instead of having this little girl grow up like I did. I'll definitely be a better father than my dad and a different breed of brother from now on.

JOE

Today is another day and Trina is late having the baby. She went from trying to have it three weeks early to being almost a week late. She has got to have this baby and have it soon or I'll go crazy. The doctor is already prepared to induce labor if she doesn't drop soon. I guess my son isn't in a hurry to enter the world.

He should be ready to get his groove on with his daddy. I'm going to spoil the hell out of my first son. All he has to do is ask daddy for whatever he wants and I'll get it for him. I'm sure I'll be competing with Trina because she spoils me. Our first child will definitely get the world. I know one thing, there won't be a lack of love for his ass.

Speak of the devil and I can hear her yelling my name now.

"Joseph! Joseph! Where are you?"

"I'm coming as fast as I can. What is it?"

"What do you mean what is it? Your son is trying to rip a hole in my ass. My water just broke."

"Trina, don't be bullshitting about stuff like that. You know how pumped up I get when I think it's time."

"Joe, I'm not bullshitting," Trina said. "If you don't believe me just put your hand under my ass and feel. Now help me up before I scream."

"Okay, here we go." I get Trina up and get her to the car as gently as possible so we can make it to the hospital without breaking the speed limit. I love this woman so much I can't believe we are finally on our way to bring a part of both of us into the world.

We arrive at the hospital and I run inside to get a nurse or doctor or someone to help. I forget all about Trina in the car with her water breaking and screaming at me for leaving her behind.

I finally get some help and we get her inside. I forgot all of the stuff I read in the Lamaze books and classes that we took. All that money went to waste because I was feeling very nauseous. I told Trina that I was right there with her. They assessed her situation, made sure our insurance was current, and whisked Trina down to the operating room. I was by her side the whole time. I was coaching my baby on her breathing and squeezing her hand and encouraging her. I felt so good while the doctors and nurses prepped everything.

The stage was set, my son was about to be born. Then all of a sudden Trina turned into Mrs. Hyde. She started cursing at me for getting her into this mess. She said some names I wouldn't even repeat. She was giving my hand the death grip and all I could do was grimace. I just started trying to get her to concentrate on the breathing and all of a sudden I blacked out. I don't remember a damn thing until one of the nurses was giving me some smelling salts so that I could go and see my brand new son in the nursery.

I got dressed in my little hospital garb and went into the nursery. The word of our son being born got out pretty fast because when I arrived at the nursery there was my dear old mother and father-in-law. They were all smiles since they were standing there holding my brand-new son before I had a chance to. Trina's father had this sinister grin on his face. He could tell this story for years to come. I can see grandpa telling little Joseph, Jr. the story of how his daddy couldn't hang when he was born.

I was so excited about having my first son, I could feel myself fighting back the tears of joy. He was absolutely beautiful. His hair was jet black and smooth as silk. He had a head full of hair, not like the other babies in the nursery. Joe, Jr. had big hands with long fingers and large feet. He was so tiny and gentle. I thought I was going to break him if I held him too hard. I just stood there holding my son. I made this and I felt a tear roll down the left side of my face.

Of course, this little miracle was not mine alone, I had a little help from Trina, but I held the gene that determined the sex. I remember that much from college. My son was going to be someone special, I could just feel it. He just lay in my arms looking up at me like he knew who I was. I was making all kinds of noises and sounds to get him to smile. He just looked up at me with this serious look on his face. Smile or not, this was my son and at this very moment I was the proudest man alive. I wanted every man in the world to experience this. The feeling of having your first child and being around to hold him, talk to him, and let him know everything will be all right is indescribable. Too many brothers are out there having children and never spending any time with them, or hell never even realizing who they are.

I thought being a daddy was amazing and special but it has become a nightmare. Joe, Jr. has been driving Trina and I crazy for about a year now. I've missed out on so much sleep. He cries like a little damn girl. He started out in a crib next to our bed and then I tried putting him in his own room. We bought one of those two-way radios so we could hear him crying. Every little whimper he made caused Trina to go in there and bring him back into our room. I can't get any sleep and sex was out of the question. "It might wake the baby up" is what she would say. Even the baby got to suck on a breast, but not me. My dear son was putting a damper on the love life. I never thought about that when I was holding him in the hospital.

Now that he is getting closer to two years old he has to sleep in the bed with us. Every night he would start out in his own room and no sooner than I think I'm going to get me some he starts crying. That's all Trina needs to hear and he is right here in the middle of us. I think he knew exactly what he was doing. How could I let this happen? I should have put my foot down the first time it happened. Trina was spoiling this boy so much it wasn't funny. I also know now what my grandmother used to mean when she would tell folks about a child going through the terrible two's. Joe, Jr. throws temper tantrums, tosses his food, and has a bad habit of saying no to everything. I know I was a bad ass kid, but my son takes the cake. I hope he grows out of this phase or he won't make it to three years old. I'm just talking trash because if I even yell at him Trina is right there in his defense. I think he's only had one beating since being born. That was only because one day he slapped Trina in the face while she was trying to feed him. She snatched his butt out of that high chair so fast I thought his legs were still in it. All I remember was her spanking him right on the butt. It had to hurt even though he had on a pamper.

That's the last time he ever tried hitting his mother. Now I was a different story. He would always come over and start hitting on me. In the face, head or wherever. Trina says it's because I always play so rough with him. I'm not that rough with him, I just pretend to be a WWF wrestler with him. I don't do it around Trina all the time. If she ever seen me pretending to body slam her son I'd be the one getting body slammed. Joe, Jr. always laughs whenever I'm playing with him. He is a happy baby even though he is a brat.

TAJ

Joe invited me to his house to watch the return of Mark Tyler to boxing. Tyler had been suspended from boxing for about a year and prior to that he was a hell of a puncher. He used to knock everybody out in the first or second round. The last fight he had he got his butt kicked pretty well.

This commentator on the pre-fight show was pumping this up to be a contest similar to David and Goliath. His return was against some rated white guy. Now that seems a bit strange. Most of the heavyweights were black. Everyone seems to want to find the great white hope. Any white guy with the stamina, punching power and guts to get into the ring with the other heavyweights of the world has immediate support. Even if he wins on a technicality it would be a feather in the cap for white people everywhere, not to mention a nightmare for bookies.

I put on some jeans and a sweatshirt and headed over to Joe's. When I arrived at his house there were already a few cars in the driveway so I parked in front of the next door neighbor's house. I went up to the front door and rang the bell. rina answered the door holding their young son on her hip. He looked to be about a year old. He was a handsome little boy and I'm glad he looks like Trina and not Joe. I met Trina before we went to our Lake Tahoe weekend.

Joe, CK, Marcus were all sitting in the living room watching an old tape of the NBA. I knew it wasn't a current game since they had just finished a lockout that almost ended the season. Joe jumped up and greeted me right away.

"What's up, Taj? Come on in. You remember CK and Marcus from the bachelor weekend."

I remembered them but I hadn't seen them since then and I was going to miss the wedding.

"What's up, Taj, how have you been, my brother?

"I've been hanging in there and yourself?"

"Nothing much."

I remember Marcus was the tallest brother, and I knew when he stood his 6'9" frame up who he was.

"What's up, bro?"

"Nothing, just waiting to see Mark kick this white guy's booty."

"That's what I'm talking about. I hope he knocks his ass out in the first round."

It was strange looking up to another brother, especially since I was a legitimate 6'6".

We continued to make small talk until Trina interrupted us.

"Joe, I'm leaving now. I'll be over my parents' house, I left the number on the front of the refrigerator just in case you've forgotten it."

"No problem, baby, I'll talk to you later."

Trina left and Joe, CK, Marcus and I changed the conversation to the fight. The pre-fights were very boring. None of us recognized the fighters and they didn't even have the women bouts, which made the fight card more interesting. Before Trina left she made sure there was plenty of beer and snacks.

The main event was about to begin and all of us had snacks and something to drink. They began the main event by doing a background story on each fighter. This was an attempt to show a why each fighter had a chance to win. They had a comparison for everything. Each fighter's weight, height, and arm reach. They also previewed each fighter's statistics from the time he turned pro. I thought Joe would have a few more brothers over to make the sideline conversation more interesting. Unfortunately it was just the four of us.

The bell was about to ring and each fighter looked ready. The referee for the fight was this controversial brother that had stopped a previous fight for a scratch, and later let some guy get beat into a bloody mess before he stopped the fight. Most people thought the bookies were paying him off. He gave his little talk to both fighters and sent them to their corners. We were all sitting there waiting for the bell to ring on the return of big Mark.

When the bell finally rang both fighters met in the middle of the ring with a couple of jabs that never landed. They seemed to be feeling each other out.

Big Mark didn't seem like the aggressive fighter that we had all come to watch. I noticed the white guy was bringing the fight to Mark. It was kind of boring and all of us kept giving Mark instructions on which jab to throw, or when to go to the body. We had watched enough fights to give detailed instructions on how to win a fight. That was barring any sudden decisions by the current referee.

We were trying to make the best of this rust-filled bout between a returning heavyweight champion and a ranked contender. From the beginning, it looked like it was going to be a pretty good rumble. Then in the fifth round it happened.

Big Mark caught the white guy with a solid right hand uppercut to the chin. Mark must have brought the punch from China. It was a textbook punch and it resulted in a knock-out. The other fighter fell into the ropes and his corner had to come out and help him. We finally had something to yell about. Joe however was a bit pissed off.

"Man, I paid almost $50 to get this sorry ass fight. I thought it would go at least ten rounds. I want a damn refund."

"What makes you think they're going to give you and the whole cable-watching world a refund, Joe?"

"Fuck that, CK, they should have a refund clause based on the number of rounds the fight goes."

"That's why they have a whole bunch of pre-fights scheduled to ensure they give you more fights for the money. If they only had one fight on and this happened I could see you getting pissed."

We all sat there wondering what to do with the rest of the evening. I thought they were going to put that old ass NBA tape in again. Someone began a conversation on women and I really don't know who it was. It was probably Joe since he thought he was the founder of all wisdom on women.

Joe thought that women fit into five categories: mothers, freaks, snobs, bitches, or lesbians. We decided to concentrate on the freaks.

Joe started by asking the brothers and I how does a woman come to realize she is a freak. I knew where this was headed. Each one of us would wind up telling a story about a freak we had met and the weird way in which she got off. I sat there and listened to Joe while I began to remember the freaks I've met.

JOE

I met this really big freak, I can't remember what her name was. It was something ghetto like Tonolesha, or Tashondaleke, or something like that. I remember meeting her at a club and asking her if she wanted to go to breakfast after the club. She said okay and after breakfast we wound up at my apartment for what I thought was going to be some serious banging. I was all set to hit that ass like a heavyweight champion. We started out doggie style since she wasn't very attractive to start with. After a few moments of this she stops me in the middle of one of my strokes and asked me to do her a favor.

Now you know what I was thinking she was going to ask, and there was no way I was going to be going down on her. I only did that shit a few times and the woman was seriously fine. She didn't ask me to go down on her. The girl wanted me to whip her ass with a belt. I couldn't believe my ears. I asked her if she was serious about what she just asked me and she said yes. I told her I didn't get into that sadistic shit, but I decided to accommodate her. I thought if she got off on this I could eventually get some head and bang her up some more.

She pointed out a nice leather belt on my closet doorknob. I went over and grabbed the belt and wrapped one end around my hand just like my mother used to do when she whipped my ass. I hit her ass with a few good licks and she just lay there like it didn't even faze her.

"Harder, mother fucker," she said

I gave her a few more lashes with the belt, only a little harder this time.

"Is that the best you can do, you faggot ass bitch?" she said very adamantly.

I was getting mad now and hit her even harder this time, however she was still talking shit.

"My little sister hits harder than you, are you gay or something?"

That was it, I had enough, and I wasn't going to let some horny, freaky ass woman punk me in my own apartment. I got a better grip on the belt and crouched down like a linebacker about to tackle the runner coming straight at him and began my assault. I hit her ass with all I had. I was bringing the belt from way above my head and aiming straight through her towards the floor. Each whip brought about more anger and fury in me. After about ten or so lashes I heard her screaming like a damn call girl.

"Yes, that's it, I'm coming, I'm coming ahhhhhhhhhh!"

This shit really freaked me out. The girl actually got off from me whipping her ass. I made her get dressed and put her ass out right away. I told her she was sick and that I never wanted to see her ass again. The strangest thing about this whole ordeal was how did she ever come to realize that's what she liked to get off. I always wonder whenever I meet a freak what happened to turn their asses out. "I know that beating her ass didn't do anything for me except piss me off."

"That's some wild shit, Joe," Marcus said. "I've got one just as freaky and her name was Debra."

MARCUS

Debra and I met through a friend of mine, who was trying to hook her girlfriend up with a date, and I was a little apprehensive at first. You know how those blind dates are, they can be some ugly ass bitches. Anyway I get with this girl Debra as a favor to a friend and she turns out to be a knockout. The girl was about 5'11" and dark as Easter chocolate. I couldn't believe this girl didn't have a date. She could have just about any brother that I knew. I started talking to her and we decided to get a movie and just chill at her place. I picked up a movie from Blockbuster Video that I had already seen so I could concentrate on getting some of this fine, tall ass. I got to her place and she was very casually dressed in some jeans and a T-shirt. She invited me in and offered me a beer and I gladly accepted. She was drinking a wine cooler and we made small talk.

It was fortunate for me that the VCR she had in the living room was broken and we had to watch the movie in the bedroom. We went to her bedroom and popped the tape in while we made some more small talk. I tried to kiss her and to my surprise she was very receptive. I couldn't believe some brother wasn't knocking the socks off of this sister. She probably spent several evenings by herself drinking her wine coolers and watching movies alone. I was thinking how good she kissed and realized I could probably get to like chilling with her.

The intensity rose and after some time both of us were naked, still kissing. She had cut the lights off and had several candles lit around the room. They filled the room with a fresh strawberry scent that actually made me more aroused. I was ready to experience her when she stopped me and asked the weirdest question.

"So, Marcus, have you ever burned anyone?" she said.

"Have I ever burned anyone? What do you mean by burned?"

I thought she was talking about me giving anyone a sexually transmitted disease. Most men say they got burned whenever some woman gives them something they didn't have when they met her, and I don't mean a gift.

"I meant have you ever burned anyone with candle wax?"

"No, I have never burned anyone with candle wax."

"Would you be willing to try it with me?"

"Sure, as long as I'm not getting burned, I'm game." She went right to work and arranged a few of the candles on the nightstand by the bed. Some were large and odd shaped and now I noticed that each had different spouts like they were small teapots instead of candles. She lay on her stomach and instructed me to pick one of the candles and empty the hot wax that was suspended in the container onto her back. I was to concentrate on pouring it in blotches, not tiny beads-that apparently wouldn't burn as bad. I noticed faint scars on her back where she had this done to her before.

I began to accommodate her and each candle had quite a bit of hot melted wax suspended in them. I went through about two and a half candles before I got the shock of my life. Debra was coming and coming a lot. I noticed how she squirmed and grimaced until her whole body shuddered like a person going into a convulsion.

She sat there shaking and grabbing the sides of her bed with a death grip. She rolled over onto her back and I continued the same ritual on her chest and stomach. She climaxed again and this time I could see a stream of her milky white excitement oozing down the inside of her thighs. The shit really blew me away and by now I was no longer excited or in the mood for sex. Debra lay there in a wax-covered state, similar to the famous statues in the wax museums. I had just gotten this girl off with some damn candle wax and it made me shake my head in disbelief. Now I knew why this fine ass sister needed a blind date. This was too wild for me and I got dressed.

"Are you upset or something?" she said.

"No, I'm not upset. I've just never experienced something like this."

"Would you like for me to try it on you?"

"No I really don't think that would turn me on. I had something a little more traditional in mind."

"We could do that now if you want?"

"That's quite all right, I think I've had enough excitement for one day"

"Will you call me or visit again?"

"Sure, whenever I'm in the mood to burn someone, I'll give you a call, goodbye."

I left and never went back to Debra's place again. How did she ever come to realize that candle wax was the one thing she needed to get such an intense orgasm? The whole thing about freaks like her and how they found their particular "thing" is beyond me.

"Damn, Marcus, I wish Debra were here right now," Joe said. "I've got this big ass candle the size of a tree trunk that Trina got from one of her co-workers. I'd burn her ass right into ecstasy heaven ha, ha, ha."

"Yeah, and I'd get a big ass belt for your ghetto freak, Joe," CK said.

_CK_

I've got a freak of the week that's perfect for this conversation. Her name was Jackie and she was the biggest freak I've met in my life. Jackie didn't like getting beat up or hot candle wax.

She loved sex in as many positions that a brother could handle. She also liked one thing that would make her mother cover her mouth in disbelief. Jackie likes the golden shower. That's right brothers. It only took one date to find this out and although I've never hooked back up with her, I've seen her out since that night.

When we first met we were at this club and she was on my tip hard. We made light conversation and it wasn't long before I knew I was going to be getting the ass that night. We went back to her place and we had some of the best safe sex I've had in a while. I thought I made her come a few times but I later found out Ms. Jackie was a better actress than I gave her credit for. After sex she started looking at me all weird, and struck up a conversation about freaky women.

The conversation led straight to the golden flow recipients. She asked me what I thought of that and I told her it was way out of my league. Now brothers say shit like this, but as long as our ass is still a virgin and we aren't getting hurt or doing some other guy we are usually accommodating. I decided to be just that and gave into her request. She jumped up and pulled this large bundle of plastic from her closet.

I stood there naked watching her place the plastic onto the bed and she straddled herself in the middle.

She told me to stand over top of her and start spraying. I knew I had to go bad and for some reason I couldn't at first. It was kind of embarrassing, like the first time you had to go while someone was watching, or the time you had to tell a woman "this has never happened before." I guess nature took over because I began spraying her like a damn faucet. I started going like I was in front of a stall. I didn't stop until I was drained. Sure enough Jackie got off on this shit.

I stood there wondering what went wrong with her. Did she accidentally piss on herself one day and then realize that's what she liked? Whatever made her so sick was not my problem and I was not about to chill with some freak that wanted you to go on her every time nature called. She was sick and I didn't have the cure for her. I'm sure there are a lot of brothers out there willing to accommodate freaks like all of the ones we mentioned.

"That's for sure," Joe said. "There are always brothers willing to do whatever a woman wants them to. Speaking of other brothers, I know you have a ton of freaky women you could tell us about, Taj."

"Hey, Taj, I'm talking to you," Joe said

"Oh, I'm sorry. I was just thinking about the freaky ass women you guys were talking about and why I'm glad I'm gay."

"What did you say?" Joe said.

"I said I'm gay and I've just realized that I'm not ready to tell some story of a freaky woman I was with."

Marcus and Ck were just standing there with their mouths open like one of those circus games where you throw a ball through a hole and win a prize.

"You're gay? And when did you get this revelation, Taj?" Joe said.

"I've been this way for a long time, I just came out of the closet, so to speak."

"What about our weekend in Lake Tahoe? You came in second place of the contest."

"That was just me buying my way into a lie and playing your silly ass game, Joe. I actually had my own contest with a few guys up in Lake Tahoe."

"I really don't want to hear about your butt buddies. You can get your shit and get the fuck out of my house."

"I guess this means we aren't friends anymore," Taj said.

"Hell no, I don't hang out with gay boys, faggots or homos," Joe said.

"That's enough of the names Joe, I'm leaving. I guess the rest of you are homophobic also."

"Yeah, take your gay ass home to your man," CK said.

"Just step your punk ass through the door, Taj," Marcus said.

<u>*CK*</u>

None of us brothers decided to really challenge Taj since he had each of us by about fifty pounds and it was all muscle. We knew that he could beat the shit out of all of us, however we had to appear macho and most of all anti-gay.

TAJ

"I'll leave, but know this: I'm the same person that hung out with you brothers and had your back whenever someone fucked with you. Now that I tell you something about my sexual preference, you throw me out the door like yesterday's garbage."

"That's right, so why don't you take your ass to the curb with the other garbage cans, Taj?" Joe said.

"Maybe one day you brothers will appreciate friendship and not pass judgment so fast."

"Whatever, Taj, just get the fuck out."

"Can you believe that shit? Big muscle bound Taj is gay," CK said.

"I always thought he acted strange, but I saw him hook up with a ton of women before." Marcus said.

"What made his ass come out of the closet tonight?" Joe said. "I don't care what the fuck Taj does as long as he doesn't bring his ass around here anymore."

"What if he does, Joe," CK said. "You know you can't beat his ass, Taj would beat your ass and then probably take some ha, ha."

"If he took this ass it would be the last piece of ass he got," Joe said. "My ass would be in jail right now. Doing time for killing Taj if he tried that shit with me."

"Me, too," Marcus said.

"Same here," CK said.

"Fuck Taj, he's no longer one of the brothers and he damn sure won't be hanging with us anymore."

_CK_

I left Joe's house and headed home wondering what the hell happened to make Taj turn gay. I hear so many stories of guys finding out they're gay, like they went to the doctor and were diagnosed.

What makes a brother get pussy his whole life and wake up one day and crave a dick? The shit really doesn't pass the common sense test. Whatever it was I hope I don't catch it because I know one thing is for sure that I love women. I'm sure Joe and Marcus are as baffled as I am at the bombshell that Taj just laid on us. I don't know how shit like that happens but it makes me want to settle down like Joe and get the hell off the market. I need to find one woman I can trust and grow with and marry her ass. Listen to me, I'm starting to sound like there's a famine coming and I need to stock up. I'm not the one with a problem, Taj is. Let him settle down with some man and live gay ever after.

JOE

Trina wants to have a birthday party for Joe Jr.'s second birthday. I of course don't think he deserves a damn birthday party, but I'm going along with it to keep the peace and possibly increase my chances of getting a piece of Trina later. His birthday is in two days, which is a Monday, however she wants to have the party on a Saturday. The only good thing about this is I get to go hang out with the brothers. I haven't seen, Marcus or CK in a while and I'm especially not going to call Mr. "I'm gay now" Taj.

I got into it with Trina earlier today about not spending enough time with Joe Jr. I told her that I don't hang out anymore and I'm always home with our son. I'm not out there creeping around with other women. Nothing is ever good enough for her. The fact that I work all day at Wal-Mart with all of the never satisfied customers isn't good enough. She wants me to come home and spend hours playing with Joe Jr.'s bad ass in his room and then make time for her. Sometimes a brother just can't win, even when he isn't cheating. I wish she would realize that I'm home every night and that's what matters. I should just stay home for my son's birthday party, but this is probably one of those rare occasions when it's better that I go out. Besides I already gave Joe Jr. his gift. I brought him one of those motorized cars that you can ride on. Trina says I buy my son to many ridiculous gifts and I spend too much money on them. There is nothing too good for my son and I know I spend time with him no matter what his mother says. I've got to clean out the garage so that the kids have

235

somewhere to play. I finished cleaning the entire garage, including putting up the decorations Trina bought for the party. I was tired as a lazy dog and decided to take a nap. My nap only lasted about an hour when Trina barged into the bedroom and woke me up.

"Joe, the other kids will be arriving soon for Joe Jr.'s party. I thought you were going to go hang out with your brothers?"

"So now you're trying to get rid of me. Is there something going on at the party I should know about?"

"Don't be silly, Joe. There's going to be a bunch of women and children doing boring stuff. I just didn't want you being the only man here. I have some really nice friends but I don't want any of their eyes on my man."

"Okay, baby. I'll get up and see what the brothers are up to."

I get up and jump into the shower. When I got out and dressed the first few kids and mothers had just showed up for the party. Most of Trina's friends worked with her and all of them must be making big bucks because they drove nice cars. My driveway was starting to look like a luxury car dealership. They also always brought nice, expensive gifts. Some of the gifts we received at the wedding were so expensive I wanted to pawn some of them and go out and buy a cheaper brand. Trina thought I was crazy for even mentioning such a thing. I knew when I was dating, if someone gave me a gift I didn't want, or if I got two of something for my birthday, I would recycle it to another woman I was dating. It sounds doggish but as long as the one who gave me the gift didn't find out it was all-good.

TRINA

Joe is really starting to get on my nerves. He never does anything around this house. He doesn't help with the cleaning or Joe Jr. at all. I can count on one hand how many times he actually changed any diapers, or washed clothes, or cleaned a floor. He thinks because he works his ten hours at Wal-Mart he can come home and pick up the remote control to the television and that is where he remains for hours on end. He watches every game on television (football, baseball and basketball), and if a game isn't on he is watching a movie. He thinks he is so much a part of his son's life, what a damn joke. Men need to realize that being a part of your child's life is more than just being at home with the fucking remote. It means spending quality time with the child by sitting down and playing, or reading with the child with the damn TV off. Also taking time to change a diaper, wash a load of clothes or even do the cooking for an evening or two. Joe's idea of cooking is take out pizza or Chinese food. When I talk to him about spending time with Joe Jr. or doing stuff around the house he says I'm nagging or bitching. I wish he would sit back and realize just how much I bring to this marriage. I work all day while Joe Jr. is in day care and I go pick him up and make it home to start dinner for my son and husband. Their clothes are always cleaned and pressed and I shop for everything in the house from toilet paper to steaks. I also make a pretty good amount of money at my job. I'm just tired of Joe thinking he is so involved. There are a lot of men out there who think they are an integral

237

part of their children's lives and they aren't. Being involved is more than just being around. Joe is no different than having an old throw rug just lying around on the floor. Sometimes Joe can't even hear me when the TV is on. I'll be talking about my day at work or something Joe Jr. did that was really cute and all he'll do is grunt. "Honey you see I'm watching the game, is all he'd say." There are days I want to buy a gun and fill that damn TV with a bunch of holes.

Men fail to realize that you can be right there under the same roof with the child and still be absent. It's almost like paying child support and having a room at the same house with the ex-wife. Maybe I should find a remote control with a button on it that reads "child-time". I'm sure that would work, unless of course there was a game on!

JOE

I picked up the phone and called my brother CK. He was home but he had plans for the evening. I wasn't calling that gay motherfucker, Taj. Marcus was home and we agreed to hook up at this new spot. They apparently had a happy hour and it was supposed to be packed with women. I said I was down, got the directions and told him I would meet him there. I said good-bye to Trina and the few friends that were there at the time.

I made it to the club just as they were getting started with the happy hour and Marcus wasn't there yet. I was just sitting there chilling out when who in the world do I run into but this freak I was kicking it with before I met Trina. It was Brenda and my nature started to rise the moment I saw her. She knew she had my ass strung out when I was messing around with her. Man, she was a freak. This was the kind of woman a brother would want his friends to hook up with just so they could appreciate what a real freak was. We made small talk and I tried my best to be the married man not interested in anyone except my wife. This would have probably been easy if I was not talking to someone I had been with in the past and knew how good it was. She was looking sexy as hell also.

Trina had put on a few pounds over the few years since we got married and she had Joe, Jr. She was still pretty shapely but I figured she was carrying about twenty pounds too much. That's a lot of weight on a small woman like my Trina. I hadn't actually slept with Brenda in almost two years. I forgot exactly how she felt but I was doing pretty well at my self-control at first. She realized the power she had on me a long time ago and I think she still had it. I was determined not to give into her advances. After all I made a promise to myself when I got married that I was not going to be one of those brothers that messed around on their wives. So far I had only had the one indiscretion in Cancun. I must admit I haven't really exposed myself to any temptation since then. Now I'm always with Trina whenever we can get a baby-sitter and get to go out. That isn't that often and we can never stay out too late.

By now Brenda is all up on me trying to see if she can get me to go home with her. I was kind of curious why a woman as freaky as she was didn't have a man waiting at home for her. Then I realized that I was once sleeping around with this woman but I wouldn't want her for a wife. I wanted someone that could cook, clean and be a mother to my child. Brenda did not fit that bill. She would probably be at home having one of those sex plaything parties. The sex was definitely good and I was starting to reminisce. This was not going too well for me and I was starting to sweat. I wished Marcus were here so he could talk some sense into me. Before I knew it I was following Brenda over to her place, telling myself I was only going to have a few drinks and go home. If that were true why did I leave the club? It was a futile attempt at trying to appear strong. I was weak and this woman knew it.

We got to her place and it was almost like I remembered it. Brenda's place was a cornucopia of toys, lotions, potions, and apparatus for the nymphomaniac. There were sex racks, chains, dildos, whips, leather outfits for him or her, you name it, she had it there. I knew I was in trouble when she went into her room and returned, wearing nothing except a pair of black high-heeled boots. This girl could model underwear or be a centerfold in Playboy or any other sex magazine. I just stood there for a moment probably with my mouth open.

She went into the kitchen and got a bottle of wine, dressed in her God-given birthday suit. I was getting more and more excited with each glance at her body. Delilah was tempting me, and I knew exactly how Samson felt. After making some more small talk Brenda took over and I cheated on Trina for the second time since we've been married. I spent about two hours at Brenda's before having to get my ass home.

I felt like shit the whole drive home. Why couldn't I be stronger? I could've just shown her my ring and told her how special Trina and my son were to me. My body showed her how weak I was and I let my mind rationalize going over to her place. Once I was there I was hers. If Trina found out it would crush her. I prayed not to be tempted again. I would simply never go out again without Trina and I was definitely never going over to Brenda's freaky paradise. All I could think about was having some marks on me that Trina would notice or Brenda's scent on me. Women are a lot like cats they can tell when some other felines' scent is on their man. I took a water-only shower before I left Brenda's place and splashed a little wine on my face like cologne. I would just smell like I had been to the club and had a few drinks. When she asked if I had a good time I would simply say something clever to make her feel good. As long as she doesn't suspect I've done anything, I'm good to go. She shouldn't think anything happened since I'm home hours before the club closes. That's it, I'll just say I was bored with the club and came home to be with her. That would also be a good excuse not to go out any damn more.

When I got home it was only about 11:30 p.m. and Trina was already asleep. I got undressed and climbed into bed with her, hoping not to wake her up. I didn't want to have to perform twice in the same night. That would be next to impossible, considering how much sex I'd had this evening. What the hell was I talking about anyway? Trina and I haven't had sex in so long it isn't funny. I can remember the time she would jump on me two or three times a day. What do women think about after getting you to marry them? Do they think you just lose your sexual drive and can just wait months to get a piece of complimentary ass? It's like they're rewarding you for waiting until they are horny enough to want some. Most of the time they get horny at the wrong time of the month. Who wants to get their first piece in months during "that time" of the month? Trina lets me know it's that time by simply saying, "Joe, I can't my friend is visiting." The first time she told me that I said, "shit, I'll fuck your friend, too." Once she explained that it meant she was on her period, I simply went back to my bachelor days of jerking off in the bathroom. That's the safest sex you could ever have especially when you don't feel like being bothered with anyone.

AFFLICTION

<u>*CK*</u>

My mouth has been bothering me a lot lately. I've got a few cold sores on the inside of my mouth and it feels like I have a touch of the flu. I'm not going to the doctor. Brothers, never go to the doctor unless we get shot or we're in such pain it makes you scream like a bitch. I'm going to the pharmacy and get some antibiotics until this shit passes. I decided to go to Smiths, which is one of those grocery stores with a large pharmacy right in the middle.

I wasn't sure what kind of medication to take. I went to the cold medicine aisle and there were about fifty different brands of cold medicine. I continued to look for something to match my symptoms. I found some Thero-Flu and some cold sore medicine for the sores in my mouth. I have to get this shit cured before the weekend. That leaves me a whole week before it's time to hang out. I couldn't go to the club with a bunch of sores in my mouth and the flu. I'd been using this medication and I must be having an allergic reaction to it. I've gotten more sores in my mouth, I can hardly talk, or swallow. I decided it's time to go to the doctor and get some strong, prescription medicine. I really didn't have a particular doctor that I usually go to. I looked through the yellow pages and located a doctor's office that wasn't too far from me. I've got really good insurance through the state, however I've never used it. I haven't been to the doctor in so long I couldn't find my insurance card if my life depended on it.

I found a clinic about ten minutes from my apartment. I dialed the number to see if I could get in today. I know how hard it is to get into these clinics. They are so filled with senior citizens that have so many ailments the doctor knows them by first names. I just needed to get in, get some medication for my mouth, and get out. A receptionist answered and wanted to know a bunch of information before I could get an appointment. I thought this was strange. I'm sure she was just an hourly wage typist who had never been to medical school but she was trying to diagnose me over the phone. I politely asked her if I could speak to a doctor or get an appointment to consult with a doctor! At this point I wanted to yell but I was in too much pain from all of these sores in my mouth.

She put a doctor on the phone and she was very pleasant.

"Hello, this is Doctor Dana-Kirby." It was a woman and I really don't know why I expected a man. I knew the receptionist was a lady and she could have answered the phone as the doctor. I wouldn't think they would let her get away with that since she really would never know who was calling.

"Hello, my name is Calvin Kelsey."

"Hello, Mr. Kelsey, what can I do for you today?"

"Well, I have a bunch of sores in my mouth and I think I may have the flu."

"Are you feeling weak, or have you had any sudden weight loss?"

"As a matter of fact, I have been feeling real weak and I think the weight loss is due to me not eating."

"How about the sores in your mouth, how long have they been there?"

"About three weeks, I took some cold sore medication and I must have had a reaction to it because they seemed to multiply."

"Well, I think you should come in and let me check you out. I just happen to have a cancellation this afternoon at 3 p.m. Would that work for you?"

"Sure, anything to get these damn sores cured, doctor, I'll see you at three."

"I do need to put you back through to my receptionist so she can get some specific information before you come in so we can start a file on you."

"That's fine and I apologize for being short with her earlier."

"I'm sure she is accustomed to worse than you could give her."

"Thanks, doctor I'll see you this afternoon." She hung up the phone and soon her receptionist came back on the line with a very sarcastic tone in her voice. She was pretty snug with the fact that I had to listen to her and give her a ton of information after all.

I left home, headed to the clinic at 2:30pm, even though I knew it was only ten minutes from my house. I got there at about 2:45 and I couldn't help anticipating what the receptionist and the doctor looked like. I had this picture in my head for both of them.

The receptionist was on the phone when I got up to her desk. She was an older woman in her mid-sixties and had probably been a drop-out in some nursing program. She had dark hair with plenty of gray steaks racing through her hair like lightning. Her nametag said Gonzales and I couldn't remember ever hearing her mention her name. She was also very healthy. I could tell that breakfast, lunch and dinner were all highlights of her day, and not to mention an occasional snack. There was one thing about her that intrigued me, she seemed very professional and genuinely happy with her job. This is certainly not the norm when it comes to health professionals and their staff. Most of the time they're about as caring as a doctor in the nearest general hospital.

I introduced myself and expected some sort of snide remark, however she was very pleasant. A smirk of a smile is all I received and a very pleasant greeting.

"Welcome to our clinic, Mr. Kelsey." she said.

"Thank you, Ms. Gonzales." I didn't see a ring on her finger so I assumed she was single or divorced. It was clear this lady was married to food.

"Could you please fill in the following forms completely and hand them back to me?"

"I sure can." I began the task of filling out the stack of paperwork. I assumed since it was my first visit this was standard procedure. I'm sure on subsequent visits I would just go right in and see the doctor. I had no intention on coming back though.

After about thirty minutes I completed the paperwork. I needed an aspirin after straining my brain to document my medical history. Some of the information was my best guess. I knew I didn't have any allergies and could take just about any medication. Except the cold sore medication that I was having a reaction to. I went to the bathroom and when I came out Dr. Dana-Kirby was ready to greet me.

"Mr. Kelsey?"

"Yes, I'm Mr. Kelsey."

"Hi, I'm Dr. Dana-Kirby, come on in."

She was absolutely beautiful. She had short black hair with a nice pecan skin color that reminded me of someone from the islands. She had blue eyes and a nice athletic figure that made her look like a choreographer instead of a doctor. She was nothing like I pictured, she was definitely all that.

She escorted me into a room that seemed very warm. It didn't have the long examination table with the long white disposable sheets. It was more like a psychiatrist's office. There was a couch, two leather chairs, and a large cherrywood desk with plenty of files lying on top. It was well lit with overhead lighting. Where would she check me out? How could she conduct an evaluation of me in this comfortable setting? There was another door that seemed to take you to another office just past the one we were in. I sat on the couch and she took one of the leather chairs and began with some questions as she looked over my paperwork.

Ms. Gonzales must have given her the paperwork when I went to the bathroom.

"So, Mr. Kelsey, when did you first start experiencing the sores in your mouth?"

"A few started about three weeks ago."

"Have you had any swelling or discomfort"

"Yes, that's why I finally decided to come and get some real medication."

"I'm sure we can give you something once we find out what caused the sores. I need to ask you some personal questions, Mr. Kelsey."

"Sure, doctor, whatever you want to know."

"Do you routinely practice unsafe sex?"

"What does that have to do with anything?"

"It could have a lot to do with your condition, however I have to ask the questions"

"No, I use a rubber every time I have sex."

"Do you have more than one sexual partner?"

"Yes, I do."

"Approximately how many sexual partners do you have?"

"Right now, I'm intimate with about five different women."

"Wow, Mr. Kelsey, that's quite a stable"

"I guess so."

"On a monthly basis, how often do you have sex?"

"Maybe ten or fifteen times per month."

"That's almost three or four times per week?"

"That sounds about right."

"My, you have quite the sex drive, don't you, Mr. Kelsey?"

"You could say that." I could tell she was intrigued by the fact that I had five women on a hook.

"On a monthly basis how many times would you say you perform oral sex with your partners"

"That's really personal, don't you think, doctor?"

"I know these questions are very personal, however they are necessary."

"I don't do it that much at all."

"Mr. Kelsey, I need to know how often you would per month?"

"Maybe once a month, if that." I said.

"Thank you. How many women do you do that with?"

"Only one."

"Okay, Mr. Kelsey, we need to take some culture samples of your mouth and send them out to be tested."

Dr. Dana-Kirby opened the door to the inner office and there was a small facsimile of a hospital operating room. It was complete with the table, tools and three cabinets filled with gauze, medication, needles and whatever a doctor required. She went into one of the cabinets and pulled out a pack of tongue depressors.

I remember them from grade school. Someone was always checking out your mouth whenever you weren't feeling well. Just open your mouth and say ah. She had some long cotton-tipped swabs and a long plastic container. I imagined she was going to send the sample out in the container.

I opened my mouth and I could tell by her pause that she was a bit astonished by the number of sores as well as the swelling that had taken place. She continued to take samples and placed three cotton-tipped swabs into the plastic container. The container was taped with all of my information and the doctor handed it to Ms. Gonzales. I could tell Ms. Gonzales knew exactly what to do.

"How long will the test results take?"

"About a week," the doctor said.

"Should I come back or just call?"

"Just call us and we can get you a brief appointment to discuss the results of your test."

"Is there anything you can give me in the meantime?"

"I think I have something to soothe the pain and swelling caused by the sores."

She gave me a prescription for some mouthwash. I thanked her and said good-bye to Ms. Gonzales on my way out of the clinic.

I drove over to a local Walgreen's and had the prescription filled. It said I had to rinse with this stuff three to four times per day. What the hell was I going to do, carry this bottle around with me everywhere?

I was off to kick back at the apartment, take my medication and a well-deserved nap.

It's been almost a week and the swelling on the sores seems to be going down. There are still plenty of them left in my mouth, I need to call the doctor and see if my test results are back yet. She probably needs to give me some stronger medication or something. I called the clinic and Ms. Gonzales answered.

"Good morning, Mr. Kelsey, how are you this morning?"

"I'm fine," I said. "I was wondering if my test results were in?"

"As a matter of fact they are in. The doctor could see you today at 2 p.m."

"Couldn't you just tell me what the results are over the phone?"

"I'm not sure what the results are, Mr. Kelsey. The lab tests come back in a sealed envelope for your privacy and the doctor is the only one who opens them."

"Okay, tell the doctor I'll be there at two. Thank you, Ms. Gonzales."

She seemed really upbeat and I thought my test results were negative since she seemed so happy. It turns out she wouldn't know anything about them anyway. I'll just have to wait until this evening and talk to the doctor. I might as well take a nap since I have a few hours. Whatever is wrong with me I know it has me tired as hell. I've taken more naps in the last month than

I did as a child. I set the alarm for 1:30 so I wouldn't miss my appointment.

The alarm went off and scared the daylights out of me. I must have been right in the middle of REM sleep. They say that is the deep sleep you're having when you're just about to start or finish dreaming. I jumped up and shut off the alarm clock. I got this little pink alarm/clock radio/tape player for subscribing to this magazine almost five years ago. I got up, showered, took some of my mouthwash and headed over to the clinic for my test results.

There was almost no one on the road between my place and the clinic. Everyone must be at work or just returning from some power lunch. I couldn't help thinking what my test results would be as I drove over to the clinic. It was probably some kind of gum disease that required a shot in the ass. I would gladly take the shot to get some relief from this pain and stop sleeping my life away. My appetite has been taking a beating and I can't afford to lose anymore weight. I'm sure I'll gain every pound back when I start eating again. A shot was a small thing considering everything I've been through in the last month. Besides I would have to undress and let sexy Dr. Dana-Kirby give me the shot, that sounded good to me.

I arrived at the clinic and got parking right out front. I went inside and there was Ms. Gonzales as bright as ever. She was really an attractive lady, if she lost 75 pounds she could be fine. I was laughing at the thought when she said, "hello," to me.

"Hi, Mr. Kelsey, you're right on time as usual."

"Hi, Ms. Gonzales, and how are you today?"

"I'm fine. The doctor will see you now." She was acting a little strange this time. She must know about my results and is trying to maintain her composure. I must be paranoid because she told me about the envelopes only being opened by the doctor. There was a well-dressed young lady with wire rimmed glasses sitting in the lobby with a large briefcase. She didn't look like a patient. I figured she was a lawyer or insurance adjuster.

Dr. Dana-Kirby came out, said hello, and escorted me into her first office. I took a seat on the couch and she took her usual leather chair. She seemed a bit troubled and I knew it had something to do with my test results. She was holding an envelope that must have had the results in them.

"Mr. Kelsey, I have your initial test results here."

"Why did you say initial test results?"

"I think we should take some more samples and send them to a different lab for results."

"Well, what were the results of the first tests?" I said.

"First, I need to let you know that I've arranged for a counselor to meet with you after we talk."

That must have been the lady in the lobby. She was some sort of counselor. I wasn't sure why I needed a counselor, but I was anxious to know what I had.

"Look, Dr. Dana-Kirby, just give me the information straight."

"Okay, Mr. Kelsey, here it goes. The test results came back positive for the AIDS virus."

"What?"

"Mr. Kelsey, you have the virus and it's possible that in a matter of weeks or months you could have full blown AIDS. I think I need to bring in Mrs. Robins and let her talk to you."

Mrs. Robins walked in and I was just sitting there on the couch like someone had just hit me in the stomach with a sledgehammer. She was very professional and soft-spoken. Mrs. Robins was probably someone's mother and was so good with handling problems that friends talked her into becoming a counselor. I was her most recent case and I couldn't imagine what she was going to say to help me deal with the news Dr. Kirby just gave me.

"Mr. Kelsey, my name is Mrs. Robins and I'm a counselor with the Department of Health. I'm with the Center for Control of Sexually Transmitted Diseases. I need to ask you a few questions and hopefully answer some of yours."

"Okay," I said.

"I must first ensure you realize that everything we do from this point on will be handled with the utmost respect for the privacy of yourself and your partners. I need to ensure we have the current names and addresses of the sexual partners you've had in the last five, years both male and female."

"What's that supposed to mean? I'm not gay and I've never slept with a man." This made me think of Taj telling all of us he was gay and the way we reacted to his news with homophobic contempt. He should be the one sitting here in this damn office answering Mrs. Robin's questions, not me. Why was this happening to me? I love women and I haven't had a gay experience in my life. I don't take intravenous drugs and I always wear a rubber for at least the first 6 months I'm dating someone. This is like a large nightmare and I want someone to pinch me so I can wake up.

"I'm sorry, Mr. Kelsey, I know these are tough questions but I have to ask without assuming anything."

Mrs. Robins continued to ask a ton of questions. Some of the information I knew right off of the top of my head and the rest I promised to give her later. Most of the information was about where I had been and the names and addresses of whom I had been with. I was traumatized and wished I could just snap my fingers and this would all be some sick practical joke one of the brothers played on me. She gave me a bunch of pamphlets talking about AIDS. She explained that they had a lot of information that would provide me some facts, statistics, and alleviate any misconceptions I had about the disease.

Dr. Dana-Kirby assured me that if the second test results came back positive there was medication that she could prescribe to help me deal with the complications associated with the disease.

Mrs. Robins finished with me and I stood up to leave. My knees buckled and I fell right back onto the couch like a sack of potatoes. She attempted to reach out and grab me to stop my fall.

The news had definitely affected me and I paused to get myself together. My second attempt at rising from the couch was successful, but now Dr. Dana-Kirby and Mrs. Robins were standing by waiting for another fall. Dr. Dana-Kirby took some more samples from my mouth and hoped that the second round of tests were negative.

I knew it was a futile attempt at consoling me and it didn't work at all. I said goodbye, opened the door and left the office. Ms. Gonzales was standing at the reception desk and we caught each other's eyes as I attempted to leave. She never said anything, just a regretful look on her face similar to someone who got news of a death in your family. I mustered up a smile and said goodbye.

The drive home should have taken ten minutes and I made it a forty-minute drive. I took a small detour contemplating my next move now that I just found out I had AIDS. I considered suicide. I thought that would be the answer and it would avoid all of the embarrassment when my family found out. I'm sure my family and the brothers would really freak out. As much as I love women dating was definitely no longer an option. I guess it's confirmed I need to take my own life.

I've read about people getting AIDS from the dentist or giving blood, but I never thought something like this could ever happen to me. I've been with a lot of women and I'm always careful about wearing a rubber and protecting myself. This should be happening to Joe who never wraps his penis or gay ass Taj. What am I going to do? I can't hope to ever have a family or get married. Soon my ass will be as skinny as a rail. I guess that's why I've been losing so much weight lately.

What was I going to do? My life is over now and I might as well do myself and everyone else a favor and make it official. How was I going to do it? Should I just go to a pawnshop, buy a gun and blow my own brains out? They probably want you to wait two weeks to process an application for the damn gun. I could slit my wrists and bleed to death, but that would be too painful. I could just overdose on sleeping pills. That's it, I'll just go pick up a bottle of sleeping pills and take the whole damn bottle.

I found one of those grocery stores with a pharmacy in it and found the aisle with sleeping pills. There were about five different brands of pills and I wondered which ones would be the strongest. I thought about the generic sleeping pills. The store brand with a white label marked "Sleeping Pills." They saved a ton of money on these labels, I could've printed them on my computer at home. They looked like the address labels you order out of the National Inquire, 500 labels for $2.00. I decided that since I was going to kill myself I wasn't going out cheaply. I found the most expensive brand of sleeping pills with the fanciest label. I noticed this bottle had thirty pills in it. That was ten less than the generic brand, however you probably had to take three generic pills for one of these. I paid for my pills and went home to prepare for my final nap.

I got home and felt compelled to make a few phone calls to some special friends. I called Tammy and she was not home, so I left a message on her answering machine. I simply said "This is CK and I called to say goodbye, I'm going away and I won't be coming back." I called Joe, Marcus, and thought about calling Taj, but thought better of it. After all, he should have this fucking disease, not me. No one was home and neither one of them had an answering machine. I guess it was safer since they were both hooked up. Joe had Trina, and Marcus was strung out over some woman named Davina.

An answering machine could get a brother in a lot of trouble. I guess it was cool that they weren't home. How do you say goodbye to your friends without them realizing that you are going to kill yourself?

Speaking of answering machines, there were a few messages left on mine. One was from Mrs. Robins and the other from Doctor Dana-Kirby. They were both sympathetic to my situation but I'm sure neither one of them had AIDS. I went into the kitchen and got a pop from the fridge. I was going to wash the pills down with pop instead of water. Mr. Kelsey was going out in style. I sat in my favorite chair with my pills in hand and my favorite soda.

I grabbed the remote control and flipped the television on, almost out of habit. The news was on and there was nothing good. There was nothing but rapes, robberies, and one murder. Someone had shot and killed a grocery store clerk while trying to commit a robbery. They had his mug on the screen. It was taken from the surveillance cameras. What a jerk, who would rob a place and smile for the camera? I thought I could've been there while the robbery was taking place and played hero. I'm sure I would've been shot and killed also. That way I could go out with some honor and chances are nobody would even find out about the AIDS. Oh, well, I could spend days trying to be in the right place when some nut decides to rob a store. I'm sure the best way to go out is sleep. You just drift off into an eternal sleep.

The television is making me even more depressed. I clicked the damn thing off and open my bottle of pills. I just sat there in my favorite chair wondering what went wrong and why did I have to get AIDS. I was determined not to live with this disease and suffer until I died. This was definitely the easy way out and I didn't give a shit. For once in my life I was going to make a decision that had some finality to it. I suddenly realized that I hadn't written a suicide note. Once they found me I wanted to make sure everyone knew why I was doing this. I got up and found a pen and some paper and began writing my final correspondence.

To whoever finds this letter,

I, Calvin Kevin Kelsey, being of sound mind and body, have decided to take my own life. I just found out I have contracted the AIDS virus and didn't want to go out like a thin, sickly, burdensome patient. I don't want a funeral and my next of kin is Mr. and Mrs. Kelsey of North Highlands, California.

I don't have many worldly possessions but I do own a few items. I leave the two thousand dollars in my savings account to my friend Tammy. I know she'll do something meaningful and creative with the money. I am leaving my Lexus automobile to my friend Marcus Harold Turner.

I wish I could see the look on his face when he has to give up his piece of shit Honda and drive a real luxury vehicle. My house and all of my other possessions should be sold with the proceeds used to pay for my cremation and the balance split between my parents and the clinic run by Dr. Dana-Kirby.

I want to say thank you to Dr. Dana-Kirby and Mrs. Robins. I know you both were only doing your job and I love you for that. I want to also thank Ms. Gonzales. You still managed to give me a smile, even when you knew the news was devastating.

Finally to all my brothers out there messing around with as many women as they possibly can, I have one word of caution for you and that is THINK! I never had unprotected sex, I'm not gay, I don't do drugs, and I have never had an operation that requires a blood transfusion. I never thought something like this would happen to me and now I have AIDS. I know the way in which I have chosen to deal with this may seem weak and cowardly, however it is what I've decided to do. Being careful wasn't enough, I needed to spend time earlier on in my life trying to be monogamous, instead of jumping in the sack every time I got the chance. If I had to do it all over again I would probably be abstinent.

I hope all of my brothers could feel what I'm feeling right now. I know given the chance I'd start by respecting the women that I've dated. I would also begin living my life and by making it meaningful. I'd start giving back to our young kids who are lost with no role models. Going into the schools and volunteering my time. Giving back to the communities and helping with the poor, sick and homeless. Whatever it takes to make my life count and become a different breed of brother. If only half of the brothers gave back our neighborhoods would be safer places to raise families and teach values. My letter has become too long already and it is time for me to end this letter and my life. I hope God will forgive me!

Yours Truly,

CALVIN KEVIN KELSEY
A Different Breed of Brother (In my next life)

I popped five of the pills in the bottle as I sat in my favorite chair and chased it down with my favorite soda. I then took another five, and chased them again with some pop. I continued this until the entire bottle of pills was gone. I sat there waiting for them to be digested into my blood. The pills must have been fast-acting because I was immediately sleepy. I just sat back in my favorite chair and started to sleep. I must have laid there an hour or so when I was awakened by the phone. I was so groggy I could hear the faint ring of my otherwise siren loud telephone. It kept ringing and ringing and I got annoyed for a moment. I was trying to die and someone was interrupting me. The answering machine came on and I really couldn't hear who it was. They must have left a message and I smiled at the thought of someone getting my note along with the message on the machine. This was some shit out of an Alfred Hitchcock film. I began to try to sleep and the phone rang again. I decided to go find the phone and take it off the hook. I was stumbling and knocking stuff over. The pills must have been taking effect since I could hardly move without stumbling like some drunken sailor.

I found the phone and it was still ringing. I wondered if I should pick it up or just wait until after whoever left a message. I picked it up, probably to stop the damn ringing that was driving me crazy. When I picked it up I couldn't even move my mouth to say hello. It was a woman on the other line and she was yelling my name.

"Hello, CK, is that you? Is that you, CK?"

"Mmm," I said. I couldn't understand it, I couldn't even talk. My mouth seemed to be sealed shut like some bank vault.

"This is Tammy, and I'm calling because I couldn't understand the message you left me. Are you there, CK?"

I couldn't even answer her. I dropped the phone and thought Tammy would just ramble on until she hung up. I decided to just let her ramble on. I stumbled back to my favorite chair realizing that I would not have to get up to answer the phone again, since I left it off the hook. I began thinking about my life, my family, my friends, and the many women I've taken advantage of. People always talk about your life flashes before you during significant emotional events. They're right. I'm thinking of everything from childhood to present. "God what have I done?"

I felt someone slap me in the face.

"CK, what the hell have you done?" she said.

I can tell someone is there and that they are hitting me in the face but I can't feel anything nor can I get anything to come out of my mouth. Those were some good pills I took. I can't even lift my arms or legs if I wanted to.

"Wake up, CK, wake up!"

I could tell it was a female's voice, but that was it. My eyes were open but I couldn't focus on who it was. All I could make out was a female silhouette. I thought it might be Tammy since she is the last one I talked to. Then I felt myself being lifted up like I was floating on air. Now the room was crowded. There were several men standing around me, looking into my eyes, poking something into my arms. I couldn't even wake up to see what was going on. I must be dreaming.

TRINA

Where the fuck is Joe? I've been paging that motherfucker for a few hours now. I'm pissed off, and drowning my tears with my third glass of this cheap ass Wild Irish Rose wine. I already have a headache from drinking this shit. I'm about to go through my second box of tissues. When I get a hold of him I'm going to kill his ass.

I bet he's probably stumbled across some old bitch he knew before we got married. I just hope I catch his ass in the act. I don't know what the hell I'm going to do, kill her or him first.

I never really trusted Joe until he decided to marry me. He used to lie and talk to women behind my back and when I found out he always had some smooth ass excuse for fucking up.

There won't be any good excuse this time. I'm sitting here in this big ass house full of furniture, appliances, TVs, VCRs, and I'm still alone except for my baby.

Joseph Jr. is a hardheaded boy that will probably grow up to be just like his father. I can see his poor wife going through the same shit I'm going through right now.

It's almost 2 o'clock in the morning and his "I'm still a player," jet-black Corvette is probably parked in some bitch's driveway while he parks his dick in her crotch. The more I think about it, the madder I get. Why did I marry this lying ass, cheating bastard?

All of my girlfriends said he was a dog and that I was crazy for dating him, much less marrying him. I didn't listen to them, I just thought they were all jealous and wished they had a man like my Joe. Look, there I go talking about "my Joe," just like he's some prized possession. It turns out he's nothing more than a possession for whoever has him at the time.

I do know why I love and am married to this man. He makes all of my innermost feelings, frustrations, and passions soar to new highs and dive to new lows. I have never met someone who I can be so mad at I want to kill him and one second later I'm making love to him so intensely it makes me cry. A lot of women are in relationships like mine. Women who don't have a man would tell you to let him go or just leave his ass. They just don't know how intense your feelings are for him.

The way he grabs me and makes me feel like this tiny little bird that will be caressed and cared for by his strong yet gentle touch. I love my husband so much it hurts. There's only one thing I won't tolerate and that's sharing! I will kill his ass and do the time in prison before I let some other woman have my husband. I'd probably kill both of them and plead temporary insanity. If I get one of those spousal abuse organizations to get behind me I'd probably get off scott free.

It's now three in the morning and no sign of Joe. He hasn't called or answered any of the pages I've sent. It's raining out and something terrible might have happened. He's stayed out late before, but at least he would call and invent some sorry ass story for me to believe. All he would do is listen to me bitch for a while and then say, "baby, I'll be home in a few minutes." It doesn't matter how long he stayed out, when he gets back home everything is all right again.

I'm going to wake his son up and get him dressed so he can be there with me when I catch his father fucking around with some other woman.

I remember a couple of old flames that he slips and mentions every now and then. It's probably that freaky bitch named Brenda. I never caught them two together, but I know she's trouble. She's the kind of woman who lives her life to steal other women's husbands.

The more husbands she steals the happier she is. She takes another husband and wears the conquest like a jewel added to her already crowded tiara.

One time we were at a party and I caught her ass looking at Joe. She was staring him down so hard I could see his clothes starting to come off with each minute she stared. She only stopped staring when I stepped into her view and looked at her like "try it, bitch."

It's a shame sisters can't see another sister with a good looking man or lose their ex-man to a sister and just let it go. They always have to see if they can play the "I don't want him, but you can't have him" role. Always trying to tempt your man into sleeping around with them so they can feel secure about him now being with you. It's almost like they want to be able to say, "I can have him whenever I want." You can clothe and feed his ass until I decide to have him again. Any woman in her right mind knows if her man can be tempted into spending one night with that other woman he can be tempted into several nights. You might as well give the other woman a key and say it's all right because from that point on he will never be all yours.

Most men don't think women pay attention to them when they're around their buddies. We pick up on shit just like the bionic ears of the 6 million-dollar woman. Men don't realize that if they even mention some other women's name while in the bathroom, or walking around the house, we'll hear it. Even if we weren't home when they said the other woman's name, the name would just hang around suspended in the walls and play back when we returned home just like a tape recorder. I'm going to go find his cheating ass.

"Wake up! Joseph Jr., wake up!"

"Mommy, why are we getting up, it's still dark outside? Don't we go to school when it gets light out?"

"Yes, you're right. We're going to meet daddy."

"Yeah, yeah, where's daddy, mommy?"

"Don't worry about where daddy is, just help mommy put your clothes on and we'll be there in a few minutes."

"Okay, mommy, I'll get dressed."

I get Joseph Jr. dressed and dash out to the car in the pouring rain. I'm getting soaked putting Joseph Jr. in his little car booster seat and seat belt. I shouldn't be lugging him around with me, however it would be worse to just leave him at home while I try and find his daddy. A baby-sitter would be nice, but who could I call at three in the morning to come and watch my kid for a few hours, or until I find his father and bring him home? I want to see the expression on Joe's face when I bust in on his ass with some other woman and I have his child with me to bear witness.

"Mommy, Mommy, why is it raining so hard?"

"I don't know why it's raining so hard, please be quiet, Joe Jr."

"The teacher at school says that when it rains the Angels in heaven are crying. Is that true, Mommy?"

"Well, the teacher at school is full of shit."

"Ooooh! You said a bad word, Mommy."

"I know I did and you better not repeat it. Rain is just one of those things that happens like the sunshine or the clouds. God created all of this just like he created you and me and your rotten ass father."

"What did you say about Daddy?"

"Nothing, honey, just sit back and be quiet, mommy is trying to drive in this nasty rain."

"Mommy, why are you crying?"

"Mommy isn't crying, honey, that's the rain on my face."

This dumb ass radio station is playing some sad music. The "Quiet Storm" is what they call it. There's nothing quiet about a storm. I'm cutting this shit off.

"Mommy, why are you driving so fast?"

"Don't worry about why mommy is driving so fast."

I know why I'm driving so fast. It's because I'm in a hurry to catch that motherfucker sleeping with his little bitch. These wipers are about as useful as tits on a bull they hardly work. I can't see a damn thing, but I know where I'm headed. What the fuck is that bright ass light up ahead?

"Oh my God, help me!"

"Mommy, what's happening!"

Screech, slam, bam!

JOE

"Holy shit! It's almost three in the morning and I'm still here at Brenda's house."

"Why are you freaking out Joe you've been over here late before and didn't have any problems, what's different now?" Brenda said.

"The difference is I'm a married man now, Brenda, and besides all of the times I stayed the night here Trina was out of town."

"What do you think she'll do?"

"She'll probably have a loaded gun ready to pull the trigger when I walk through the door."

"You're not really serious, are you?"

"I'm serious as a heart attack. The only thing saving me is we haven't had a gun in the house since my son was born. She's been paging me like crazy. Look at all of the times she's on my pager."

"I know, I shut your pager off so you could sleep."

"Why did you do that shit, you're going to get me killed. She would kick your ass also if she knew I was over here."

"Why would she ever suspect you were over here?"

"You don't know Trina, she has a way of finding out shit without appearing to know anything."

"Do you want to call her?"

"Hell no! If I call her ass from here and your number shows up on her caller ID, she'd be over here in five minutes."

"I have my number blocked, so she won't know where you are calling from."

"What about that *69 call back? I'm telling you the woman is so resourceful she would call the operator back and say her husband just called her from a number and she thinks he is in physical danger. The operator would send a police car over for my ass and Trina would probably follow the sirens to your house."

"What are you going to do, Joe?"

"First I've got to get the hell out of here and get my ass home. If I make it before daylight I can say I was drunk and stayed over one of my partner's houses."

"Which partner?"

"I don't know, I could use any of the brothers as an alibi, they will all back me up."

"It's raining like cats and dogs out there why don't you wait until the rain lets up a little?"

"I can't, I know she's steaming mad by now. The last page I got was about two-thirty this morning. I know she's probably up waiting for me to walk in the door."

"Will I see you again soon, Joe?"

"Let's not talk about that right now, Brenda. I'm trying to think of what the hell I'm going to say to my wife so she doesn't ask for a divorce."

"I thought that's what you wanted anyway?"

"I can't get a divorce right now, especially when she's pissed off. She'll make sure I never see my son again and I'd be paying some outrageous amount for child support. She would go home crying to her rich ass daddy and he'll hire the best lawyer in the country to ensure I pay for making his precious daughter miserable. I need to slowly work into that divorce shit. It needs to be a mutual decision where we both decide to go our separate ways."

"Are you sure you're going to be okay?"

"I'll be fine, see you later, Brenda."

"Goodbye, Joe, drive safely."

"I'll drive safe, all right, look at this damn rain."

It's coming down so hard Trina would understand if I didn't want to drive in this shit. The first thing out of her mouth would be why didn't you call. Most of the time if I just call her and listen to her go off on me for a few minutes everything will be fine when I got home. I'm just going to have to figure out a massive lie to tell her when I get there. This rain isn't helping me think. I have to concentrate on this road and all of the nuts on the road that drive like it's still hot and sunny out. Damn, it sure is pouring down.

I knew the first time I messed around and slept with Brenda after I got married I would always be thinking about getting some more of that ass. She is nothing but trouble. Cutting my pager off while I was asleep was a dirty ass trick. She knew I would have hell to pay when I got my ass home, after staying out all night. She probably thought Trina and I would argue and I would just leave and come back to her place.

My self-control is definitely gone when it comes to her temptations but I still love my wife. I'm determined not to ever mess around with Brenda or any other woman again if I can just get myself out of this last jam. Why the fuck didn't I just carry my ass home after I banged Brenda the first time last night? That was a rookie ass player move, to lay down and go to sleep after sex with the other woman. Brothers know that once all of the blood fills your penis there isn't any left in your brain for rational thinking. You only have instinct to rely on. Instinct should have picked me up, put my clothes on, got me in my car, and been home before The Cosby Show finished airing last night. I'll think of something, I always do. It's taking forever to get home in all this rain. It usually only takes me about 15 minutes to get home from Brenda's place. There's no sense in speeding in this weather. I might run into something and never make it home. At least I'd have a good excuse for not coming home. Oh shit a damn detour up ahead, now I'm going to be even later. Some asshole probably thought the rain meant go faster. Looks like some big ass truck took out somebody. Truckers think they own the road anyway. In weather like this it pays to stay out of their way. A lot of times they can't even see a car until they are right up on you and then it's too late.

There's a bunch of firemen and police officers around. They were all scrambling around, talking on radios, measuring the pavement, and taking notes. They must be doing an accident investigation. They always respond to accidents in droves. I guess it's so they can take advantage of the live training they get at multiple car accident scenes. Man, it looks like it was a terrible accident. You can hardly see what's left of that car on the side of the road. Wait a minute that's a white Honda Accord. Trina has a white Honda Accord. It couldn't be her. She would never be out this early, especially with Joseph Jr. Besides she would have to get someone to watch him. She would never leave him home alone either. She also would never drive in this kind of rain. She hates driving as it is. I'll just pull over and make sure it's not her. Lord, my heart is pumping a mile a minute. What if it is Trina? What if she had Joseph Jr. with her? I don't know what I would do if I lost my wife and child. Please God don't let it be them.

I get up to the yellow tape the police always put around every accident scene.

"Sorry, sir, this area is off limits, can't you see there's been an accident."

"Look, officer, I see there's been an accident, I just need to make sure that isn't my wife over there."

"Wait just a minute! I'll get one of the detectives over here."

He makes a call on his two-way radio and this large friendly-looking guy comes over wearing a trench coat.

"Hello, I'm Detective Moorhead, can I help you?"

"Yes, you can help me. My name is Joseph Ronald Williams and I believe my wife may be involved in this accident."

"Why do you think it may be your wife?"

"My wife drives a white Honda Accord similar to the one over there on the side of the road."

"Can you describe your wife for me?"

"Why the fuck do I need to describe my wife for you?"

"Calm down, Mr. Williams, this is standard questioning. We aren't in the habit of letting everyone that passes by, thinking one of their loved ones is in an accident, into a police accident scene. If you just bear with me a minute we'll be able to tell if your wife was in this particular accident or not. Now please describe your wife for me?"

"She's about 5'5", dark-skinned, with brown eyes and a very athletic body."

"Would she have had anyone else in the car with her?"

"She might have had my son in the car with her, but I doubt it."

"How old is your son?"

"He's two years old. Now can I just go over and see if it's her?"

"Do you have any reason to suspect she would be driving around in this weather at three in the morning with her son in the car with her?"

"No, detective, I was just on my way home and saw the accident, and thought I would make sure it wasn't her."

"Don't you think you should call home first and see if she answers the phone? It would save us a lot of time and you a lot of grief."

"I wasn't thinking about that, I just pulled over."

"Here is my cellular phone, feel free to call her right now."

I could feel my heart racing with each number I dialed. I almost dialed the wrong number because I was so scared. I thought about rushing right past this detective and seeing if it was Trina's car. I realized there were so many paramedics, policemen and firefighters that I would never make it five feet. I finally got all seven digits dialed and pushed send. The phone began to ring. This was one of the first times I wish Trina would pick up on the first ring. Sometimes when she's upset and waiting for me to come home she would answer the phone on the very first ring. The phone was on about the tenth ring before the answering machine came on. It had a loud crying message from Trina. "Joe, I hate you, where the fuck are you? It's three in the morning and I'm on my way to find your ass and I'm bringing your son with me. I want him to see just how much of a whore his father is. I could just kill........." Just that quick it cut off. I could now feel the stream of water rolling down my face. When I went to wipe my face I realized it was tears because the rain had finally let up. It was soon going to be daylight. I handed the detective back his phone and said thank you.

"Well, was she home or not?"

"No, she wasn't."

"What is it? Why are you crying?"

"She left a message that she was leaving home with my son to find me."

"Do you know what time she left that message?"

"She said it was three in the morning."

"You weren't home at three this morning?"

"Apparently not, detective."

"What time did you leave home last night?"

"I left home yesterday about six in the evening. I went out to a bar for happy hour and ran into an old friend."

"Yeah, I know the routine, one thing led to another and you forgot about the wife and kid until this morning."

"That's none of your business, detective."

"I think it is my business, since the lady and child you just described were just taken from my accident scene to the Sacramento Presbyterian Hospital ten minutes ago."

"Why didn't you say something? I could have been there already."

"Wait, Mr. Williams, I'll have one of the officers take you. I don't need you speeding over there all upset and I wind up with another accident on my hands."

"Okay but please hurry. I hope they're okay. Did the paramedics say whether they were alright?"

"No word, they just rushed them right out of here as I drove up."

The whole time the police officer is driving me over to the hospital I kept praying that God would spare the lives of my wife and child. I was the one messing around behind her back and if she weren't out trying to find me they wouldn't even be in the hospital. We would all be safe and sound in bed at home. I wished this was some bad dream that I could awaken from and I would never cheat on Trina again.

Just as soon as my wish for this to be a dream, we arrived at the emergency entrance to the Sacramento Presbyterian Hospital. The officer opened my door for me to get out and I couldn't feel my legs to lift them out of the car. My body was so weak from the shock of what could be. He finally reached out his hand to help me. I was glad to reach out and take his help. He never once tried to be patronizing or coy. He remained silent and supportive about the whole ordeal. I entered the emergency room and tried unsuccessfully to locate Trina and Joe Jr.

I finally cornered a nurse and she directed me to some doctor down a hall and through some large double doors. There were three letters on the door, which read ICU. I remember watching an episode of ER and I knew that meant intensive care unit. I just wanted to see my wife and child. The doctor immediately assured me that they were doing everything within their power. I asked if I could see my family and he politely said, "It wouldn't be a good idea right now." My wife was in surgery and my son had been given a sedative. He suggested that I go up to the front and begin filling out the large amount of paperwork that was required for them to continue treating my family. I followed the doctor's directions like he had just given me a prescription.

The paperwork they gave me was about as thick as a local telephone book. I decided to just begin and maybe they would come around soon and give me some information about Trina and Joe Jr. I began concentrating on the large stack of paperwork and before I knew it an hour had passed. I completed the paperwork just as the doctor came around the corner and gave me the second worst news I could ever want to hear.

Trina had slipped into a coma. Joseph Jr. was going to be okay. He just sustained a few scratches and had a broken arm. It turns out Trina was not wearing her seatbelt. She was thrown from the car and hit her head on the ground. The doctor said she could've been speeding when she got thrown from the car. I wondered why she didn't have her seatbelt on, but she took the time to put Joe Jr.'s seatbelt on. She was probably so upset with me she forgot to put it on. The weather was so terrible last night, that it must have made things worse. There she is upset and driving in the pouring rain looking for her cheating ass husband. She ran head on with an 18 wheeler truck. It's all my fault.

"Please God, just give me another chance to make it up to my sweet loving wife." Here I was praying again when faced with a significant crossroad in my life. They let me go in to see my son and he was just resting peacefully. I just rubbed his head, told him I loved him, and kissed his forehead. I wondered what would I do if I had to raise him all by myself. I left his room crying like a baby. The doctor finally allowed me to go into Trina's room in the intensive care unit.

They had performed surgery on her head to release a blood clot in her brain.

When I opened the door to her room I could hardly recognize her. Her head was bandaged, she had several stitches and her face was swollen. Look what I did to my beautiful baby. I immediately remembered our wedding day and how I just stared at her face before we kissed. It seemed like yesterday. I called her name but she just lay there as still as a corpse. My tears got heavier and heavier. Why would I risk such a wonderful family just for a few hours of pleasure with another woman? It doesn't make any sense. I thought about Brenda and realized that even if I were to divorce Trina I would never be with her.

Women who allow themselves to be the one on the side or the mistress will never be the main one. Men don't respect the fact that you were willing to play second fiddle. The women who refuse to allow themselves to be the other woman will always have their respect. Let's face it, without respect you're not really a woman. Here I am, calling myself respecting the woman that I love, and here she is lying in the hospital in a coma because of me.

I wish God would allow us to trade places. I just fell to my knees and began to pray, again.

"Dear God, I know You know why I'm praying to You today. I want to know what it would take for me to get Trina back and have us be a family again. You were clearly trying to get my attention and you have it now. I promise that I will do whatever it takes to keep us together. I know it seems like You only hear from me when I'm tempted or in trouble. I also promise that this won't be the last time you hear from me. I will pray more often, go to church, do volunteer work, whatever you wish me to do. Please bring my Trina back to me, please!"

Now I was faced with another difficult task. I had to get myself together and call her parents to let them know about her hospitalization.

They knew something was wrong since I had never dialed their number the whole time Trina and I have been together. Her father answered the phone on the second ring.

"Hello, Higgins residence," he said.

"Hello, Mr. Higgins, this is Joe, how are you?"

"What's the matter, Joe? Where is Trina? Is Joe Jr. all right? Where are you?"

I couldn't get a word in from all of the questions. I interrupted and said, "Trina and Joe Jr. were in an accident."

"An accident, oh my God! Are they okay?"

"Not really."

"What the hell do you mean not really? What exactly does not really mean, Joseph Williams?"

"I mean Joe Jr. is okay, but Trina hasn't recovered yet. She's in a coma, sir." I heard the phone drop on the other end. There was a long silence and then it came. Her mother let out such a shriek that I thought I was going to run and hide. Her father finally realized I was still on the phone and picked up.

"Which hospital do they have our baby in, Joe?"

"She is at the Presbyterian Hospital downtown."

"We'll be there as soon as possible."

I don't know how they took what should have been a 25-minute ride and cut it down to 15 minutes. They were standing in front of me in record time. Trina's mother was so hysterical I thought they would admit her soon. Her father actually shocked me, he was serious, and very business like. "Which doctor is working on my baby?" I showed him the doctor and they went into a room to talk. I imagine her dad was just letting the doctor know how well off he was and that money should not be an object in treatment. He seemed to think money would somehow make Trina wake up in a few hours. The doctor was already doing everything he could for Trina. Maybe her father thought that once the doctor knew that her father was loaded he would now give her some wonder drug and Trina would rise up out of her bed and walk.

We went to Trina's room where we found her mother sobbing like a baby. Mr. Higgins just went over and began comforting his wife. I decided to go down to Joe Jr.'s room and see if he was awake. He was awake but still a little drowsy. He tried to talk and I could hardly make out what he was saying.

"Hi, Daddy, where were you? Me and Mommy were driving in the rain and saw a bright light."

"I know, son, don't try to talk too much, get some rest."

"Are you going to be here when I wake up, Daddy? You know Mommy cries when you're not home?"

"I'll be here, son don't worry."

Soon my in-laws were in Jr.'s room. Trina's father must have overheard Jr. and I talking because he had this interrogative look on his face.

"Joe, I still would like to know what my daughter and grandson were doing out driving in the pouring rain in the wee hours of the morning," he said.

"Can we talk about this some other time, Mr. Higgins?"

"Sure, only don't think I'm just going to let this go."

"I'm sure you won't. I just want my wife and child to be okay. We can talk about what happened later."

I left my in-laws to attend to Joe Jr. They were pampering and fussing over him. They were treating him like he was a little baby. I wish my parents were still alive to see my son. I was so young when they died I can't even remember them.

I knew Trina's dad wanted to eventually get to the bottom of what exactly happened to his sweet young daughter. I was not about to offer up any information and I hoped they would not decide to interrogate my son. I went back to Trina's room to find a bunch of flowers and cards. I couldn't understand how the word got out so quickly. Her parents must have called the "I've been in a wreck hotline." I'd been at the hospital for about 3 or 4 hours now. I went out to the nurse's station only to find more flowers recently delivered for Trina and Joe Jr. A few hours had passed and the flowers and cards were getting ridiculous. There was no room for all of them and the hospital staff was starting to get upset. You would think they had a celebrity in the hospital. I tried to figure out what to do with all of the gifts, flowers and cards. The first person I thought about was the wedding planner we used for our wedding. Why was I thinking of that expensive old bag? I think I just recently got over her bills. One thing was for sure that she was very good at organizing and controlling an uncontrollable situation. I went into Trina's room and found her daily planner in her purse. I looked up the number it was under W for wedding. I called her and explained what had happened and she arrived at the hospital within the hour. I was impressed since this was a Sunday. I thought she would be resting, or shining her combat boots. She took charge from the moment she arrived. She arranged to take one of the hospital storage rooms over. A desk was put in front of the room, and every gift, card and flower was chronologically logged in and accounted for. I now felt comfortable about any gifts or money being collected. I did realize that she would come with a fee. Her fee was the last of my worries. I just wanted Trina to be okay. That would be worth every dime I had.

We stayed at the hospital, in shifts, Trina's parents took the day shift and I took nights. There were strict instructions to call the other shift if anything changed, no matter what time. I was able to take Joe Jr. home with me on Tuesday. We kept a vigil on Trina for the next four days. I arrived at the hospital on Thursday around 6 p.m. for my twelve-hour shift. The muffled tears of her mother and the blank stares of her father greeted me.

"My baby, my baby. What have you let happen to my baby? You did this, Joe, you son-of-a-bitch, you did this to my baby!" she said.

"What's going on, Mr. Higgins? What is it?" He just held his wife and stared off into space. I rushed through the hospital to Trina's room. She was not there. I found a nurse and insisted she tell me where my wife was. No one was saying anything. My heart was beating so hard I thought it was going to explode. I was sweating so bad it looked like someone had thrown water in my face. I found the doctor that was treating Trina and, almost out of breath, asked him how she was?

"I'm sorry, Mr. Williams. We did all we could. The trauma to her head was too severe. Your wife died about 30 minutes ago."

My legs got so heavy I just fell to the floor. I lay there and cried out, "noooo"! "Trina come back I love you baby, please don't leave me, please!" The pain of what he just said was so severe it felt like someone had just jabbed a hot sharp knife through my heart. I was on the floor holding my face in my hands, crying like a baby.

I felt a strong hand reaching down and grasping my shoulder. I could hardly see from the tears. I thought the Lord himself was about to take me to join Trina. I wished that were the case, however when I looked up it was Mr. Higgins, Trina's father.

"Get up, Joe, I know now that you loved my daughter as much as I did. I resented her marrying you from the start, but now that she's gone we have to stick together. You, my wife, and I are the only family that son of yours has left. Come on, Joe, get up, son."

He never called me son. Why was he trying to comfort me? I just killed his daughter.

"We still have to think about Joe Jr."

My son just lost the only mother he knows and he wants me to just get up and shake it off. I couldn't get my legs to stay sturdy enough for me to stand. I finally got to my feet and leaned against my father-in-law. He felt like a rock. I was crying and babbling about losing my sweet Trina. He had this look on his face that seemed indifferent. He remained the strong adhesive that would hold any family crisis together. We went to the lobby and he went over and held Trina's mother as we both woke up the hospital with our cries of sorrow.

None other than the wedding planner made the funeral arrangements. She wouldn't even allow Trina's father or me to pay her for her services. She insisted that the advertisements on the programs would bring her enough business to justify her services. She was slowly becoming a friend. For the first time since I met this woman I had grown to hate, we hugged.

Her next greatest challenge was the funeral arrangements for Trina. I now realize there was no way I could put something like this together. It was so traumatizing to imagine what it would be like to pick out caskets, burial sites, a picture for the programs and whatever else it took to arrange a funeral. I was completely distraught and so were Mr. and Mrs. Higgins. I really miss Trina, it's starting to hurt so much, but I must remain strong for Joe Jr.

I didn't have to lift a finger, the wedding planner told me that the money collected from the hospital was more than enough to cover the funeral expenses. I didn't know how to thank her. She reminded me how special Trina was to her and she didn't need to be paid anymore money for the job she was doing. I contemplated what I would do for the next few days prior to the funeral. I went downtown to the K street mall and picked out a nice new black suit from some men's clothing store. It was nice and I paid a pretty penny for it. Money didn't matter at this point, when you lose someone close to you all of a sudden material things don't mean that much. I would give any amount of money to have Trina back. The next few days were filled with people still bringing cards and gifts for Trina. I didn't even realize how many people knew her. She must have touched a lot of people's lives. I wished she could just wake up and see just how many people love her, especially me.

The morning of the funeral arrived seemingly overnight. I got Joseph Jr. and myself dressed. By the time we were ready to go, the wedding planner was in front of the house in a long black limousine. When we got down stairs Trina's mother and father were already inside. Her mother was crying and her dad just sat there with this blank look on his face. I said hello and hugged Jr. by my side. This was going to be one of the toughest days for me to get through. We arrived at the church and everything was in place. She did a very good job arranging the funeral. It was very stylish, complete with several black limousines outside of the church for the families to ride to the gravesite. The same preacher that married us, Trina's long time pastor and Godfather, Bishop

Walker gave the eulogy at the church. He gave a spirited eulogy, which moved every one in the church to tears. He talked about how spirited she had been from a little girl. There was a peculiar story he told about a time he had to intervene when Trina was about six years old.

He had gone out to his car for something and saw Trina outside yelling at some little boy. He walked up behind the two children, and before he could do anything Trina had socked the little boy right in the eye. The little boy was much bigger than Trina was and it almost made him laugh. He grabbed the two children and took them inside and had one of the deacons tell their parents that they were both fighting. It wasn't much of a fight the way he remembered it. Trina had so much fight in her even then.

I just sat there with tears rolling down my face and my heart hurting something awful. All of the memories of our life together and the way she would slap the shit out of me made me crack a smile that parted the tears streaking down my face. My sweetheart was gone and there was no one there for me to blame but myself.

The church was packed. There seemed to be more people here than at the wedding. There were even people standing in the rear of the church. I looked around and to my surprise I saw the one person I never wanted to see again in my life, Brenda. There she was standing in the church at my dead wife's funeral like she was invited. The nerve of her ass, I wanted to go over and physically throw her ass right out of the church. That would cause too much of a disturbance and someone would figure out I was messing around with her. If that happened I might as well leave the church with her. My ass would be dead. If Trina's father didn't kill me, one of her family members or girlfriends would take pleasure in taking my mistress and me out. I'll deal with her ass later.

There were so many people wearing black to mourn Trina. It made me feel even worse that Trina was loved so much and it was my indiscretions that resulted in her death. There were family, friends, loved ones, and some of them might have been those professional mourners. They show up to funerals and cry and bawl like they actually knew the person lying there in the casket.

Trina would make even a professional mourner seem for real. She looked far more beautiful than I've ever seen her before. The funeral director did a wonderful job on her makeup and I picked out this nice dress that she loved to wear on special occasions. It was a nice full-length navy blue dress that almost looked black. It had one of those fancy collars that looked like it was made of cardboard. It folded over real neat and was cut just enough to be sexy, but not revealing. The cuffs matched the collar and I would just admire her whenever she wore that dress. Her shoes matched the outfit, and as I stood in front of the casket I broke down again and yelled out "Trina!" She was officially gone out of my life. My sweet wife looked so beautiful and I noticed Joseph Jr. standing next to me crying. I turned, leaned down and picked him up.

"I'm fine, Daddy. I wish Mommy would wake up so everybody would stop crying and we could go home and eat."

This made the tears accelerate down my face and my heart fell like a broken elevator dropping ten floors. He was so innocent and sincere in his words. He actually thought his mother was sleeping. I wondered how I could let him know that she would never be coming back home. When the funeral was over we all climbed into the black limousines and led a long procession of cars to the gravesite.

I couldn't tell from the front limousine, but judging from the amount of people that actually went to the gravesite, it must have been a ten-block procession of cars. All of them were coming to pay their respects to my wife. The ceremony was short and sweet. I remember watching Joseph Jr. throw the handful of dirt he picked up onto Trina's casket. He was looking so strong and I could tell he wasn't really sure what was going on. He was just following everyone else. They lowered Trina into the ground and I had to go back to the limousine. I climbed inside with Jr. and waited for Trina's parents to join me.

The funeral procession headed for the wake, which was held at a banquet room rented by the planner, and the spread was enormous. There was so much food. Everyone could eat, take a plate home, and there would still be more food left. Even Trina's side of the family couldn't eat this much food. We ate, mingled, and everyone seemed to keep coming up to me expressing his or her condolences. This made me feel even worse.

I received a lot more envelopes, most of which had money in them. I just knew it was enough to put a student through a local state college for at least 1 year. Everyone hung around until very late at night. I was so tired I could hardly talk anymore.

Joseph Jr. was knocked out on a chair, someone had found a pillow and put it under his head. I went over to get him so we could leave and I just looked at him lying there so peaceful and he reminded me of how peaceful his mother looked at the funeral. I picked him up before I started crying some more. My tear ducts were probably almost drained by now.

We had the limousine driver drop us off at home and I put Jr. to bed. I took a long hot shower in hopes that would help me relax. I sat back on the bed where Trina and I used to spend so many nights making passionate love. I was holding a picture of Trina from the wedding. I had found it a few days ago while going through some of her stuff. I hugged the picture and closed my eyes real tight to try and imagine she was right there holding me again. It worked because I fell asleep almost immediately and was emerged in a dream with my sweetheart making love to me again. It was so real I didn't want to wake up. She was as beautiful as ever talking shit about how she was going to rock my world. We were making love so intense and all of a sudden I heard someone crying.

It wasn't Trina because she was with me. I suddenly woke up to Joseph Jr. crying in the next room. I rushed in and heard his painful cries.

"Mommy, Mommy, I want Mommy!"

"Joseph Jr., Mommy isn't here."

"Where is she, Daddy? Tell her to come home."

"She can't come home; she's gone to heaven."

"Can we go see her?"

"Maybe someday we will see her, son, maybe some day."

Joseph Jr. threw his arms around me and I thought my heart was going to be ripped out of my chest. I just held him tight and realized how selfish I had been. All of the lying, cheating, and the games I've played on Trina and every woman I've ever dated. My whole life has been a big joke. I have never been committed to anything except pleasing my own selfish ass. I was even praying to God to give me my wife back, I never once thought about Joseph Jr. My selfish fooling around has taken away my son's mother. He's going to have to spend the rest of his life wondering why she had to die so young. I don't think I could ever tell him what really happened and I pray he doesn't remember anything about that night. All he has in the world right now are Trina's parents and I.

I began to cry along with my son. We just sat up on the bed, crying together, father and son. We would have to lean on each other through all of the tough times we would go through from now on.

I'm going to dedicate my life to being the best father I can be to him. I owe that to Trina and Joseph Jr. There won't ever be anything too good for my son. I guess some people would say that I'm attempting to pay my way back into the good graces of my wife or God. I'm sure they are both watching down on me from heaven and wanting me to bring our son up to be God-fearing and decent.

I'm going to do my best to do that, and one thing is for sure, he will never mistreat a woman in his life. I'll make sure of that. I'm going to teach him all of the things I never did when it comes to women. If I have my way he'll be the exact opposite of his father when it comes to women.

The only thing I ever did right in my life was meet, date, and marry Trina and have my beautiful son by her. I'm going to have to spend the rest of my life dealing with what led to her death. I don't think I will ever forgive myself. I just wish I could tell all of my brothers out there, lying and cheating on their woman, my story. I would make them see how empty my life is without Trina. Also the price I paid for my indiscretion was more than I was ever willing to pay for a piece of ass.

If more brothers stopped and thought about the possible consequences of their actions there would be a lot of fathers still at home raising their children. There would also be a lot of empty jails and prospering communities. It's too late for me to bring my wife back. There might be a brother on his way to the other woman's house right now. Hopefully by sharing my story and how much it cost me it would make them reconsider and stay home. Any brother that changes his mind will be grateful in the end. Also he will still have a loving sister at home to keep him warm, safe and dry from the rain.

I must concentrate on raising my son as a single parent now and if God decides to send someone else into my life as special as Trina, I know for a fact I would not mess up a second chance. Joseph Jr. and I will visit his mother as much as possible and especially on her birthday and put some fresh flowers on her grave. I'll make sure he grows up knowing the type of woman she was and how much she really loved him. He was the first child for either of us and she was my first real love. I only hope he grows up to be the man I never was. If I have my way my son will definitely be a different breed of brother....

DEMISE

TAMMY

What the hell is going on with CK? He just left the weirdest message on my answering machine. I'll just call his ass up and see what the hell is going on.

That's strange, CK just left the phone off of the hook and all he said to me was "Mmm mmm." Something is definitely wrong. I'm going right over there and see what's up. On the way over to CK's place I couldn't help thinking of the worst possible thing. I would walk in the door and he would be dead. The thought made me drive faster, oblivious to the other cars on the road or the chance of getting a speeding ticket. Right now a policeman is exactly what I need. I get to CK's house and ring the bell. I tried the door and it was unlocked. I went into the room and there was CK lying in his recliner with an empty bottle of sleeping pills in one hand and a can of pop that had spilled onto the floor. I ran over to the phone and called 911. I explained to the operator that my friend had just taken an overdose of sleeping pills and was unconscious. She wanted me to stay on the phone with her until the paramedics arrived.

The operator tried unsuccessfully to coach me into checking to see if he had a pulse. I had seen people do this on television but this was real life and I was petrified. My heart was beating a mile a minute and I felt so helpless. I should've taken that CPR class or those life-saving courses offered by the Red Cross. I always thought you needed those courses when you were around a bunch of old people. Hell, CK wasn't even thirty years old yet. The operator was telling me to just slap him and see if he responds. I was glad to accommodate her request since I was getting mad that CK would put me in this situation. I pulled back and slapped him and I have to admit it felt good. He moved slightly and it appeared that he was trying to open his eyes and focus on me. I called his name and slapped him again. It was no use, he was definitely out of it and I didn't know what else to do. Just then I heard the siren of the ambulance and knew help was on the way. I remember holding CK in my arms and telling him to hang in there, help is on the way.

Four paramedics came busting through the door with cases, and two carrying a stretcher. They began wrapping his arm with a blood pressure reader, sticking a needle in the other arm, and flashing a flashlight in his eyes. I was getting even more worried. A policeman came in, pulled out a pad and pen, and began asking me questions. CK was unconscious and wasn't going to be much help.

"What is your name?" he said.

"My name is Tammy."

"Tammy, what is this guy's name?"

"His name is CK."

"Could you please give us his full name?"

"It's Calvin Kevin Kelsey."

"How many pills did he take?"

"I don't know. When I got here he was lying there just like that."

"Did he talk to you today and say anything about what would make him take an overdose?"

"He called me and left a message on my answering machine saying goodbye."

"Goodbye?"

"Yes, he said he was leaving and he wasn't coming back. I guess this is the trip he was talking about making."

"Is there anything else you could tell me about Mr. Kelsey?"

Right after the officer asked me that, I saw something sticking out from beneath the couch. It was almost hidden and it made me pause for a moment.

"Excuse me, Tammy, is there anything else you could tell me about Mr. Kelsey?"

"No, I don't know anything else." I pointed to the paper on the floor and the officer put on a pair of plastic gloves and picked it up. He took a few minutes to read the note CK left and just stood there shaking his head. He looked over at the paramedics and told them to be careful since he just found out CK might have AIDS.

"AIDS? What makes you think he has AIDS?"

"Never mind, Tammy, I think you should go now."

"I want to know what that note says."

"I'm afraid I can't let you read the note, Tammy," the officer said.

"Look, my friend is lying there dying and he called me to say goodbye. I'm the one who dialed 911 to get help, the least you could do is let me read the damn note he left." I could tell the police officer was contemplating this and he must have been having a good day. He asked one of the paramedics for a pair of plastic gloves similar to the ones he had on. He handed me the gloves and I put them on like I was a nervous first year medical school student. Once I had the gloves on he handed me the note. I read each line like I had to store the information in my head for a pop quiz later. Each word ran through my eyes, then my brain, and finally my heart. CK's final words pierced through me like a razor sharp sword. I felt the tears rolling down my face after reading my name. His words about mistreating women made me think of the reasons we broke up. The note wasn't that long, but it took me forever to get to the end. I was crying like a hungry infant when I handed the note back to the officer. I told him thank you and went into the bathroom to find some tissue. I could probably use a towel at this point.

I couldn't believe CK had done this. How did he find out he had AIDS? How did he get it? Should I get checked? We dated for about a year and I felt like I needed to get tested. I thought about finding the doctor in the note and find out what happened to my friend.

The paramedics had taken CK to the hospital and I decided to stop worrying about myself and go down to the hospital. The police officer offered to take me down to the hospital and I gladly accepted his offer. He was able to maneuver his way around traffic and go a lot faster than I could, and he had a siren. They took CK to the Sacramento Presbyterian Hospital. This was one of the best hospitals in Sacramento. If CK was going to make it they brought him to the right place. We got to the hospital and I rushed into the emergency entrance looking for CK. A nurse stopped me and began asking all kinds of questions. What was his name? Was I family?

I was glad when the police officer came in. He took the lady over to the side and began talking to her about the situation. She instructed me to wait in this room and a doctor would come out and speak to me when they finished working on him. It turns out CK was in the operating room at that very moment. They were probably pumping his stomach or trying to push something through his system to counteract the sleeping pills. I wish I knew how many he took. Now that I know why, I wish I were home when he called. I could've made it to his house sooner and maybe given the doctors more time to work on him.

I waited in the lobby for what seemed like hours. When I looked at the clock I realized that I was only there a little more than an hour.

The doctor came out and as he came towards me I could tell the news was not good. He was drenched in sweat like a runner finishing up a marathon. His forehead was wrinkly like a person trying to figure out a difficult math problem. He seemed to be coming towards me in slow motion since I could read everything about him. About forty years old, with some early gray on his side burns that made him look particularly distinguished. His glasses were large and thick and I didn't think he could get another pair with that prescription in an hour from Lens Crafters. He stopped along the way and talked to the nurse who initially stopped me when I came in. They talked for a few moments and I saw her pointing in my direction. The doctor then proceeded to come in my direction. I remember taking a deep breath in hopes of keeping my heart beating while I heard the news he was bringing. He got closer and closer and when he was close enough he put his hand out to shake mine.

"I'm Doctor Marqueur."

"My name is Tammy. Is my friend CK all right?"

"You're a friend? I thought you were a relative"

"I'm all the family he has here in town. You can check the note he left and see who he talks about, me."

"Well, Tammy, I'm sorry to say that Mr. Kelsey died a few moments ago. We tried our best to save him and nothing we did would help him. I believe he took between twenty and thirty pills about two or more hours ago. Most of the medication was already into his blood system, which caused him to have a cardiac arrest, and he died. I am so terribly sorry."

There I was, hearing the news I never wanted to hear. CK was dead. I started replaying the note in my mind and I broke down and cried, again, aloud this time. The nurse was right there like clockwork grabbing a hold of me. It was good that she did since I felt my knees buckle and I could hardly breathe. My friend was gone. Just like the message he left on my machine. He was leaving and not coming back. Why couldn't he just get some counseling? Why couldn't I have been home? Why did the doctor tell him he had AIDS without letting anyone else close to him know? Where were his so called brothers, Joe, Taj or Marcus, who he left his car to? I can't handle this, it's just too much. I'm bawling like a baby now and I know they probably want to give me a sedative or something.

It's been less than a week since CK died and his funeral is today. Just like he wanted there wouldn't be a casket, just his remains in a large vessel. His parents are having his funeral at this little funeral home around the corner from where we both went to lunch together a few times. I'm trying my best not to be too emotional during this ordeal, but I must go and pay my respects to my best friend. The drive over to the funeral home was long and tumultuous. I caught myself wanting to beat the crap out of several drivers on the road. I was having a serious attack of road rage. When I arrived at the funeral home I couldn't believe my eyes. There were over a thousand people standing in line to enter the place. There were absolutely no parking spaces and there were TV news cameras everywhere. I never realized CK knew so many people or maybe this was one of those opportunities for the local news to do a story on the repercussions of promiscuity. I remember reading a small story on CK's suicide in one of the local papers but I didn't think much of it.

There were all kinds of people out in massive numbers. There were Blacks, Whites, Hispanics, Gays, with signs promoting everything from abstinence to free sex.

I was dreading having to wait in line to get in. I noticed CK's parents' limousine pull up and I caught his mother's eye. She recognized me and motioned for me to join them. I went inside and was impressed with the inside of the funeral home. It was very small but quaint. There was only room for about a hundred people and I couldn't fathom all of the folks waiting outside gaining entrance. I was glad to be inside myself. CK's remains were at the front of the church with two six-foot posters on either side of this large container, which probably contained his ashes. The poster on the right was a large blown up picture of CK. He was wearing one of those black Lycra shirts, dark slacks and his usual glowing smile. The other poster caught me off guard. I didn't expect to read those words again in my life. It was a very large copy of CK's suicide note. At first I thought this was a little morbid but I read his words again and there was a definite message in his last words that CK wanted to get out. I realized this would be something he would approve of. He wanted other brothers to read and take heed to his words.

I noticed a few of his brothers squirming around trying to fight back tears. I had met most of CK's friends and thought there would be more of them at the funeral. I remember this very tall brother named Marcus, this really bright brother Joe, who I knew was a whore. He fucked over a few of my girlfriends. Then I noticed the finest one of all of CK's friends, Taj. Damn, he was fine, I could see myself mounting that large frame of a man. I had to bring my attention back to the funeral for my best friend who is no longer with us.

CK would not be calling me again, we couldn't go out together anymore, and we would never get to hold one another again. The tears started rolling off of my checks as I sat and thought about all of the special things we did together, when I wasn't pissed off at him. I read his words on the large poster one more time and reminisced watching him lie there with all of the paramedics working on him. That is one scene that will be etched in my mind forever. I was doing exactly what I was trying not to do, get emotional. I seized this opportunity to make my discreet exit. I was able to escape without being noticed.

I found my way back to my car and just sat there for a while crying. After about ten minutes or so I found some tissues in the glove box, wiped my face and took an alternate route away from the funeral. I went home, fixed myself a nice hot cup of tea, and took a long, well-deserved nap. I thought that when I woke up I would be rested and better able to handle CK's death. I wish he was here now and I could be the woman he hooked up with after his revelation and before he decided to end his life. Here I am a lonely woman with a career, no real close friends and especially no man. In some ways I think CK is a lot better off, however I'm not going to take my life to see. I'll probably just make an appointment and make sure I don't have AIDs. It hurts to know CK couldn't handle the news. I'm not sure what I'll do if I have it. I know one thing whether I have it or not, from now on I'll be one of the biggest advocates for AIDs research. It's too late for CK, however maybe they'll find a cure someday that will benefit someone else.

"God, I pray that you take my friend CK into Your arms and allow him into heaven even though he took his own life."